My African Rose

A Memoir of
Love and Devotion

DAVID FARRELL

KINGSLEY
PUBLISHERS

First published in South Africa by Kingsley Publishers, 2025
Copyright © David Farrell, 2025

The right of David Farrell to be identified as author of this work has
been asserted.

Kingsley Publishers
Pretoria,
South Africa
www.kingsleypublishers.com

A catalogue copy of this book will be available from the National
Library of South Africa
Paperback ISBN: 978-0-6398420-1-1
eBook ISBN: 978-0-6398420-0-4

Also by David Farrell

The Chameleon
Where the Birds don't Fly

Jeanne Mendonca, you reignited my passion for writing and have forever altered my world. You taught me how to love and to be loved. This fictional memoir expresses how you make me feel.

Prologue

My name is Rorke Wilde. Most are familiar with me as Rory. You may know me from my memoirs in *The Chameleon* or my writings in *Where the Birds Don't Fly*. Both depict my travels across the globe in search of a home.

My African Rose is a story set in a pub and restaurant owned by my partner Rose and me during an interesting time in South Africa. The country was in its third year of majority rule, and the Springboks had won the World Cup the previous year. Life was good. Positive change seemed possible for all, but just as silver linings exist during difficult periods, dark clouds threaten sunny times. The government's questionable dealings unnerved the fledgling nation, troubling many for the future. Hope was the overriding aspiration. History was less so, alluding to the folly of neighbouring bankrupt countries.

This is not a truth story but rather a perception influenced by my experiences and prejudices. There is no intention to apportion blame or preach a political agenda. I have not adjusted my words, thoughts or actions to meet the demands of political correctness or conspiracy theories. That time in history was how I perceived and experienced it. Your own beliefs will determine what's right or wrong. All are relevant.

The book reflects my love and adoration for my wife, best friend, and saviour, Rose Wilde. Without her, I am nothing. Our achievements stem from our unwavering commitment to one another. She inspires me endlessly, but enough of my sentiment. Allow me to show you the gem that she is.

Inspired by the release of Nelson Mandela. My return to Africa after seven years in England kick-started my subconscious revolution. The United Kingdom was not a suitable fit for my family. I had to find something for both them and me.

Selfish?

Yes, but inevitable. I searched for answers.

Who am I?

Is this the life we want?

Are we happy?

We needed to challenge who we had become and where we were heading. Our dissatisfaction with life stemmed not from others or each other.

Father Time was not a patient entity. Mother Nature showed no mercy. The law of karma was inescapable. We had to act now or be consumed by the voracious appetite to right all wrongs.

The year was 1996.

France stopped nuclear testing in the South Pacific as a gesture of global disarmament.

Britain battled mad cow disease by feeding the national herd meat and bonemeal. This was a neurodegenerative disorder transferable to humans via contaminated meat.

Book of the year in relationship psychology: *Men Are from Mars, Women Are from Venus.*

Independence Day, a blockbuster doomsday movie, was filling cinemas.

OMC *How Bizarre* played on the car radio on my home from work.

> *It's making me crazy*
> *Every time I look around,*
> *Every time I look around,*
> *Every time I look around,*
> *It's in my face.*

I wondered what advice my mentor Themba, whom I had left behind in Zimbabwe ten years earlier, would give us if he were here.

I benefited from his guidance and counsel every minute that

passed, how I missed him. With the traffic at a standstill, I opened my wallet and pulled out a note he wrote me when I was at boarding school. It read.

> *Howzit, Mr Rory, I am fine to thank the Gods.*
> *The house is quiet without you.*
> *I am sure a tokoloshe (evil spirit) has taken your place.*
> *Everyone is too busy to see the truth.*
> *I cannot miss you when I sit by the fire because you are ever with me in my soul, but I miss our talks.*
> *Terrible things are coming, my friend.*
> *The country does not talk.*
> *People are not praying.*
> *That is why they sent you away, to learn to fight.*
> *My son, Sipho, wants justice, as do his comrades, and I can't stop the boy's ideas.*
> *How I wish we could enjoy God's world sitting around a fire worshipping the world and its people.*
> *The spirits are not happy.*
> *But you and me, with God's help, will sit again soon to sort this madness out.*
> *Our ancestors say it must be so.*
> *Kumele ngihambe khathesi.* (I must go now)
> *Size sibonane njalo.* (Until we meet again)
> *Lihambe kuhle jaha.* (Go well, son)
> *Themba.*

The paper, two decades old, was thin as tissue, his words as relevant as when he wrote them. I'd promised to keep all his writings to me in my private tin box at home.

I glanced at the traffic behind me through the rearview mirror, and saw the same jam ahead. Like always in Johannesburg, the vehicles inched along the motorways.

On that long-ago first night at boarding school when I was eleven, I remembered Themba's last words as I closed my eyes.

You are our gift, Zulu warrior. Now, let us celebrate your first day with boundless joy. Tomorrow, we will call on our memories to ward off the agony of absence.

My heart heaved. 'Where are you, Themba? You promised,' I say under my breath. *Thank goodness I have Rose and the family.* I pondered our next steps.

We did not choose this life or identity. We were far from our goal. Our crossroad awaited.

Could we find what we were looking for?

Join us on our pilgrimage.

Chapter One

I first set eyes on My African Rose in a retail outlet I was managing in Johannesburg. I like to believe it was on Boxing Day because the place was mayhem. Customers were buying everything in sight, and the checkouts were heaving. Around lunchtime – and forgive me, Rose if the timing is inaccurate – a beautiful, petite redhead approached me as I walked down the store's main aisle.

'Excuse me. Are you the manager?' Emanating from a smile came the sweetest voice I had ever heard before.

'Yes. I am. How can I help?' I asked, more pleased with this request than the dozens I had received already.

'I was looking for one of those TVs you had on special, but the salesperson tells me they are all sold out.' A dainty hand pointed to an empty shelf. 'I was just wondering if you had a spare I might have.'

Her subtle, do-not-mess-with-me tone caused me to blink, but I closed my mouth when she continued. 'Us retailers always have spares somewhere, don't we?' She gestured towards a familiar logo on the pocket of her golf shirt.

'Let me…um…let me see what I can do for you.' I stammered, 'You carry on with your shopping, and I'll track you down in the store when I get back.' I tripped over my two left feet, adjusted my tie, and lurched for the stockroom. *Get a grip, Rorke Wilde.* I admonished myself for my unprofessionalism and teenage awkwardness. *You're thirty years old, man.*

My delightful shopper was right. As with all specials expected to sell well, I had put one aside for each of them for this very circumstance. Wow, did she qualify? *Calm down, Wilde, she wouldn't look at you once, never mind twice.* I placed the boxed item in a trolley and sought her out on the shop floor.

'Hello, there. I found a spare set for you.' I said, pushing the television to her.

'I knew you would. Thank you so much.' She gave me her hand.

I grasped her ever so soft fingers and felt somewhat giddy. *Hold it together, dipshit,* my brain chastised my beating heart. The two were seldom out of sync. 'My pleasure. Have a good day.' I stormed off in a tizz, annoyed at myself. *Oh, crap, I didn't offer to help her to the car with it.* I did an about turn and asked as she waited in the queue.

'No, that's okay, thanks. Someone is waiting outside for me.'

I nodded and sauntered off as if unperturbed. Never had somebody affected me the way she just did.

The encounter was brief, and I think it did not bother me again until I saw the logo from her shirt on an empty shop window in the same mall. I speculated whether she would be involved in the opening or running the store. *Wonder what the chances are,* as that fine woman crept back into my conscious once more. A note next to the 'soon-to-be-opened' sign advertised vacancies, including that of a manager.

I applied for the position – I admired the brand for their innovative approach to retail in the country. I'll have you know nothing to do with the customer I had served the week before, and I'm sticking to that version. There was also the potential to become a regional manager.

A few days later, the HR department scheduled an interview at the new shop. I would meet the Merchandise Director and Operational Director there. *I wonder? No, it's too coincidental.* My inner voice debated with my logic. *Fat chance, Wilde. There's no way she'll be there.*

At the prearranged time, I told my existing team members I would welcome the new brand to the mall. I knocked on the papered windows and entrance, but there was no response. I tried the door, which opened, so I let myself into the building. The floor, covered in brown paper to protect the lino, had pallets of stock strewn across it.

'Hi, Mr Wilde.' A short, balding man in his mid-thirties greeted me from the other side of the space. 'I'm Karl, the operations director.

Pleased to meet you.' He put out his hand in greeting. 'I believe you have met our merchandise director, Rose?'

'So, we run into each other again, Rorke Wilde.' Rose also shook my hand. 'Great customer service, by the way.'

Elated, I clasped the same tender yet firm grip. 'Wasn't expecting you.'

I stumbled over my words, expressing gratitude for her compliment, but I couldn't look away from her eyes. The two executives directed me to three white-plastic garden chairs in the middle of the floor.

'So, tell me about yourself,' Karl offered around a box of cigarettes, lighting one for himself when everyone else refused. Rose widened her eyes ever so slightly and tilted her head in anticipation.

It was an informal chat to determine the ideal manager profile. I met most of their requirements. It ended with Karl excusing himself to take an important phone call and Rose glancing at me with a soft smile. 'We'll be in touch, Mr Wilde. Thanks for stopping by.'

'My pleasure. If I don't succeed, best wishes to you all. A brilliant concept,' I said, and left the building.

Within the hour, Rose called me back to offer me the job of, which I accepted on the spot. I was over my current position, the bureaucracy of corporate compliance being too much to bear. A professional decision, I'll once again have you know. Albeit less convincing.

A month later I joined the team, and I was the national retail manager within a year.

Rose was in her element. Director of the nation's fastest-growing baby store chain, she was pioneering the way in retail by opening warehouse outlets instead of the traditional boutiques. Mountains of disposable nappies lined the floors. Stack upon stack of bargains for the baby enticed new and expecting parents. The latest strollers and prams, toys and nursery equipment on the market. Something for everybody, no matter their income.

I travelled to the stores to ensure we fulfilled housekeeping compliance, team engagement, and service levels. My years of retail experience in Britain stood me in good stead.

I lacked her entrepreneurial skill and social adeptness, but I compensated her with tenacity and attention to detail. Combining our skills meant we worked well together.

My initial post-school job was at a bank, which turned out to be an unsuitable environment for me. Counting wads of cash while sitting across the table from someone who bored me to tears.

I then worked as a clerk in a government organisation that featured a level of bureaucracy and political manipulation I have not seen again. I first encountered entrepreneurs in England when I joined a family of brothers operating in a small town in the Cotswolds. It was not until I left them a few years later to join a corporate equivalent that I realised where my niche was.

Another seven years passed, and after moving to South Africa I found myself with Rose and the amazing organisation she was running.

With a handful of branches, we exploded onto the scene, opening twelve more outlets across the country. Without organisational limitations, every outlet became more attractive, efficient and, above all, unique. The aim was to serve the local community best. Seldom were ideas played down, with most coming from the team no matter their station.

Rose and I bonded during these shop openings as we merchandised and improved upon the previous store. Her eye for colour, contrast and ambience complemented my appreciation of space. We spent many hours working together before the openings – creating, debating, disagreeing and laughing. Then, weeks thereafter analysing and preparing for the next.

My evenings were short as I slept, exhausted but pleased. I woke excited about starting a new day and couldn't wait to start again. Perhaps a little eager to be in Rose's company, but that was my only compromise to my professionalism.

An opening party of thanks celebrated each branch, and this was where Rose, and I got to know each other better. Our professional demeanour was always clear when working. Our true selves took a while longer to emerge, though we often saw what was beneath our business hats through a mutual creativity of merchandising and decorating of the branch. I savoured the moments when Rose revealed a softness and vulnerability behind her smiling eyes and tender smile.

'Oh, Mr Wilde, I do like that,' Rose said, admiring a display I was sweating over.

I froze, anticipating more and relishing it.

'If you alter these colours, you will have more impact.'

And there it was. 'Thanks, Rose.' I answered. 'Didn't see that.'

'Men rarely do.' She gave me a saucy look, switching the colours.

I watched in awe and could not deny being smitten.

Chapter Two

The Rugby World Cup 1995 was to me – and still is some thirty years later – a pivotal event in South African history. A year after gaining independence, the majority now ruled the country. The World Cup served as a welcome sign and reward, confirming South Africa's membership among the world's nations.

Many people accepted the need for change and tried to embrace it. The past showed an impatience for this, which further hampered meaningful integration. However, as we have seen in recent politics, there were always extremist groups competing for power.

The tournament refocused the nation as the Springboks edged towards the highest accolade as the best rugby team in the world – a title that resonates with people in the southern hemisphere. The focus shifted from politics to supporting their squad against the ultimate archenemy and much respected All Blacks. Individuals from most, if not all, ethnicities are united to watch games on TV screens in pubs, and clubs are united in watching games on TV screens in pubs, clubs, and shop windows. They shared cigarettes and celebrated even the smallest victories.

On June 24th, the host nation, The Springboks, played against the powerful All Blacks. The ABs had a secret weapon named Jonah Lomu, who was intimidating and scored tries by steamrolling through players. Many locals took solace that at least we were in the final. It's not bad for a country excluded from world sports events for decades. Finding tickets for the game was the challenge, as Ellis Park stadium was a mere fifteen minutes from our hometown, Germiston. Others travelled across the region to lay their hands on the limited tickets available. The illegal market was inundated by desperate stalwarts.

Rose returned to the office the morning before the final after a long day of board meetings. 'I'm glad it's Friday, Rory. That was a tough week.'

She ducked into the staffroom to make a coffee. 'Can I get you one?'

'No, thanks. Pleased you're back,' I called after her down the passage. 'What are you up to tomorrow? Are you watching the game? Having a drink or two, maybe?'

'Nah. I've better plans than watching the telly,' she answered, sipping on her hot drink. The chills of the winter were making their presence felt early that year.

'Not sure what I'm doing.' I shrugged, fishing for her thoughts.

Rose pulled a pair of cards from her jacket pocket, fanning herself with them. 'Guess what these are,' she said, grinning from ear to ear.

'Movie tickets?'

'Try again.' She bent her knees and sprang upwards, tossing the tickets.

I stooped, picked one of them up, and read *Rugby World Cup* with smaller type saying *Cup Final.*

'What the ....' My voice shook in disbelief. 'How?'

'Because I'm amazing.' Rose fluttered her eyelids with a cheeky grin. 'No, seriously. The boss only wanted to watch England in the final, so now he doesn't want to go.'

'I can't believe it.' I gave her an enormous high-five. 'That is incredible.'

'That's not all.' Rose picked up the valuable fare. 'He gave them to me for free.'

'What's the catch?' I shot her a doubtful glance, somewhat jealous.

'Absolutely nothing.' Rose held out her arms, showing the palms of her hands. 'I swear.'

We had a fun afternoon, teasing and laughing with each other. Rose couldn't wait to share the news with everyone and enjoyed their playful envy.

Before we left for the weekend, Rose walked over to my desk and handed me a ticket.

'For me?'

'Of course. No one better than you to accompany me. Also, I wanted to thank you for your recent hard work.'

'I don't know what to say.' I stuttered, getting up from my seat, and hugged Rose awkwardly.

'Ooh, Mr Wilde,' she whispered with playful demureness.

I looked at the carpet, kicked at my heels, and asked, 'Maybe we can have a couple of drinks this evening to kick the weekend off before we go to the game?'

She tilted her head to one side, looking straight through me, and offered me her hand. 'Deal. What time?'

Excitement and nervousness overwhelmed my mind, and I have no memory of the ensuing conversation.

'Okay, so meet you there around seven.' Rose waved me goodbye and left the office.

'Yup… yes… cool. See you then.' My less the suave answer hung in the room.

We met as planned later that day. Rose was dressed in faded waist-high jeans, a white crop top that revealed little from behind, a black bomber jacket and matching combat boots. Her look is complete with a resplendent fluffy nineties' hairdo. The lights of the cocktail lounge emphasised the red in her long locks.

'So, what are we having?' I asked, offering Rose a seat at a table in the corner.

'A beer to start would be great, thank you.' Rose lit a cigarette and offered me one.

'Thanks.' I lifted the candle burning at the centre of the dinner table to light hers, then mine. 'It'll be quicker to grab those drinks ourselves.' I looked around for a server before heading for the bar. 'Won't be long.' I left her with a smile.

We spent the evening talking and getting to know each other over beers and cigarettes. An older man crooned in the corner, creating a pleasant ambience.

'This has been nice, Rory. Thanks for coming tonight.' Rose touched my hand, resting on the table whilst clutching a beer. The split-second touch caused us to readjust ourselves in our chairs. The spark was undeniable.

'No – thank you, Miss Rose,' I replied with the affectionate nickname I used when we first worked together. A mark of respect without the formality.

'It's been great catching up and chatting, but it's best we head back, given that it's such a big day tomorrow. Can't wait.' *You're such a wuss, Wilde*, I scolded myself, looking into her eyes. *What are you saying? What's she going to think…*

'For sure.' Collecting herself, Rose stood.

I escorted her through the door, my hand at the base of her spine. She looked into my soul then dug for her car keys from her tiny bag before giving me a peck on the cheek.

'I'll pick you up around eleven?' she said before pulling away. I could taste the aroma of her perfume and the warmth of her breath.

'Look forward to it. Thanks for a great evening.

June 24, 1995, started with a glorious dawn. Shards of sunlight warmed the birds into song. The dew stirred the aromatic soil with the sweetness of resonate flora – characteristic of our beloved Africa.

Too eager to eat, I drank volumes of coffee and dunked Ouma's rusks as I readied myself for the match, though I was more thrilled to see Rose. *More so than the rugby? What's happening to me?*

Diagnosis, debate and crystal ball gazing by *fundis* (experts) and commentators filled the TV, radio and newspapers – the air buzzed with anticipation.

'Right,' I said, patting my jeans pockets. 'Wallet – check. Cash – check. Gum - check.'

I stood outside and waited for an eternity for Rose to arrive, but I was told it was a mere five minutes.

'Hi.' Rose waved the tickets at me, then tucked them into her sports jacket should the weather turn. 'Let's do this, Rory Wilde.'

'You got it.' I took my chance, kissing her a good morn on the forehead and jumped into the passenger seat.

'Didn't think I'd be a wreck like this - the nerves.' Rose adjusted her seatbelt.

'I know, me too,' I answered, noticing she looked flushed. *You've still got it, Wilde,* my ego yelled at me.

'It feels as if the entire country is holding its breath, and the rest of the world is watching.' Rose shuddered from the goosebumps running up her neck. 'This is history in the making, Rorke. I can just sense it.' Rose used my full name, which she only did in rare moments.

Maybe not, my conscious disagreed with my ego. *It's the occasion, not you, dumbass.*

'Time will tell.' I heard myself tell my dear Rose how that time has flown in the blink of an eye. Our thirty-year-old selves were oblivious to the inevitable passage of time. 'Come on, let's enjoy the day no matter the result.'

We drove to a predetermined parking lot and walked the rest of the way, with the crowd of spectators thickening on our approach to the stadium. Rose gripped my elbow as we funnelled towards our allotted entrance, close to where our seats were. The noise of the audience was intoxicating, so we took our places and looked at the field. Not the best tickets, but far back enough to witness rare harmony. The singular sway of a collective happiness. Nerve-tingling roars of approval. A rise of shared disappointment and the pulsating joy of folk in song.

'So many people of all races,' Rose whispered to herself. 'Just amazing.'

'They reckon sixty thousand,' I answered. 'I bet it's more. That would be the official count.' I smiled at Rose, who nodded back. South Africa's growing corruption-tainted our humour.

The entertainment began with a troupe of people dressed in yellow, green, red, black, blue and white, each with a handful of matching-coloured balloons floating above their faces. They pranced to the middle of the field and joined, forming the country's new national flag to the eruption of the mass crowd. The fans quietened when a rumble on the distant horizon approached, a hint of fear in everyone's eyes considering recent history. Heads turned upward to see a South African Airways Boeing 747 jumbo jet with its trademark orange tail thunder close overhead in celebration.

A group of Zulu dancers dressed in traditional attire sneaked onto the field while releasing the balloons distracted the crowd. Others were adorned in wild animal clothing - every race represented. They danced to the beat of the customary hide drums, the men's chant and the shrill of the women's voices exhilarating.

The audience hushed, their excitement now one of retrospection.

Singers replaced dancers with each act, with a visual display of colour, acrobats, and smoke across the field.

Five helicopters in tight formation flew by with flags of the participating countries below. The crowd cheered.

Rose gripped my arm, a tear running down her cheek. A parachutist with a plume of fog landed in the middle, followed by the haunting World Cup anthem *World in Union,* sung by P.J. Powers and Ladysmith Black Mambazo.

The two rugby teams jogged onto the field and lined up to prepare for the national anthems. The anticipation was both audible and visual.

'Look at all the flags.' Rose tapped me, pointing to the crowd waving the colours. 'So many new South African flags.' Her voice faltered as she looked at me. The glimmer of hope in her eyes reflected that of millions of South Africans on that day.

Tears flowed when Nelson Mandela walked onto the field wearing the much-adulated captain of the team's number six Springbok jersey. It was a stroke of genius that tipped the balance in favour of the New South Africa. The crowd sang *Ole, ole, ole,* heard at European soccer matches. Now at the podium, Mandela raised his Springbok cap to the sixty-two-thousand-strong audience, who cheered and chanted Nelson, Nelson, Nelson. It was a moment when I believed Africans could rebuild this country. Rose hid her face in my shoulder. I coughed at the lump in my throat, realising that that happened this day. One for the country, another for me.

Even today, thirty years later, while I am recounting this day for you, tears stream down my face. My heart is now broken and packed with pain and a sense of loss at losing my beloved Africa.

While we were singing the national anthems, the fighter jets flew by. The future irony of hearing the New Zealand anthem for the first time stirs a fateful notion within my soul.

The game was about to start, and the crowd broke into the traditional miners' song *Shosholoza* and moved as one to the African rhythm. I will not share the match that ensued with you, for every rugby fanatic knows it all too well, and those of you who are not won't care.

Nothing wrong with that.

The all-consuming two-hour ordeal had an unfathomable result. South Africa's first World Cup, and we were the champions. Enough said.

Rose and I reacted and interacted with every action on the field. From handwringing and holding to hugging and jumping. To Rose asking for my jacket and hiding behind it.

Post-match on our journey back to the vehicles and -joy and patriotism abounded in the streets when we arrived in Germiston. Cars, taxis, and buses hooted their horns as people of every race hung out the windows, cheering and waving flags. Strangers high-fived each other and shared liquor and rolled tobacco. Music of all genres filled the sidewalks, and folks jived in celebration.

'It's been a long time since we've walked in the streets after dark,' Rose said, zipping up her jacket. 'What's happening, Rory? This is something very special.' She took my hand and bounced in high spirits along the sidewalk.

'It sure is,' I replied. 'In more ways than one.' I smiled, looking down at our clasped hands.

Rose beamed, flushed with excitement, ignoring my comment.

Throughout the night we ate and snacked, enjoying the atmosphere of nationalism and assumption.

This just might work, my internal monologue whispered.

We drove back to Rose's home, leaving the celebration for the party animals. They would continue nonstop through to the morning and into Sunday.

'Thanks for a wonderful day, Rory. Take my car if you want and pick me up later tomorrow.' She tossed me the keys.

'Sounds like a plan. Thank you for the extraordinary time. Can't believe we were so lucky to experience this.' I bent forward to peck Rose on her cheek. She turned her head and kissed me on the mouth.

'See you later, Rorke Wilde.' She tossed her red hair and spun around, and disappeared into the house.

I have no idea how I got home. My mind was elsewhere, bouncing about in joy, self-doubt and apprehension.

What a day. One that would prove to live with me for eternity.

Chapter Three

Following the Rugby World Cup, the country was on a high. Hope emerged victorious. The Rainbow Nation endured. The possibilities seemed endless.

In 1996, South Africa created the Truth and Reconciliation Commission to address the injustices of apartheid. Desmond Tutu chaired the commission, and Nelson Mandela supported it. The commission asked victims of human rights violations to share their experiences and held public hearings for some of them. Those who committed violence could testify and request amnesty to avoid legal consequences.

South Africa also ushered in a new constitution.

Rose and I had become closer, with similar ideas for business and life. Over the next couple of years, that friendship developed into a relationship of constructive collaboration, friendship and love.

With the company we worked for being sold to a corporate conglomerate had an opportunity to think about personal change. We discussed the future, our dream roles, and our goals. There was no better time to transform our lives where we could make a difference to ourselves and our family.

The Rainbow Nation was tarnishing, with the ruling party in disunity and Mandela's influence curbed. The impatient and corrupt sought personal gain and quick-fix solutions that did nothing but make matters worse as it had in Zimbabwe.

Rose and I were over being corporate cogs and fuelling financiers' pockets. The new government was making efforts to address past imbalances in the country. This meant that they would consider our skin colour, gender and background. Whether true or perceived, that was our belief, confirmed by many we knew seeking employment.

Although we knew that our most valuable commodity, time, was slipping by, we decided to wait until the right opportunity showed itself. Rushing in the wrong direction invites misfortune and thus puts our happiness at risk. As part of our search for a lifestyle change, we spent the weekends travelling with friends and family to the smaller towns of the country.

Rose's nudge in my ribs replaced the jarring sound of my alarm clock.

'Out of bed,' she said. 'It's eight o'clock and Billy's expecting us for brunch.'

'Only had a couple of hours,' I muttered from under the pillow.

'Well, I'm up. Help me load the car. Let's go.'

'Okay, okay.' I threw back the covers and tottered into the bathroom in my boxer shorts.

'Just look at the state of you. You were tossing and turning all night.' Rose giggled at my dishevelled hair and drowsy eyes.

'Couldn't sleep a wink. Nightmares churning over on what we stand to lose if we dare change our lives.' I yawned and rubbed the bristle under my chin. 'I'll just have a quick shower and some breakfast.'

'You'll have to settle for cereal. There isn't time to cook.'

'Mm,' I grumbled over the hiss of the water. 'Can't we make an excuse? Say we're not feeling well or something?' I screwed up my eyes and cringed at my girlfriend's reaction.

'I won't dignify that with a response. Besides, we've exhausted all those excuses. Now hurry.' She banged on the door.

I didn't answer, resigning to the inevitable.

'Rory.... RORY? Are you ready?'

'Won't be a minute.' I rolled my eyes and shook the water from my hair.

I haven't felt this way since my first year at boarding school. Endless work challenges and exhaustion. I relived the bullying from senior students, the turning of blind eyes by the masters, and the fear from the unrest in the country. *Maybe this isn't so bad.* I applied some perspective and, along with the refreshing shower, felt reinvigorated.

'*Rorke.*'

'Coming.'

'So is Christmas,' Rose smiled.

'Ready to go?' I said, clapping my hands.

'Heading out for the weekend, Mrs Wilde?'

'Ahh. Morning, Mrs Naidoo, just off to visit my sister-in-law in Balfour for the day.'

'Balfour, hey?' Mrs Naidoo's head bobbed back and forth behind the garden fence. 'That's a sweet little town. I have family there, too.'

'You don't say,' Rose answered, pretending it was Mrs Naidoo's first mention of the fact. 'That's very nice. Can we drop something off for you?'

'Why, thank you, Mrs Wilde. I'll be back soon.'

We watched her disappear in a flurry of colour, her sari swirling. I heard Rose say under her breath, 'It is only a few samoosas, but they love them.'

Before Rose could respond to my raised eyebrows, our neighbour bustled out the back door, clutching a brown paper bag. 'Here you are, Mrs Wilde. It's only a few samoosas, but they love them.'

Rose gave me an I-told-you-so look.

'Oh, hello, Rory. Nice day for a trip to the country.'

'Sure is, Mrs Naidoo,' I answered.

Rose waved in acknowledgement as she expelled Mr Bigglesworth, the cat and locked the front door.

Mrs Naidoo was still holding the bag. 'As I say to Mrs Wilde, it's only a few samoosas.'

I said wickedly, 'Don't tell me. They love them?'

'Well, yes, Rory, they do.' She looked a little affronted but recovered. 'It's very kind of you. Shall I give you their address?'

'Don't worry,' Rose said. 'I remember from the previous times.'

Mrs Naidoo feigned embarrassment. 'Oh, Mrs Wilde, you are such a tease. Have a lovely trip.' She waved and disappeared indoors.

'Why can't we have normal neighbours?' Rose muttered. 'This lot are not *lekker.*'(right)

'On all sides,' I agreed, pointing at each perimeter of the garden.

'How come she calls you Mrs Wilde, and I'm just Rory?'

'It's about respect.'

'Oh, thanks for that.' I smiled back at my partner.

'They are a sweet family, but never pass on a chance.' Rose laughed, climbed into the car, and donned a pair of oversized red sunglasses.

I followed suit and started the engine.

The modern architecture of Johannesburg and her luxurious suburbs gave way to flat, open fields of corn. Dust devils danced amongst the rows and jumped the single-lane country road to the next pasture. Farm stalls sold produce ranging from fresh vegetables to homemade jams and pickles. Signs hand painted in whitewash – *Konfyt and Blatjang te Koop* – beckoned passers-by.

'Why did we have to visit the family today?' I asked.

'Don't start. You know very well it's your sister's birthday,' Rose answered, tapping my hand resting on the shift gear.

'I know, but I hate visiting them.'

'No, you don't. You just aren't bothered. Will your dad be there?'

'Don't know. I haven't spoken to him in a while. Hope not. He's a bigger pain in the arse than ever,' I said, without taking my eyes off the road.

'That's true, but it's not your sister's fault.'

'Maybe.'

'Besides, once there, you always enjoy yourself, and it's good to keep in touch with your sister.'

I nodded, wondering yet again why my once best friend Billy – now my sister's husband – insisted on living in small towns where nothing ever happened.

Welcome to Balfour. The bright orange words emblazoned on the side of an enormous corn silo greeted us.

'Unbelievably, this place, just an hour from Johannesburg, feels like another world. A different dimension.'

'You are a ball of fun today, aren't you?' Rose glanced at me. 'We're here now. Let's make it a nice day for your sister, please.'

Combine harvesters and tractors replaced car dealerships and malls. A police constable napped on a park bench at the town's intersection, sheltered by a jacaranda in full purple bloom. Cape Dutch buildings, as did the many butcheries and home industries, highlighted the town's history. A single row of shops connected the town centre to the village suburbs that contained only twenty thousand residents.

'Talk about dumb names,' I scoffed under my breath. 'Balfour. Why would anyone call a town Balfour?'

'I have an idea, but I won't say.' She hid a smile. 'It's the sort of place Billy likes. He says it suits him better.'

I crossed my eyes and pulled a face.

'There's no need for that. He's married to your sister, after all.' Rose gave me a disapproving stare.

'Well, that's her fault, isn't it? I warned her years ago.' I bit on my lip.

'That may be so, but it doesn't alter the fact now, does it?'

'Suppose not.'

'Oh, come on, we'll have a lovely day.'

'You're right.' I lifted my sunglasses onto my head and smiled.

'Hey, Cara. How are you doing?' I hugged my sister and shook Billy's hand on our arrival.

'We're good, thanks. Same old, though.'

We walked across the sparse yellow grass on their lawn, pulled open the flyscreen door, and entered the house.

'So, what's new?' Cara asked, tucking her legs under her as she sat on the brown velour lounge chair.

'Nothing much. Looking to make some more changes in our lives. You know how it is,' I said.

'Don't I just,' Cara tutted.

'What does that mean?'

'You know what I'm saying. You keep turning everybody's lives upside down.' My sister tossed her blonde hair at me. 'Always thinking of nobody but yourself.'

'That's rich coming from you.'

'Oh, don't start, Rory,' Rose interjected.

Billie cringed at the interaction, pretending not to notice it as he peered at the local newspaper in his hands.

I almost continued but then silenced myself and surveyed the room. The soft feel of the floral carpet underfoot belied the loudness of the print and the clash with the furniture. When we were children growing up, we got over our disagreement, but as the years passed, our closeness diminished to one of toleration.

The day meandered through small talk and reminiscing about our days in Rhodesia and Zimbabwe as if they were different places. The evening involved the customary *braai* (BBQ) with a lager, which helped to enhance the subsequent movie-watching experience. A mutual squeeze of our hands showed it was time. Rose and I bid the hosts good night.

'We'll be leaving early morning, so don't worry about making brekkie,' Rose said.

'Oh, okay,' Cara answered. 'I'll have the kettle on for a nice cup of coffee before you leave.'

'Thanks. Night, all.'

'Night, night.'

'Glad that's over.' I collapsed on the bed in the spare room. 'We've just got so little in common.'

'But it's your sister,' Rose answered.

'Yup, but don't forget I was sent to boarding school at eleven and then left the country straight after finishing school.'

'I suppose so.' Rose brushed her hair, ready for sleep.

'Sad in a way, but it doesn't really bother me.' I puffed up my pillows and put my hands behind my head.

'It's because you don't know any different. She stroked my head. 'I'm sorry, Rory. Sleep tight.'

'Okay, guys, have a pleasant trip home. Thanks for coming.' Cara gave a false smile and waved from the driveway as we pulled away the following day.

I hooted in response, then tapped Rose's knee. 'At least that's done.' I blew through pursed lips.

She ignored me, putting her head on the window and looking out.

Our drive home took us through the centre of Balfour town. On one side of the main road, was a row of downsized and rather tired-looking national-branded retailers. Faded signs and shop fronts in dire need of repainting hunkered behind a sidewalk full of potholes and overflowing rubbish bins. Street hawkers plied their trade alongside the fresh vegetable stores with wares displayed on trestle tables.

It was the weekend, so across the road, the taxi rank was quieter than its usual hustle and bustle, transporting workers back and forth. Ragamuffin kids kicked a ball around in their bare feet and raggedy clothes. The lack of upkeep and poor maintenance of public domains suggested strained council budgets.

'So sad,' Rose said, staring out the side window of our German car. 'We should do more to help, Rory.'

My lips moved, but I had no words. Finally, I sighed and answered, 'You're right. Perhaps we can dedicate time to do what's right as part of our new beginning.'

'I think so, Rory. Let's not leave everything to others and institutions.'

In silence, we passed through once-white suburbs featuring large homes, swimming pools and affluence that stressed the gulf between the haves and the destitute. Guilt accompanied us all the way home.

'We must stop pontificating,' Rose said, staring into the distance through the parked car's windscreen when I pulled up at our home. 'Let's stop talking and start doing, or it won't happen.' She spoke to herself as much as to me.

'You're right. Maybe it's time for deadlines and timelines,' I said, looking for her reaction.

My best friend, my girlfriend, raised her eyebrows and answered. 'Rory, we need to initiate or purchase a business by year-end. What do you say?'

'Damn right. With Christmas only a few months away, we must start moving.' I gave her a thumbs up.

Rose broke into laughter. 'You're such a dweeb, Rory, but I love you for it.'

'I love you too, Miss Rose.'

We traipsed indoors.

Chapter Four

We often met after work for a meal and some personal time. A Cobblers Bar & Grill sign flashed above the entrance on the corner of an ageing building where shops serviced a well-to-do suburb of Germiston, with a butcher, greengrocer, real estate agency and a bar. A smaller, less glamorous, unlit notice next to it warned of the dangers of excess consumption and prohibited underage drinking.

The pub contained diverse cultures and political beliefs, from patrons to employees. An imitation teak bar dominated the room, surrounded by tall wooden stools with leather padding. Behind the bar, a wall of glass shelves and mirrors display alcoholic drinks. The higher the shelf, the more expensive the tipple. Large tap levers towered from the tavern's rear, showing off their famous wares, from beer to stout, lagers, and ciders. An area of polished concrete served as a dance floor or could accommodate additional seating on busy nights and special events. Advertisements covered the walls, praising popular brands, some even promoting cigarettes as stylish.

Germiston was a town famous for processing much of the world's gold at the Rand Refinery plant. This was the largest precious metals smelting complex on the planet. The countryside bore the scars of mine dumps and polluted waters from an industry with little respect for the ecosystem. Even a century later, nature's wounds were still raw and infected from the mining, her eventual recovery questionable.

An old myth spurred the building of immigrant settlements clinging to Johannesburg's slag heaps. The streets were not, in reality, paved with gold. People from struggling countries north of the border—like Mozambique, Zimbabwe, Zambia, and Namibia—came here.

Artisans, labourers, civil servants, and miners made up the Germiston community. As a conservative town, it found the changes brought by the Rainbow Nation difficult. Outdated ideals of segregation and persecution faced resistance from young people. Race, culture, and religion conflicted, and the truth was a painful revelation. That's how it ought to be.

This big, diverse village near Johannesburg expected hard work. The community had little else to brag about. Our intolerance and a fragile, fearful facade, used to hide our shortcomings and ignorance, mirrored how we saw and treated others.

I entered the Irish-styled bar after buzzing at the security gate. Guinness and Kilkenny stouts were popular choices, but Jameson and Black Bush whiskeys catered to a more refined palate. Gaelic music and South African accents blended while a thick fog of tobacco hung in the air. Laughter from small groups mingled with the clinking of glasses and the ringing of cash registers. The old-fashioned gold and red patterns on the bottle-green carpet and the surrounding noise caused me to grab the door for support. I looked around the room, hoping to see someone I knew. Cigarette smoke billowed out the doors, clinging in desperation to the ceiling to remain inside. The unmissable sweet-leather odour of cigars permeated through the air.

From the far corner, a delicate hand waved, and, adjusting to the dim light, I raised my eyebrows in acknowledgement.

'Hi, my girl. Good to see you.' Transfixed by Rose's smiling green eyes, I kissed her beloved light red hair—something I'd never got used to over the years.

'Hey there, Rory. How did your day go?'

'Tedious and drawn out. I've been waiting for this all day.'

'That's so sweet,' Rose said, caressing my cheek.

'This place is different. Not our usual kind of jaunt. Has it been here a while?' I asked.

'No, it's relatively new. I heard the town's buzzing about how great it is, so let's give it a shot.'

'The carpet tells me otherwise.'

Rose smiled. 'That's more about poor taste than time.'

'Great. You want a beer?'

'Please. Grab some smokes while you're there.'

Approaching the bar, the bartender, mid-conversation with a patron, smiled at me before excusing himself. 'Mr. Else, that is quite fascinating. I'll be right back after assisting this gentleman.'

Ignoring the bartender's attempts to leave, he told Len, 'My wife wants dinner tonight.'

'We can set up a takeaway for you once you place your order.'

'Oh no. She's going to know I was here. She thinks I'm out walking the dog.'

'We'll come up with a plan soon. This customer requires my attention. Please excuse me…?' Before the grey-haired gent could reply, Len dove toward me.

'Sorry, *boetie.' Brother*. The barperson smiled.

Mr. Else, a cigarette dangling from his chapped lips, waved from across the room; I acknowledged him with a raised finger.

'First time here?' the keep asked.

'It is. Nice place.'

'That's great to hear. I'm Len. I'm as much a part of this place as the furniture. Tell me your preferred potion, and I'll have it ready for you before you even take a seat.'

'Oh... okay... thanks.' I smiled, unsure how to respond.

'What can I get you?'

'Two lagers, please.'

'You bet. Lion, Castle, Black Label? Do you want me to bring them over to your table?' He waved across at where Rose sat.

'No, don't worry. I'll take them when you are ready. Castle will be great, thank you,' I answered. 'Can I also have a pack of Stuyvesant, please?'

'Sure, twenties or thirties?'

I showed him three fingers.

'Coming right up.' Len smiled and spun on his toes.

I waited, watching the barkeep glide over to the lever to pull the draft beer from the keg.

'Thanks. I've been dying for this.' Rose took the slim glass of lager. 'I see you've met Len?'

'Yeah. He knows his stuff.'

We watched Len in skin-tight jeans, a white blouse, and calf-length cowboy boots. His immaculate close-cropped hair stressed a beak of a nose that balanced a tiny pair of horn-rimmed spectacles.

'You two okay over there?' he asked from across the restaurant.

'Fine, thanks.' Rose lifted her half-empty glass.

Surprising to see a gay bartender in this neighbourhood, I thought.

'He's renowned in Germiston, having worked extensively in the hospitality industry,' Rose said, reading my mind, then changed the subject. 'I believe the homemade pies are amazing. Should we?'

'I reckon.' My eyes lit up at the sound of food.

'Chicken or beef?'

The food arrived on a food trolley, served in two large ceramic pots with handles on either side by the waitress. 'Hi, my name is Sheila. Can I bring you anything else?' she asked without looking at us, wiping the tabletop before she placed the plates.

'No. We're all good, thanks,' we said in unison.

Rose showed the proper way to eat the pies by flipping the top of the pastry onto her plate. I followed suit, burning my hand on the steam from the meat and gravy inside. 'Now pour the contents onto the crust. Delish.' Rose held a snippet on the end of her fork. 'Oops, we forgot the peri peri sauce.' The spicy chilli in it adds a bite.

I lifted two fingers at Len behind the bar for more beer.

'Here we are folks, enjoy.'

After our meal, we chatted and took in the atmosphere of Cobblers. My fascination was in watching people, seeing what triggered behaviours and surmising why. It's a pastime I've done since I was a child, so I can now read the room and body language.

'This place is just like this song' I swayed my glass in time to Billy Joel's *Piano Man* playing on the jukebox.

Sing us a song, you're the piano man
Sing us a song tonight
Well, we're all in the mood for a melody
And you've got us feelin' all right

Businesspeople chatted at the bar, some intent with a furrowed brow, others flushed and snorting in merriment. Families took to the table and chairs, deciding on what to eat and drink. Teenagers played at the dartboard in the far corner, self-conscious as they explored the legal age of socialising. The outside world shut off for the time being as punters interacted with one another, with the music and their insecurities.

'It's lovely, Rory. I've always wanted one of these places.'

'What do you mean, one of these places?' I looked at her in horror.

'You know. A pub, restaurant.' Rose opened her hands at the room to me in explanation.

'You've got to be kidding?' I answered. 'I've always hated these things, even as a kid. Discos were a nightmare.' I smiled at her. 'I've always kept away from nightclubs, busy bars, concerts. Just too many people where the music's so loud you can't hear yourself think.'

'Oh, Rory. You're such a loner. If only others knew.' Rose laughed.

I raised my eyebrows and my drink, grinning.

'Well, I can dream, can't I? Come on, let's have a dance.' Rose pulled me by the hands to the dance floor. We swayed to the music, but my mind pondered Rose's wish to own something in hospitality. *You'll need to step up, Wilde, if you hope to keep this lady,* I ridiculed myself as I watched Rose move to the music – happy. *You cannot be an old fart in your thirties. You've taken risks before, dumbass - emigrating and changing jobs. The reward for getting this right is greater than ever. Foreverness.* Decision made; my focus returned to enjoying ourselves.

'You, okay? You look a little distracted.' She wrapped her arms around me as we shuffled to a slower song.

'I'm good... No, I am more than that,' I answered. 'Because of you.'

Rose put her head on my chest and whispered, 'Thank you. Me too.'

Life got even better.

We refreshed our drinks before returning to our table. Jess and his partner turned up and joined us for a minute before hitting the dance floor.

'He's such a character,' I said about her brother.

She snorted and agreed. 'A clown at times, though.'

'You know, it's a long weekend. Why don't we head out to Sun City tomorrow? Spend the night gambling. My treat.' I couldn't believe the words coming from my mouth. *You've flipped, Wilde. This lady is making you crazy, but I love it.* My internal dialogue chastised me.

'I would love that.' Rose flung her arms around my neck and kissed me. 'It's not like you to be so spontaneous, Mr Rorke, but I like it.'

'I know, but I feel we deserve it,' I answered as convincingly as I could.

'This is so exciting. I enjoy going to Sun City,' Rose said the next day, packing her second despite a pre-agreed single overnight case. 'Just in case.' She shot me another of her infamous, wide-eyed, don't-mess-with-me look.

'Maybe I'll put a change of underwear in with your lot. What do you think?' I gave her a cheeky smile, waving my toothbrush. 'I'll shove this in my pocket.'

'Can we at least try to fit in? The place is posh?' She grabbed it from me and deposited it in a toiletry bag. 'You're such a pleb sometimes, Rorke Wilde,' she snickered to herself, then began mumbling away about not forgetting this or that.

'It's why you love me.'

'Don't push it.' She placed her hands on her hips and narrowed her eyes. 'You ready?'

'Just about. I'll load the car and check everyone is okay and everything is secure.'

'Great. I made sandwiches and got Cokes for the drive.' Rose produced yet another suitcase, this time a cooler bag.

'Hope it all fits in the boot. We're only going for the night, I teased.

'Whatever *poepal*.' Afrikaans slang for a likeable but foolish person. 'Thanks for helping us out, Ouma,' Rose called and waved to her mother.

'You're welcome,' she said, waving from the steps. 'Enjoy yourselves.'

'Bye Ouma. Will bring you a pressy.'

'I've already got her list,' I whispered to Rose in the car.

'Of course you have. That's Ouma for you. She's so sweet.'

After a three-hour trip, we booked into the chalet just outside of Sun City, stopping off along the way to savour the scenery. A one-night stay in the resort would have been ten times the price we were paying for a decent self-catering facility, which came with a pool. The savings made the short drive to and from the entertainment worthwhile. We could spend more time on ourselves at the casino and go to multiple restaurants and live shows.

Rose did a quick inspection before opening her arms in delight. 'This is perfect. Much better than I was expecting for the price.'

'Yeah, not bad at all.' I threw the luggage onto the closest bed. 'A quick shower, then I reckon we head for Sun City.'

'Speak for yourself. I need a bit of time to get ready, mister,' Rose said, unzipping the bags. 'We're styling tonight. Take a swim if you want in the meantime.'

'Don't feel like it I'll wait outside in the sun until you're ready.'

'Are you sure you're okay, Rory?' Rose looked into my eyes.

I shrugged and shook my head, turning my mouth downward. 'I'm good.'

We dined at the best seafood restaurant we could get into. Sublime African Portuguese, spiced, flame-cooked fare. The platter we ordered included Cape Rock lobster, large Mozambique prawns, fresh Knysna oysters, Saldanha Bay mussels, and the unequalled, sweetish Kingklip white fish.

Rose used her winnings from the slot machines to pay for an extravagant live show, complete with fancy drinks and well-dressed servers. We watched professional gamblers puffing on cigars and pipes in front of whirling roulette wheels and the desperate opportunists vying for an elusive win on the card tables to turn their world around.

Despite my enjoyment of the lavish, I observed another level of human degradation I had not witnessed before. The casino was a step up from the average tavern or drinking house we frequented. The gambler's plight was obvious, their fight intense, their flight predictable.

'Wow, what a night.' Rose slumped into a chair outside the casino, away from all the commotion.

'Amazing, but exhausting.' I joined her. 'Its hard work being pampered.'

'Do you know what I fancy right now?' she asked.

I bounced my eyebrows at her.

'Behave yourself, Rory Wilde.' She gave a small grin. 'A swim in that pool at the motel. To relax and chill out.'

'I'm all for it.' I paused. 'Now?'

'Yup, let's go.'

We arrived back at our room in the early hours. All was quiet. Other tenants slept or gambled.

'Oh, shit, I forgot my costume.' I rummaged through my backpack.

'Well, there's only one thing to do then,' Rose said, clad in a towel. 'Last one in makes the coffee in the morning.' With that, the towel dropped, and she streaked outside and dived into the pool. 'Ooh, it's lovely. Come on, Rory.' She bobbed in the water.

'What the hell?' I ripped off my shorts and did the same.

Before we had time to enjoy the moment, we heard the approaching sound of a vehicle.

'Sshh. What's that?' Rose held a finger to her lips. 'Is it coming here?'

'Not sure, but it's more than one car.' I peeped over the edge of the pool to see two sets of car headlights arriving at the motel.

'Don't move. Hopefully, they won't even notice.' Rose clung to me, both of us snickering like children.

We could hear loud voices and laughter with the engines turned off, making me take another surreptitious peek. 'They're not going inside,' I whispered in Rose's ear.

A short look of shock crossed her face as the lights in the pool were turned on. A shriek of laughter followed her expression as she hauled herself from the water, flung her towel around herself and disappeared into the motel room. Somewhat slower to react, I hightailed it to the room to the cheers and wolf whistles of the new arrivals.

Following my usual routine, I woke up at dawn and left the room to avoid disturbing Rose. After a brisk walk, enjoying the countryside,

I woke her a few hours later, switching on the kettle to make her a coffee.

'Hey, Rory.' She smiled without opening her eyes.

'Morning.' I placed the mug on her side of the bed. 'Time to make a move. We have to be out of here before eleven o'clock. Gives us an hour.'

'I have a better way to spend that time,' Rose purred, stretching under the sheet.

'Don't tempt me, but we can't.' I stroked the hair from her face. 'Put on something nice, and I'll take you for a *laanie* (posh) breakfast.'

'Sounds delicious.' She gave me a suspicious look before turning her head to the window when we heard a loud noise outside and someone cursing. 'Wonder what's going on?'

I jumped to the closed curtain and peeked outdoors. 'Nothing. Just the garden service doing their job.' I lied.

Rose went to the bathroom to shower and change, uncertain about my nervous disposition.

After booking out of the chalet, we climbed into the car and headed towards Sun City for breakfast – or brunch.

'Which restaurant are we going to?' Rose asked, enjoying the scenery out the window.

'I'm sure we'll find a decent takeaway there.'

Rose did not respond; instead, she rested her head on the glass.

We parked and entered the resort, where I walked Rose and me to a hotel terrace. 'Where do you want to sit?' she asked.

'Over there.' I gestured towards an open Land Rover with couples seated in the back.

'What are you playing at, Rory?' Rose said, following with reluctance.

I smiled and took her hand. With the other, I gave the driver our tickets.

'Great, we are all set to go, guys.' He grinned at us all. 'Fasten your seatbelts. We'll be there in about an hour, depending on what we see on our way.'

Rose's eyes brightened in delight. 'Oh, Rory, you're taking us on a game drive? How sweet.' She put an arm through mine and laid her head on my shoulder. 'I thought you were up to something.'

The Pilanesberg National Park is a six-hundred square kilometre wildlife reserve where tourists can see the most iconic animals and enjoy the African savannah. Nothing more than dirt roads in four-wheel drive vehicles. The visitors at one with the countryside.

'We've got one of the big five left to see.' Rose counted on her fingers after several hours' game viewing. 'Lions, rhino, buffalo, and that beautiful herd of elephant. Just the leopard left.' A glimpse of colour in the distance ahead of our Land Rover distracted Rose's attention. 'What is that?'

'Not sure,' I lied again.

'Oh, my word.' Rose held her hands to her face. 'You are kidding me, Rory Wilde.'

The vehicle pulled alongside the three hot air balloons tethered to the ground by rope. They guided us to the central airship and requested that we climb the short ladder into the basket.

'You are shitting me.' Rose's eyes filled. 'Oh, I love you, Rory' she hugged me, then took the hand of the person flying the balloon.

'Welcome aboard,' he said. 'I am your aeronaut today. Enjoy.'

Within a few minutes after our safety training, we were lifted into the wide African sky. The views were beyond stunning, and a reality set in of our inconsequence as a species. With just the roar of the burner above, the silence was absolute, apart from the odd, inquisitive bird who flew close.

'Would you like to take control?' our tour operator asked Rose, who jumped at the opportunity. After a while, he announced it was time to return to earth and pointed to the tiny collection of vehicles we had left behind.

Rose turned towards me to find me on my knee with a ring in one hand. 'Will you do the honour of marrying me?' I asked. Her answer seemed to take forever as she digested what was happening above the planet.

'Yes, yes, yes, Rory,' she cried through tears of joy. 'But of course.'

'Fantastic', the aeronaut chirped in, taking paperwork from his flying jacket. 'This is where I come in.' He handed Rose a Bible.

'What's going on?' Rose asked.

'He's marrying us now,' I answered. 'If you're not ready or prefer to do this differently, we can stop.'

Tears streamed down each of our faces.

'You're crazy, do you know that?' Rose laughed.

'You make me crazy. I used to be quite normal before I met you, or so I thought.' I said, hugging her.

Chapter Five

The aeronaut, now our marriage officer, performed a brief ceremony and witnessed our legal vows, then said in a most official tone.

'My name is…'

What was that? I didn't catch his name. My thoughts interrupted my concentration.

He paused, gave me a serious look, then continued: '…and I am duly authorised by law to solemnise marriages according to law and to officiate at your marriage today.' He added with all pomp and ceremony: 'I take this opportunity to wish you both much happiness in your future lives together.' Prompting us for the next part.

'I, Rorke, take you, Rose, to be my…' I watched my soon-to-be wife smile and cry all at once as I made my vows.

'I, Rose, take you, Rorke, to be my…'

My heart filled with the same mixed emotions. A joy so powerful it brought tears to us both. The words were lost on me again.

Our matrimonial pledges were identical without genre, tradition or prejudice.

We kissed before Rose pulled away and asked. 'Is that it? Are we married?' She glowed like I had never seen before.

'Technically, no.' The flyer winked. 'As soon as we land, you will sign your marriage certificate and two witnesses. Then you'll be officially married.' He smiled, offering us a handshake. 'Congratulations. I wish you everything you dream of.' He put his papers away and returned to operating the balloon.

Mr and Mrs Wilde leaned against the wicker basket, embracing while we admired Africa's resplendent scenery. Mother Nature's masterpiece. Wide open spaces and distant horizons, where the Kalahari Desert transformed into savannah veld. A bounty of different thorn trees and shrubs where the north-facing slopes of the hills were dryer from longer exposure to an unforgiving sun.

Africa's ability to instil humility stems from our insignificance in the universe. I was reminded of my childhood days in the nineteen sixties, when I spent most of my time playing in the African bush. Where I would leave home before sunrise and only return at sunset. I ate what I found in the flora, rested in the arms of giant baobab trees, and drank water from rivers—contracting malaria because we did not consider taking quinine and catching bilharzia from the freshwater – a parasitic worm that enters the bloodstream through the skin. Infection leads to symptoms like rashes, itchy skin, fever, chills, cough, headache, stomach pain and muscle aches. I learnt to respect all the wild animals, keeping my distance no matter how cute they were whilst avoiding the poisonous at all costs. And feeling a contentment I'd experienced nowhere else in my travels.

I hear parents howling in protest and cringing at the very idea.

Was it right or wrong? I believe it to be a bit of both. Parenting left a lot to be desired, but is that any different today?

What are the long-term health issues of such an upbringing? I suspect little, as modern immune systems seem weaker, and maybe that's why Boomers live long.

My background created a means of survival against all aggressors. Can we say the same now?

Both generations have their attributes and challenges. Neither is better nor worse. Just different.

'Brace yourself, newlyweds.' Our aeronaut broke our silent musings. 'We are heading back to our base.'

We descended to the applause of the staff running the hot air ballooning business and a handful of people preparing for their turn. We signed our marriage certificate along with witnesses on disembarking, and then we were whisked away.

'This way, please,' the aeronaut who married us said. 'There you go.' He waved his arms. 'Enjoy yourselves. Take your time, and there is no rush.'

On the edge of the hill where we stood was a wooden table covered in a white cloth, holding two glasses of Buck's fizz - orange juice and champagne. From our vantage point, the view was how nature intended – not a hint of human existence. Wild animals roamed beneath, monkeys played in the surrounding trees, and birds soared above.

We sat in the two chairs provided, enjoying the solitude when a server placed a tiered serving dish full of appetisers before us.

'So excited.' Rose clinked our glasses together.

'Not more than me. I was worried you wouldn't like to get married this way.' I said, dishing us each a plate of the snacks. 'We can always do it again differently if you prefer.'

'No way. This is amazing, Rory. You make me incredibly happy.'

We whiled away the hours watching the balloons take off with their new passengers. Most of them were tourists from abroad. Then, when time ran out, we climbed onto the rear of the Land Rover and headed back to Sun City.

'We should stay another night,' Rose suggested on our arrival.

'Not a chance. We can't afford it.' I unlocked our car.

'That was a short honeymoon if ever I saw one.' My new wife threw me a look of daggers.

'We've got to get back. Ouma is expecting us and –'

'I get it, Rory. I get it,' Rose said, getting into the passenger seat.

'I'm sorry if I upset you.'

'I'm not upset. I just don't want this to end so soon.' Rose held my hand.

'I'll make it up to you, I promise,' I said, easing the car onto the road to Johannesburg.

Rose napped for most of the hour-long trip home, waking when we hit the traffic in the city. 'Back to this shithole,' Rose said, her mouth twisted down in disgust.

'Feel more refreshed after your sleep?' I asked her.

'I do, actually.' She sat upright and started sorting out her hair. 'Better dress the part when we tell Ouma and the rest of the family our news.' Rose turned the sun visor down to look in the mirror. 'I wonder how she'll take it?'

We travelled south until we got to the Germiston turnoff and arrived at our destination a few minutes later.

Rose looked at me, confused. 'Why are we stopping here at Cobblers?' She asked. 'Do you need a drink before we face everybody at home?'

'Just a quick one. What do you say?'

'Okay, but you're getting weird again, mister. What are you up to?'

I ignored her, exited the car, and held the pub door open.

'SURPRISE.'

Rose jumped from the shock of the cheer from the family hiding inside. Len, the barperson, hung a sign outside the gate before shutting it.

Closed

Private Event

'Again, Rorke Wilde?' Rose looked at me in disbelief. 'Again?' She opened her arms to the crowd, walking up to Ouma, her mother, holding a large helium balloon with Congratulations written on it. 'You knew all the time?'

'I sure did, my Rose,' Ouma said, embracing her to more applause.

Brother Jess took us to the little stage where the entertainment played and asked for everyone's attention. 'Friends and family. I present the bride and groom.' He lifted his glass, eyes brimming with pride. 'To Rose and Rory Wilde.' The clan repeated the toast.

Food of every description filled the tables in the restaurant. Portuguese peri peri prawns. The delicate spices of Indian Biryani. American ribs, sausage rolls and finger snacks. Kids chased each other around the restaurant while close and distant families caught up with one another.

The atmosphere was a joy to behold. A memory we shall remember forever. My delight heightened when I saw my African Rose so happy with those she loved. As was my want, I sat back and observed, with the niggle of doubt raising the question: *For how long?*

The festivities continued until late into the evening, reaching their peak with the entrance of a five-tier wedding cake, eliciting oohs and ahs from the attendees. Reducing Rose and me to tears.

My heart was full of this wonderful person. She showed me countless places I would never have dared to go, and there are still many more I am willing to explore with her. How lucky was I? How blessed am I three decades later?

Chapter Six

The pub became a cherished getaway from our daily routines.

'Rorke, we need to talk,' Rose said on a quiet Sunday evening as we enjoyed our sundowners there.

My heart missed a beat. She never called me by my full name unless I was in trouble or something more serious was going on. 'Is everything all right?'

She smiled. 'I've been thinking.'

'Sounds ominous. What's up?' I asked, putting down my Guinness stout and wiping away my froth moustache.

'I love this place. What say you we give it a go?' Rose asked, waiting for my reaction.

'Are you bringing up that one again - opening a pub?' My heart turned cold at the idea.

'No. Making an offer on Cobblers Bar & Grill. I hear the owners are thinking of selling.'

'Maybe because they're not doing well?' I asked with a touch of sarcasm.

'Could be, but I believe they want to return to the UK.'

I examined our surroundings with a new perspective. An older man sat reading a newspaper, sipping a brandy and Coke. A couple watched the races on the television, their faces reflecting that their horse of choice was not performing as hoped. Len's replacement for the day polished glasses before loading them onto shelves, his eyes darting around the bar to see if anyone needed a refill.

'What do you say, Rory? Stop ignoring me.'

'Don't know. Haven't thought about it.' It was all I had – I was still trying to find a reasonable objection.

'It's a chance to leave corporate life and start something new. We work well together.' Rose held my arm, her gaze searching mine. 'This may be the opportunity we need.'

I couldn't resist those eyes, nor could I deny the excitement of running our own business. 'No harm in talking to the owners, I guess.'

'Great. We're meeting with them tomorrow for lunch.'

'Of course we are.' I gave Rose a playful nudge.

'It was just a thought, Rory Wilde.'

The change I waited for may have arrived. With the family settled. This was our moment – my chance to do something different. To challenge my norm. The voice inside my head deliberated with my commonsense. 'Do you know what, Rose Wilde? Let's do it. If that is what you want.'

'Are you serious?'

'Fuck them all. We'll do it for us.' I spread my arms across the barroom.

'Fantastic, but you must want to do it as well.' Rose clapped, laughing aloud. 'I'm so excited.'

'What have we got to lose? Apart from everything.' I widened my eyes in jest. My gut told me otherwise, but the heart won over. *Never a truer word spoken in jest*, I chastised myself.

A Scotsman, an Irishman and two South Africans walked into a pub.

They had little in common.

The Gaelic stalwarts hailed from a generation we did not understand. Boomers, by all accounts. Nothing wrong with that. Their cultures were worlds apart, just as our home countries were at the opposite ends of the globe.

'So, you kids think you want to buy Cobblers then?' the barrel-chested Scotsman pointed to a table.

'We are considering a few options, Granddad.' Rose took a seat, not backing down from his ageist insinuation.

'You got a fiery one there, laddie.' His partner, the lanky Irishman, grinned at me but changed tack when he saw Rose's disapproving look.

'I do not own her,' I stated. 'She tolerates me and controls both the money and the intelligence.'

'You don't need to build me up, Rory.' With her chin on her hands and elbows on the table, Rose reassured everyone, 'I got this.'

'She's up tae high doh.' The Scottish owner whispered under his breath, surprised at how riled Rose was. Neither of us understood a word he uttered.

The two partners sat silently in unison, scanning the room for any prying eyes.

'What can I get you guys?' Len broke the silence, and small talk ensued.

Then Rose brought the meeting to order. 'So, gentleman. Let's get down to it. How much and when?'

'Yay dinnee like to blather – *you don't tolerate bullshit* – Rose Wilde. I like that.' The Scotsman tilted his head towards his friend. 'Take no notice of the auld skinny malinky, longlegs Irish bastard and me. We dinnee mean no disrespect. Aye, we are a pair of *crabbit* (grumpy) auld boys. Sorry?' His Scottish lilt was soft. *'Whit's fur ye'll no go by ye!'* What happens will happen. 'But let us see if we can work out a plan for the sale of our baby, Cobblers.'

'You are right, my highland eejit. I too apologise.' The other's Irish brogue differed from that of the Wilde family I had met in Northern Ireland.

'Sounds good to me, gents. Now, can I have the price and timeline?' Rose recognised the tactics and was the sharper tool.

'Well, it all depends?' Scotty eased a rounded cheek off his chair, his three chins set with intent. 'We're not willing to let go of everything inside.'

'I tell you what,' Rose said. 'Give me a list and a value for fixtures and fittings. Understand that goodwill affects the selling price. I expect to get just that if I'm paying for goodwill.'

'Aye. We can do that,' they said in chorus.

'Great. Let me have it within a week, or there's no deal.' Rose stood to leave.

'A week is not long enough,' Paddy spluttered, his facial hair, wiry fringe, and lengthy neck matching his Irish Greyhound physique. 'We need –'

Rose interrupted. 'I'm not willing to negotiate or participate in a bidding war. We have the cash. We are ready to go.' She leaned forward and looked at their gaping-mouthed faces in the eye. 'Boys. Choose who you want to sell to. This is no game.'

I jumped to my feet and said to the owners. 'Put that in your pipes, gentlemen. I presume you will pick up the tab?' I swigged the last of my beer and gave them a silent toast with the empty glass before placing it on the table. The two men sat motionless.

We walked away, maintaining our composure until we reached our vehicle.

'You were amazing.' I said to Rose, hitting the steering wheel with open hands and whooping in delight.

'It's all about knowing your audience.' She blew the nails on her one hand and polished them on her shirt in fake self-adulation.

'Oh, excuse me.' I high-fived her and started the car for home.

A week later, we reconvened for another meeting.

'How's the *craic*?' Paddy said, getting to his feet when we arrived. 'How are you doing?' he translated for our benefit.

Scotty did the same, offering his hand in greeting. 'Thanks for joining us here.' He referred to the restaurant where the negotiation was to be held. 'Just thought some neutral ground would be beneficial. The rumours have already started in the pub.' He smiled, showing us our places.

'Rumours?' Rose asked.

'Aye,' the two responded in unison.

'The words out with the Cobbler lads that you guys are interested in buying,' Paddy added.

'Good idea. Germiston is a small town.' Rose took her seat.

'Can I get you two a drink?' Paddy asked.

'Let's keep the drinks for after business.' Rose smiled at the Celtic men across the table. 'We can then either celebrate our success or drown our sorrows.'

'Fair enough. Let's look lively then and get this done.' Scotty opened his hands in invitation.

'Sounds good,' Rose said. 'Well, we know the price you are asking, the value of the fixtures and an estimate of the stock. Which leaves the goodwill.' She paused for dramatic effect. 'How did you come up with that amount?'

'Feek. Where do we start?' Paddy used the more polite Irish version of the F-word. 'It's been a long, hard slog from when we opened two years ago.'

Scotty joined in, saying. 'That's true, and the goodwill doesn't recuperate all that we have spent getting it where it is today.'

'It has been difficult, but now it is time we sold. Now it is time for us to sell up and return to our homes in Ireland and Scotland,' Paddy added.

'Och aye, that is the plain truth.' The Scottish dialect was thick from his partner.

Rose raised a finger to get a word in. 'It is not for us to help you recoup your expenses but to pay a fair rate for what the business is worth. As I've said before, we are cash buyers and can move within days. We request a ten percent discount and will keep an additional twenty percent for a month in case of issues.'

The table quieted, digesting the offer.

Scotty started to say something when Paddy gripped his shoulder and spoke. 'Five per cent. For both.'

Rose and I looked at each other, and then she answered them. 'We'll need some privacy to discuss that, so we'll head to the cocktail lounge. If you wouldn't mind.'

'Haste ye back.' Return soon. Scotty tried to fold his arms across his chest, but his pot belly got in the way.

We watched our sellers from a distance as we chatted about what changes we would make to the drinking establishment, excited by the opportunity. They snuck glances when they thought we could not see. Their body language told us what we had already expected. At one point, it appeared they were bickering, then later sulking with each other.

'Let them sweat for a while longer,' Rose said with a cheeky grin. 'They're getting a taste of their own medicine.'

I lifted my glass of wine. 'Cheers, Miss Rose.' My role was just to be there – a witness to my wife's impressive skills in emotional intelligence and negotiation. Something that had benefitted us in the past did now in the present, and no doubt would in the future. An ability to see and seize upon an opportunity.

At that moment, the sight of two uncertain publicans approaching our retreat caught our attention as they made their way towards us through the hazy, smoke-filled room.

'Bloody hell. Looks like the Laurel and Hardy show,' I muttered from behind my glass.

Rose wiped her mouth with a napkin after almost choking on her drink. 'Hello, gents. What can we do for you?'

Paddy opened his lips, his Adam's apple running up and down his long neck, his John Lennon round glasses steaming up. 'We've been.... thinking.' He stuttered over his words. 'Deciding. We... umm...'

'*Haud yer weesht,*' Scotty interrupted and translated his Scottish outburst, seeing our confused expressions. 'Be quiet.' He put a hand on his friend's forearm. 'Yer lookin' a bit *peely wally*. Do you need to sit?' He turned to us, showing his friend looked frail.

'Go away out of that. I'm fine.' Paddy answered.

'I wasn't joking, mate.' Scotty said, shrugging.

'Sorry to interrupt you, gentleman, but is there a point to this?' Rose refocused the bickering couple.

Paddy persevered, talking over his pal. 'We'd like to make you a counteroffer.'

Pretending to show annoyance by the silence that followed, Rose interjected. 'Which is?'

They glanced at one another.

'Spit it out, boys.'

'Five per cent discount and paid in full upfront.'

Rose took her time looking each of them up and down as they stood awkwardly in front of us.

'That's worse than your previous offer. Why would this appeal to me in any way? I tell you what, Paddy and Scotty. What say you we have those drinks now? Rory and I will get back to you in the morning?'

For the briefest moment, they looked at her, aghast, then broke into smiles.

'Sounds good.' Scotty answered.

'That it does. We're close to making the deal.' Paddy agreed, trying to squeeze out a little hope that we were interested.

After a couple more drinks and chatting, Rose asked, 'I know you guys want to return home overseas, but why are you selling Cobblers?'

'To be honest, we are exhausted and don't have the time to run the place and go to work,' Scotty said with a slight slur.

'It doesn't make enough to support our families,' Paddy said, joining in. 'Besides the long hours, the customers can be very demanding and high maintenance.'

Rose sat back with a faint smile on her lips, listening to the two present her with more ammunition for when we got to her final offer.

'I've been in South Africa for quite a few years and do not like where it is heading now,' Paddy said, his accent thickening with each swig of Irish whiskey. 'Since elections, this country has gone downhill.'

The two men launched into a negative diatribe, running South Africa down until Rose declared it was time for us to leave. 'Thanks for your time, gents.' She ducked an attempt at being hugged and put her hands through my arms. 'You ready, Rory?'

'Sure am,' I said. 'Thanks for meeting with us and for the drinks.' I shook their hands.

'Goodnight.' Rose gave them a wave, then stopped and turned towards them.

'Last offer for Cobblers Bar and Grill.' She named her new, lower amount. 'This includes a ten per cent discount paid in full upfront when we get the keys, but excludes the stock, which we will count together and agree on a value.' She didn't wait for them to answer as they stood open-mouthed. 'Offer ends a week from today,' Rose called over her shoulder as we departed.

We sat in silence in the taxi, reliving the evening to glean all we could from the meeting, working out what we would need to do financially and literally to adapt to being self-sufficient business owners. Should it fail, there was no funded social security system to fall back on. We stood to lose everything, even our home, should we not pay our mortgage, lights, etc.

I squeezed Rose's hand. 'Scary but exciting, hey?'

'If anyone can make a go of that business, it is us. Germiston needs a nice place for people to relax and let their hair down,' she answered. 'Especially these days.'

'Absolutely. That was a fun evening. Those two weren't the same cocky shits we've come to know at Cobblers.'

'You got that right.' Rose laughed. 'They're bigshots when they're with their mates and full of liquor. Let's see if our plan worked.'

'Our plan?' I asked. 'You smashed it all on your own. Excellent job. Proud of you.'

We stayed away from the bar and maintained silence as the days ticked by.

'Well, it's day seven, and there is still nothing,' I said when the deadline ended. 'Maybe they've had second thoughts.'

'No. I think if that was the case, they would have been in touch.' Rose answered, drawing the curtains for the evening. 'Reckon they'll wait until the last minute, hoping we'll crack first. I got news for them.'

'Yup....' Rose's phone cut me short before I could finish my sentence. Cobblers Bar and Grill flashed on the screen.

'Here we go, Rory.' She blew me a kiss before answering. 'Rose Wilde speaking.'

Her eyes wandered through the room as she listened, adding sounds of encouragement. 'I see. So, what's the bottom line, boys? Uh, huh? Okay, we'll give you another twenty-four, then the offer is off the table.' She turned her mobile off and looked across at me. 'They're buying time. Maybe checking out other offers.'

'Glad you gave them a final deadline – otherwise, this could drag on forever.'

'Thanks, Rory. Let's see what tomorrow brings. I'll call them if I don't hear from them by lunchtime.' Rose paused. 'Actually, let's have lunch at Cobblers tomorrow. Put the pressure on.'

She smiled and turned her attention to the television to relax for the night.

We walked into Cobblers as per the plan the next day. The usual crowd was in, and there was an audible hush upon our arrival from certain parties.

Len welcomed us and gave Sheila our food order before pouring us a couple of sodas and bringing them to our table. 'Here you go, folks. Good to see you again,' he said, wiping the table with his cloth. He stopped, looked about the room over his glasses, and then stooped towards us. 'Just an FYI. Scotty and Paddy are hiding out the back. They hightailed it when they saw you guys pull up.' Len giggled and turned red. 'Loving this. I hope you buy the place. It so needs trendier owners.' He swished away in delight.

'Looks like the proverbial is hitting the fan, Miss Rose.'

'Too right, Rory, exactly what we want. The unpredictability of emotion.'

We took our time eating lunch and ordered coffees to go once we had finished. On the ride home, Rose indicated she would call Scotty when we arrived. 'Enough is enough. It's time to bring this standoff to an end.'

'Sounds good to me.'

Before I parked the car, Rose was already dialling on her cell phone. 'Hi, Scotty. Please call me back when you get this message.' She held the bridge of her nose. 'I'll give him an hour, then will text them both.'

Sixty minutes later, Rose sent a text:

Hi, gents. We are withdrawing our offer to purchase Cobblers Bar & Grill. We cannot wait any longer and need to move on. Thanks, Rose Wilde.

Within a few seconds, Rose's mobile rang. 'That'll be them.' She lifted it to her ear. 'Hi, Scotty. Long time no hear. … That's all right. What have you got? … Great news. … Yup, we can meet you there. Let me know when.' Rose smiled at me with a thumbs-up. 'Sounds awesome. Drinks it is Friday evening. Take care.' She put the phone down and jumped into my arms. 'We are soon to be the owners of a pub.' She whooped with excitement.

'That's amazing. Excellent job,' I responded.

'Celebratory drinks are on Friday after we've been to the lawyers with them.'

'So, it's all go, then. There's some work to do.' I thought out aloud.

'Finance, plans, resign from our jobs. There will be no going back.' I looked at Rose with raised eyebrows.

'Bring it on, Rory. This is our chance to make the changes we spoke about.' Her eyes sparkled. 'This is for us.'

'Damn right, it is. Let's get those resignation letters typed up.' I kissed her on the top of her head as we hugged.

'To us,' I toasted that evening.

'To you and me,' Rose replied. 'I know this is tough for you, Rory. We're going to be all right.'

'I was a little anxious, but now that we've committed, I'm really looking forward to the challenge.' My stomach was in a knot. My safe space was challenged. Not a terrible thing.

Chapter Seven

We studied how our employees and customers interacted at Cobblers while working our notice periods to learn what worked and what did not. We established the basics of running a business and talked about desires and enhancements, feeling we were ignoring a large part of the community. Our goal was to create a fun and inclusive space for everyone, regardless of consumption, despite what the previous owner may have intended. Rose and I sculpted our model into four pillars - ambience, food, drinks and entertainment.

We continued to frequent the establishment, not revealing that we had purchased the business until the official handover.

December the first marked the big event. We arranged a soft week-long takeover to meet the staff and customers before taking charge.

'Right, Mr Wilde. Are you ready for today?' Rose asked, dressed up for our first day at the bar.

'Sure am. A tad nervous. How about you?'

'Terrified but excited. This week is about getting acquainted with everything and everyone. It's the one after that is scary.' Rose pulled her lips to one side in concern.

'We couldn't have chosen a tougher time. Christmas is going to be crazy busy,' I said, grabbing the car keys. 'Come on, let's get this show on the road.'

'Right behind you, mister.'

'Tonight, I will teach you four of our top cocktails.' Len beamed at Rose and me, loving the opportunity to impart his expertise.

'Be gentle with us, Len. This is only our third day on the job.' Rose laughed. 'Though I can't wait. I just love cocktails.' She gave me a nudge.

'She sure does,' I answered. 'More of a beer or wine fan myself.'

'We'll soon change that.' Len shot me a mischievous look. 'What wine takes your fancy?'

'I like a Sauvignon Blanc.'

'Len?' Rose said, to refocus him.

'Oh, right.' Len grinned at his audience, lifting a bottle. 'Amarula is a local cream liqueur. Its key ingredients are sugar, cream, and the fruit of the African marula tree, nicknamed the elephant tree or marriage tree. He paused for effect. 'Right.' He held up two cocktail glasses in his other hand. 'The first one is the easiest to make and the most popular around here.' He paused for dramatic effect. 'The Springbok shot, with its green and gold colours, is a beloved and patriotic South African drink inspired by the national rugby. This minty and smooth shot mixes Amarula, made from sugar, cream and the Marula fruit, with crème de menthe, a sweet mint-flavoured liqueur.' Len filled the glasses and passed them to us.

'Mm.' Rose's eyes sparkled. 'Always enjoy a Springbok. So fresh.'

'Next. The Amarula Brandy Alexander cocktail for those who love creamy, caramel, after-dinner drinks. This beverage combines Amarula for a delicious blend of fruity and caramelised flavours.'

We both nodded in approval after taking a sip.

'We won't finish them all at once,' Rose said, placing her glass alongside the half empty Springbok. 'If that's all right, we'll enjoy them after our training.'

'Up to you guys.' Len spun around to introduce his next concoction. 'The Dom Pedro is a thick and frothy drink and is a dessert in a glass, with an ice cream base and a choice of either Amarula or Kahlua coffee liqueur.'

'Delicious,' Rose and I said, licking the sweetness off our lips.

'Ahh, but now the pièce de résistance.' Len was now beside himself with excitement. 'My favourite. Milk Tart Liqueur.'

'Shut up,' Rose blurted with great enthusiasm. 'Never heard of that one. Love melktert.'

Len held up his finger for attention. 'Inspired by the renowned

South African custard pie, this one is a sweet and creamy cocktail. Just mix sweetened condensed milk, evaporated milk, and a touch of cinnamon to achieve a smooth texture in this vodka drink.'

He sounds like a TV advertisement, was the first thought to cross my mind.

After thanking Len for his time, Rose and I took our alcoholic loot and sat at our favourite table with a packet of salty chips to offset the sweetness of the drinks.

'That was fun, hey?'

'It was all right for you. You aren't all thumbs like me.' I said, showing my hands. 'Some of those glasses are tiny. When the pressure is on, I'm going to make one hell of a mess.'

'Nice try, Rory Wilde. You'll need to pour cocktails when it gets busy, just like everyone else.'

I shrugged and toasted Rose. 'Cheers.'

Our first couple of evenings after a full day's work in our current employ passed in a whirlwind of information and meetings. Sales representatives plied their wares from alcohol to food and consumables. Seasoned clients told us what they thought we needed to do, and others warned us to be careful not to change the existing atmosphere – causing customers to have unpleasant disagreements amongst themselves. After our eight-hour day shifts at work, we went straight to Cobblers to put in another six hours. Sleep was a luxury; instead, we napped when we could.

Like other business owners, we faced challenges that felt draining like jet lag. The constant availability and demands caused our corporate routines to collapse, replaced by a tiredness yet a sense of achievement, no matter the scale of the issue. A gratification of ownership and the unmatched adrenalin rush that comes with it.

The pillars supported a delicate and ever-changing ceiling - the customer, a less tangible asset we spent many an hour observing, cogitating over and arguing about, we noticed a different dynamic, even though the same regulars were there, drinking the same and sitting on their favourite stools. What intrigued and dared I say baffled us were the extras, the hangers on, the surprise visitors. Why did they select that day to join us? Why were they there? How did we persuade them to make more frequent visits?

The training week passed, bringing our first evening alone with the regulars and the Cobblers team.

'At least we have Scotty and Paddy watching over the place during the day,' Rose said, getting ready for our debut.

'Yup,' I replied. 'Gives us three weeks' grace before we're there full time.'

'I'm looking forward to it. I don't like those two standing over me.' Rose gestured over her shoulder.

'Suppose so. Thankfully tonight's quiet so we can get our feet wet without too much drama.'

Rose smiled and agreed. 'Best we let the team get on with their jobs. We'll be in the background in case they need us.'

'Sounds like a plan. You ready?'

'As I'll ever be.' Rose joined me outside.

We took turns serving behind the bar, pulling pints of Irish keg beer, pouring shots, and even concocting the simpler cocktails. Learning how to operate the till and give the right change. Clearing tables of dirty crockery and cutlery and interacting with our patrons. Checking the toilets were well stocked, and cleaning floors and walls of all discharges when necessary.

The first month of ownership proved to be a social shock wave for Rose and me. Customers understood the establishment better. They continued to provide us with unwelcome advice and did not hesitate to suggest how to solve issues or point out what we were doing wrong.

Friends assumed that we would give them special privileges, which included discounts and unlimited access to all areas. Dare I say, even the odd family member sought preferential treatment at the bar or eating in the restaurant.

We were no longer the carefree couple they once witnessed, unaffected by opinions or influence. A small group of people who were admirers of the previous owners seethed with hostility, condemning every change we made.

'What do they know about running this place?'

We received direct communication from them and comments in the background, audible to everyone. The devotion to the previous owners of the institution was hard to overcome. It would take time to swing things in our favour. Loyalty was a hard nut to crack, made easier through inclusion and empathy.

Christmas Day was a highlight during those tough times. We closed earlier than usual on Christmas Eve, then set about preparing the dining area for our private celebration the next day. A grand affair of immediate and extended family, each of whom brought a specialist meat and vegetable dish. It filled the tables with various food options like pork, chicken and turkey, along with tongue, ham and breyani. We shut off access to the bar so we could keep tabs on the alcohol, and nobody could sneak an expensive malt whiskey or the likes. This was a business, after all.

Glasses tinkled, quietening the joviality of the family, when Rose's brother, Uncle Jess, called out, 'Speech. Speech.'

Rose, quick on the uptake, turned to me, saying, 'Yes, Rory. Christmas speech.'

I shot her an ironic glance. 'Thanks.' Then I laughed and spoke to the gathering. 'Raise your glasses. To each one of you, a Merry Christmas.' They drank and hailed the yuletide. 'Thank you all for your support. Rose and I are grateful. First toast to our dear Ouma. You are our world. The family salutes you.'

The family cheered, much to Ouma's embarrassment. She blushed and flapped her hand for us to stop. Her grin was so wide as she sat at the head of the table.

'And let us also toast absent friends and family.'

'Friends and family,' they called out in unison.

Jess stood to draw our collective attention. 'Just wanted to say, sis, I'm proud of you and Rory's work here. I know it's difficult, but you guys will be great. Thank you for tonight on behalf of the family. Cheers to a joyful Christmas and a fantastic New Year for both of you.'

The family cheered and clapped as they stood, music playing for dancing.

'How sweet,' Rose whispered to me. 'We can't let them down.'

'We cannot allow ourselves to fail, either,' I added. 'Let's dance.

We'll worry about all that later.'

A cousin played at the piano in the room's corner. Laughter and popping of Christmas crackers filled the air.

Other days were not so pleasurable. Paddy and Scotty's farewell in particular.

They explained that Irish whiskey and Scottish whisky are not just spelled differently, all the while drinking a lot of both. They argued about different Celtic types' tastes, strength and lasting power.

'Hey, laddie.' A random haggard Scotsman yelled out at me through his orange-flecked white beard. 'Dinnee just stand. More drinks, man.'

I bit my tongue and jumped in to help the busy bar staff. 'What can I get you?'

'You need to ask? Aren't you the boss?' He leered in my face. 'Any owner worth his salt knows everything about his customers.'

'I will in time. Just trying to lend a hand.'

'Feekin hell,' his lip snarled. 'Good luck to you and the missus if you think you can do as well as these two.' He slapped their backs, attracting their attention. Scotty laughed and turned to his crowd of well-wishers.

However, Paddy was having none of it. 'That'll be enough from you, Jim boy. Give them a chance.'

'A chance is all they're getting. After that, I'm heading back to my *auld* jaunt at the hotel.' He mentioned an old and rundown hotel downtown that was just an inn with shabby rooms for rent.

'I'll bear that in mind, thank you,' I told him. 'What can I get you to drink?'

'Time for some of your top shelf single malts for me and these old codgers.'

'Sure thing.' The last laugh was mine, as I poured expensive whiskey and bantered with the Celts over which was better.

Besides reassuring our clients, we wanted to ensure any changes would not impede what attracted them to Cobblers Bar and Grill. We needed to do the same with our employees. Change is an uncomfortable part of life we often choose to avoid, and no more so than making decisions that affected people's income. In line with our plan to prevent too much disruption, we decided everyone should keep their existing hours and shifts until we could decide on any changes.

Our first Christmas was an interesting time because we were busy, albeit not as much as we had expected. Business parties dominated with companies treating their workers to a meal and a chance to let their hair down. In the last few days before yuletide silence reigned except for a handful of loners at the bar. Families busied themselves with organising and buying for the big day. Christmas Eve was both eerie and sad with coloured lights flashing yet lacking goodwill or cheer.

In contrast, New Year's Eve was an absolute nightmare of excess and odd behaviours from people we least expected. There seemed to be a need, if not a collective sense, to let it all hang out in the name of celebrating the end of the old year and welcoming in the new. We struggled, already shellshocked by a torrid week of hospitality issues – staff not turning up for their shifts, clients intolerant of the smallest of delays after ordering their drinks, suppliers running short of essentials and our family struggling with our lack of routine.

But after Christmas and New Year's festivities, we were eager to implement our business ideas. It promised to be a tough project. People viewed changes as criticism and the instigators as arrogant. A no-win situation until and unless the modifications brought about improvement.

Chapter Eight

Our daily routine involved alternating chores and shifts, often resulting in limited interaction. A hello or goodbye in the passageway or a wave from the garden gate. Stilted conversation at three o'clock in the morning to discuss finances and issues, or just to hold each other.

Rose's expression made it clear she was unhappy when I returned to the pub one morning after a run for supplies. She and the others had been preparing for opening time.

'Rory? We can't continue funding these bar tabs. Some are over five hundred rand?' Rose's hands were filled with till records.

'Oh, shit. Where did you find those?'

'In this folder that was beneath the cash register.' Rose showed me a lever arch file full of till receipts, a plastic sleeve per customer running on tick.

I looked at the first one. 'Is this Gary's, our part timer?' I asked.

Rose nodded, blinking her eyes in agreement.

'But he works for us. Why is he racking up a tab?'

'Who knows, but it has to stop,' Rose snapped.

'Damn right.' I scanned through the rest. 'Oh crap. Closing some of these will be tough.'

'Not really. They'll understand once we explain. I mean, who runs bar tabs these days? Hello. This is the late nineties.' Rose crossed her arms. 'You take half. I'll do the rest.'

I turned to our head barkeep. 'Oh, my word, Len, what is going on here?'

'The previous owners also run tabs, guys. They told me you would be okay with it.'

'Let me make it clear.' Rose stepped forward. 'From this moment, everyone will pay for their drinks as they get them. We only run one kind of tab and that is for food, and it must be settled after they finished eating.' She glanced around at the rest of the team. 'Is that understood? Good. Now get this place open. Trade well, people. Remember to sell those snacks and shooters. Money in the bank and all that.'

'The old owners need to be notified,' Len said in a quiet voice. 'They still think they have free rein here. Especially when you're not around.' He changed the topic the second clients started entering. 'Morning, gentlemen. The usual?' Len in his element, the pensioners in theirs.

Rose moved away from the bar, and I followed. 'Rory, we need to plan for the changes and let the customers know what we are doing. That way, we can avoid shocking the regulars too much when we cancel their tabs.'

'I'm listening,' I said, taking a seat at one of the food tables and stapling each customer's receipts together, then adding them up on a calculator. I wrote their name on the slip from the machine next to the dollar value showing.

'What are doing with that?' Rose asked, watching me pick up the slips with names on and putting them up on the board above the cash register and card swipers.

'If they don't pay their tab, everyone will see it. I'll inform them all that there is a one-month grace period for settling their bill.'

'Nice, Rory. Good job. Some won't like it, but tough. We have a business to run, and we will not finance people's drinking habits.'

'Yeah, well, those who object aren't the customers we want to hold on to anyway. *Skomgat.*' I used the derogatory Afrikaans slang for a loser or ruffian. 'What's next?'

Rose thought for a moment, pen resting on her lips. 'I believe there are three top priorities. Big rocks. One.' She held up a finger. 'Entertainment. A cover band who sings popular and retro hits. Two. Redecorate the pub. I know it's an Irish-style tavern, but this place needs some updating, especially because of the awful decor we have here. All these dark wooden chairs, tables, bar, walls, and poor lighting make it look like some seedy joint in Hillbrow.' A now squalid area in downtown Johannesburg. 'A few extractors would help get rid of the smoke haze too. And do not get me started on those bloody purple velour curtains and the dowdy nicotine-stained magnolia walls.'

She waved away my look of concern. 'I'm thinking we start in the dining area by replacing the tired table and chairs. Instead, we could have cubicles painted in cerise and padded with matching tartan cushions. So much more a modern feel.'

I sat and listened, not wanting to break her line of thought and creativity. I had learnt that lesson before. Well, it took a few times, but I got there in the end.

'Three,' she continued. 'Food. Fish 'n' chips and burger 'n' chips just don't cut it, and by that, I mean we must also offer salads, pastas, etc. All must relate to the clientele we have as well as the ones we hope to attract.'

'That's a lot of work, not to mention cash,' I said but nodded in agreement.

'The refurbishment maybe, but if we do most of it ourselves the cost won't be so harsh. I'll make pamphlets and wall posters telling the customers about the changes and to ask them to share their thoughts and ideas.'

'Is that wise?' I asked.

'We'll get a mixed bag of suggestions from them, but at least they'll feel they are part of the revitalisation. We can put a positive spin on it.'

'I will leave it in your gifted hands. Just tell me what you need me to do. I will make a start on recovering funds from the outstanding bar tabs. Wish me luck.'

'What are your thoughts on changes re operations, Rory?'

'Ssshh.' I put a finger to my lips. 'That's corporate speech. It's banned around here, remember?'

'You know what I mean,' Rose said, a little miffed.

'Just teasing,' I smiled, and thought of what I would like to alter. 'A couple of things right off the bat along with the stopping of running drink tabs. We've got to stop people bringing in food to eat, whether they're sitting at the bar or in the restaurant area.'

'That's a no-no for a start.' Rose butted in. 'I haven't seen that yet.'

'Seems to be the lunchtime crowd. They pop in for their lunch hours, eat their packed lunches, and buy only a soda.'

'Good one. I'll leave that with you. What else?' Rose asked.

'The same applies to bringing drinks in. Caught a lad the other day, pouring brandy from a hip flask into the cola he'd bought. Charged him for it, though.'

'Corkage. Nice, Rory.' Rose waited, knowing there was more.

'Dress code is something we must consider. Bare feet are a step too far. Excuse the pun.'

'Droll, but I agree,' she said with a hint of sarcasm.

'The only other thing that comes to mind,' I continued, 'is that we need to set up a diary for event bookings. You know – birthday parties, farewells, bachelor parties, stork parties, and suchlike.'

'Yup. I've got that one down here, too. Leave that with me.'

'Meeting over?' I asked.

'Done and dusted, Mr Wilde. It's a start to sorting this place out. Now for the fun and games. People.' Rose lifted her eyebrows.

I sat back in my chair and blew a silent whistle. 'That's going to be an interesting one.'

'Yes, but at least we have a strategy. We just have to set it in motion.'

'Set it up so we begin afresh next week with a new roster?' I asked.

'I think so.' Rose nodded. 'Len head barkeeper, supported by Gary and Sunette, to cover the seven days.' Rose spelt out the plan on her fingers. 'Sheila runs the kitchen and serves the food. Then we find a couple of casuals to take extra shifts and to replace *Ballie* and Peggy.'

'All right then.' I sat forward. 'Let's set up meetings for those two and let them know they aren't staying. When best suits you?'

'We can tell them now, then organise it for the end of the week, so they have time to get used to it.' Rose shrugged. 'Love you.' she concluded the meeting and went.

I picked up the phone to set up the meetings for the employees who would not be part of the team.

'*Ballie* didn't seem all that fazed when I mentioned we needed to talk about his employment,' I said to Rose, who was preparing a table for our meetings with the two team members. 'Reckon he was half expecting it, to be honest.'

'Agreed. He hasn't approved of us taking over, plus he never turns up for his shifts anyway,' Rose answered. 'Peggy, not so much. She looked a bit taken aback.'

I nodded. 'Will have to play that by ear. See how Peggy responds.'

'A quick visit to the loo before the first one arrives.' Rose stood up to go, but her phone buzzing interrupted her. 'Hello. Oh, hi, Peggy.' She turned to look at me. 'Are you certain? We can talk about it if you like.'

I studied my partner's body language for clues about what was being said.

'Well, if you are sure. We'll leave the invitation open until the end of the week should you change your mind.' Rose widened her eyes at me. 'Take care and catch up soon. Bye, Peggy.' She lowered her mobile. 'One down. Peggy's resigned – says she's found another job.'

'Is she okay?'

'She says she is. I gave her some time to think about her decision, but she's adamant. She asked for a reference, so maybe it's fine for all parties.'

'We've got an hour then until *Ballie* turns up. Fancy a coffee?'

'Thanks. That would be great.'

Ballie arrived ten minutes late for his appointment, as was his want. He nodded at our greeting but didn't say a word. Just sat himself down, his eyes switching between Rose and me.

The room was silent, apart from his deep breathing. His white beard grew about a foot below his sallow chin. Thin purple veins decorated his dry cheeks, black bags hung from below his slitted eyes, and bushy grey eyebrows competed with the intense wrinkles on his forehead. An awkward silence ensued until he broke the quietness.

'Let me save you the effort.' He raised the palms of his hands. 'We know I'm not fitting in here. In fact, I don't like what I am seeing.'

Rose and I waited, allowing him the time to have his say.

'My nickname is *Ballie*, for a reason.' He looked as if he was enjoying having the floor. 'To my friends it means father. To others who are not, it's old man. Some see me as grumpy. For me, it's all about straight-shooting.' He paused for dramatic effect, then continued. 'So, here's what I'm saying. You two can stick your job where it doesn't fit.'

'That's a bit harsh, *ou Ballie.*' I leaned forward, highlighting the Afrikaans for old before his nickname.

Rose touched my arm, gesturing for me to back off. 'We're sorry you feel that way.'

He glanced at us both again, then wiped his face with his hands. 'I will only get worse if I stay, so I'm doing us all a favour.'

'If that's what you want, but I hope we keep you as a customer.' I gave him a grin.

The corners of his mouth quivered in a slight smile. 'You couldn't keep me away from here on a Saturday, watching rugby with all my buddies.'

The meeting concluded with handshakes. Rose called to Len behind the bar, 'Please buy this man a drink, then another, and charge it to my account.'

'Yes, ma'am.' Len took *Ballie* with him to sit with his pals.

'Well, that went better than I thought it might.' Rose touched my shoulder with her head. 'What say you?'

'Could have been worse, that's for sure,' I said. 'At least it's over now.' I gestured to Len behind the bar. 'We are out of here. You okay to lock up?'

'For sure. You two head out. You've had a tough day. We are all fine here.' Len patted the back of Rose's hand. 'Rest up. Tomorrow's another day.'

'Thanks, Len,' Rose mouthed across the room as we left the building.

He raised his glass napkin in acknowledgement.

In what was becoming our usual relaxation and reflection time, we were sipping coffee in bed in the early morning hours. We spoke about the team we had chosen for the renovations we were making, the impact the changes were having, and those that might still occur. We didn't always agree what was best for the bar, but we never allowed our differences to affect our relationship.

I'd had doubts about the business for that is my nature, and all that it stood for could not be further away from my personality. Yet Cobblers Bar and Grill solidified my love for my African Rose. If we could survive and even thrive, then we were meant to be. Of that I was certain.

Chapter Nine

The effects of liquor on people and how it influenced their actions struck us. A large factor in the type of response type depending on the environment in which inebriated person was found. There was not much we could do about their consumption other than to limit intake, but we could do something about the atmosphere. For each shift, we assessed the gathering of partygoers so that the next team coming in knew what to expect.

Mere observations were derived from past experiences, both rewarding and vexing. Seldom did we get it wrong.

We identified our clients based on seven predictable behaviours that are more relatable to the Brothers Grimm than Disney. Alcohol was the evil witch, with innocence nowhere to be seen.

The **Joker** talked about the past. They spoke of how lucky we were to be alive and that fun was just over the horizon. Laughing at everything, whether or not humorous, turning the mundane into dramas, and seeing the sad as an opportunity for exploitation. Whenever they felt melancholy or vulnerable, they donned a cloak of liveliness to cover it up.

Weirdos could not keep their hands or romantic inclinations to themselves. Disrespecting personal space by touching and kissing anyone nearby. Portraying a veil of kindness so not to reveal their evil intent. Predators of the weak and susceptible. More prevalent than most care to acknowledge, let alone combat. They were my nemesis, who hounded my dear Rose week in and week out. My impulse was to evict them aggressively, but I had to respect Rose, who could look after herself. It did, however, invoke a deep-seated testosterone instinct within me, and that is no slur, a driven desire to protect. Even now.

Doom and **Gloom,** identical twins that were impossible to tell apart, expressed the dire straits we faced in the future. They viewed any act of goodness with scepticism, believing it to be a cunning ploy by an ambiguous higher entity. Politics, religion and cultures were all fair game to their dour persona. Harmless floaters of the public venues in search of whoever might listen.

We found **Sloth** in the most unusual positions and locations, oblivious to their surroundings, whether on a quiet evening or at raucous parties. The quantity of drink consumed was unrelated to the eventual consequence of slumber. The serial sleeper succumbed after a glass of wine or a few beers—a subliminal need to rest within the safe confines of the public.

Truther. The secret plot terrorists set the world right according to their perceptions and prejudices. They judged contrasting views as conspiracy theories or the work of the extremist, be they fascist or communist. They lived in a flat world where the first moon landing was fake. They were vehement in their belief the 9/11 Twin Towers attack was a coverup and that aliens had crash landed at Roswell. They doubted life was real. Never offering a solution or standing behind a principle with any integrity or fortitude. Their ambition was to complain and point fingers.

Balsak, Afrikaans for ball bag (scrotum). An ignorant bully of limited intellect who attacked the weak or a perceived threat – be it living or inanimate – with force. They imposed their will with physical and mental purpose, irrespective of whether their victim is old or young, family or friend. This one was the most prevalent of all our caricatures, apart from the regular and pleasant majority frequenters.

Finally came the **Kugel.** This is a South African Yiddish slang word for those driven by material possessions and status. Who drank without altering their personality or behaviour. We were still waiting to meet this person in Cobblers, although many believed it to be themselves. This persona's downfalls were to hide their faults by pointing out others. They travelled along the spectrum of drunkenness from Joker to Doom at a whim. The loose cannon. A temperament with no logical pattern.

Each was a negative human propensity for good reason. We did not need to be on the lookout for the happy, calm and socially apt. Communal gatherings were full of interaction, and alcohol made that more difficult. Drinking houses were dens of iniquity, places of shameless behaviour. Challenging situations cropped up because of a lack of simple goodwill and an abundance of influence and were often unplanned. The traits we identified can now be seen on the internet but with a different intoxicating stimulant.

I shall not always label the characters you meet along the way, though I may refer to them that I will leave for you to spot. Humans do it all our lives – watching, assessing, and then reacting, not unlike the rest of the animal kingdom. This brought a comforting sense of security that assured our well-being in the environment we were about to step into.

Running a bar and grill was a pleasure, thanks to the gems who outweighed the seven Cobbler's distorts. The majority were South Africans seeking safety and survival. One such person who frequented our establishment was Philemon Dlamini, the author. He minded his business by sitting in the same corner of the room each day, drafting stories. order a meal which he often forgot, being lost in his world, and eat it cold. If someone took his favourite spot, Philemon Dlamini would sit nearby, clutching his backpack and waiting with a saint's patience. Never so much of a peep from him but the manners of a gentleman. He never braved coming in of an evening or when the bar was crowded, for not only did he risk being singled out, but it would mean he would have to be social. That he was a writer intrigued a side of me I had buried since leaving school, too busy with my life, too scared to share my scribblings.

Reality hit Rose and more so me the first morning we opened our new business, which came after a hectic night. We arrived ahead of time to get acquainted with the layout, count stock, and determine cleaning needs.

'Morning, Rose.'

'Morning, Sheila. Thanks for joining us so early.'

'That's okay.'

Rose opened the door and flicked on the lights.

'You never get used to this,' Sheila said, gesturing at the wasteland before us.

Rose and I stood where we entered, our minds reeling at the sight of empty bottles and glasses strewn across the bar. Discarded cigarette ends were among the litter patrons had thrown on the floor while leaving dirty crockery on tables. The smell of cigarette butts and overfull ashtrays mixed with the odour of stale beer and putrid leftovers turned our stomachs. I have no words for the rancid state of the toilets. The men's aim was non-existent, and the women's bathroom was littered. A shudder ran down my spine, akin to first seeing the death and destruction of war in my younger days in Zimbabwe.

'Oh, my word. Look at this mess.' Rose broke the spell that returned us to reality.

'How weird is this?' I asked her.

'What do you mean? You're the, strange one.' She tutted me. 'This is normal. Get used to it. Welcome to the world of hospitality.'

Sheila leaned against the wall behind Rose and stared at me with deep, brooding eyes and a slight smirk. She blinked, then pushed herself upright and disappeared into the kitchen.

'To be this bad is just unacceptable,' Rose said, pointing to the cluttered bar top and messy tables. 'Our customers shouldn't have to sit amongst this. What is the bartender doing or not doing?' She shook her head. 'They don't have to clean so much as tidy as they go along. Bloody hell.'

'Morning.' Philemon removed his hat as he entered and, without another word, found his way to his favourite corner, removing his backpack. Before taking his laptop out, he pulled a handkerchief from his pocket, dipped it in a half jug of water from the previous night, and wiped the tabletop. Oblivious to the mess around him, he started the rituals that were his writing. We weren't open yet, but Sheila fetched his obligatory morning coffee.

With cleaning tools, we scrubbed, washed, disinfected and spruced up Cobblers Bar and Grill.

'Mr Dlamini, are you ready for your toasted sandwich?' Sheila asked him as she finished vacuuming his corner. 'Won't be long before people arrive.' She waited for a response.

Without looking, he lifted his right hand above his head with a thumbs up, then brought his arm down as he peered deeper into the screen before him.

Sheila gave him a look and muttered in her language, shaking her head as she bustled off to the kitchen. Philemon glanced at her and gave a shy grin.

We kept up this routine every day. The scent still evokes nausea when I step into a drinking place, even now. The odours hiding behind the backrooms of establishments spark unpleasant memories in my mind. Rankness lurks in each crevice and behind every door.

Later that same day, after a quick shower and change at home, we returned refreshed for the evening. It was a time when most of our regulars dropped in after work, and these were the worst offenders on running a tab. Instead of sitting on the customer side of the bar, we joined Len and helped with serving drinks and supplying packs of cigarettes. This enabled us to address the issue and find a solution together.

'But I've always run up a bill. That's why I come here.' The first one we confronted protested. 'You won't keep your regulars if you don't look after them.'

'True.' Rose answered in a sweet tone. 'It's just that if no one pays their tab, the business can't buy more stock. No stock equals no customers anyway.'

The punter paused in thought, then raised an eyebrow. 'I suppose so. How much do I owe?'

'Six hundred and fifty-two rand.'

'Oh, shit. That much?' His face reddened. 'I am sorry. Here's a cheque.' As he went to hand it over, he held it for a moment. 'If I pay my tab every Monday, will that be okay?' he said, smiling at Rose.

'As long as it doesn't exceed a hundred rand.'

'Done deal, miss.' He raised his beer tankard and then turned to the rest of the bar. 'Come on, peeps. Play the game. These kids are doing a fine job. Cheers.' He swigged his drink and carried on with his colleagues.

The after-work crowd shuffled out, and evening revellers seeking comfort in food and each other replaced them.

Len drew my attention to a customer complaining at one of the dining tables. 'Kugel in the house,' he whispered, passing me by.

'What do you mean I can't put our meal on our account?' a pouty woman scoffed at me. 'How are we meant to eat otherwise?'

'Your bill is over a thousand rand.' I spoke to her out of earshot of her friends and family.

'Is that a lot of money to you, young boy? Shame.' She looked down her beak at me, pushing aside the tousles of her grey-streaked fluffy mane. Her large earrings clinked as she shook her head.

'It is, actually. If you could pay half now and settle the rest in a couple of weeks, that would be great.'

'I've never been so insulted.' Her eyes protruding from her face, she huffed and puffed, pulling out a credit card from her minuscule handbag. 'Here, pay the account.'

'I'm sorry you feel that way, but we must protect the business so we can offer you the service you deserve,' I said, placing her card for the full amount on the manual imprinter known as the zip-zap machine.

Later the same evening, after Kugel's loud and animated table required a lot of attention, she called me over. 'Hey, sweety.' She handed me her credit card with one hand, saying, 'As promised, I'm paying for dinner,' and put the other on my chest. 'Oooh, you must work out.' She winked at her table, who snickered. 'Open a few buttons, young man. You might get a bigger tip.' The transformation from Kugel to Weirdo was instantaneous.

I accepted the card, pretending not to hear her. 'Thanks. Hope you all had a great evening.' I left to caterwauling in the background. I knew that if I'd confronted them with their actions when they were sober, they'd be mortified.

Len took delight in the recouping of funds from customers he had a close rapport with that we lacked. The last thing they wanted was to upset the barman who placed their favourite tipple in front of them before they reached their stool or table. Who lit their cigarettes as they raised them to their lips and refilled their bar snacks without charge. The same ones he kept company on long winter evenings or consoled going through personal issues. Forever listening and giving sage advice or not, but always caring.

We lost a few customers, but we suspected not because of the changes we had imposed but because they could not pay their bills. Their tab remained stapled to the wall for others to see so they would not do the same and might even chastise the offenders. There is no tougher decision as a business owner than to accept the money was lost.

Chapter Ten

'What? Len hasn't pitched up again?' Rose said down the phone. 'All right. Can you hang around for half an hour while we find him or get hold of Sunette to replace him? Thanks, Gary. Appreciate the call and for helping us out. See you as soon as we have this sorted.' She replaced the receiver. 'Rory. No guesses for who didn't come to work again?'

'I heard. New boyfriend?' I changed my clothes and grabbed the car keys. 'Let's find him, hey?'

'He hasn't told me anything, so it might be someone new.' Rose lifted both hands. 'I'll just change my shoes. He only keeps that job because he's a great bartender, but boy, does he push his luck.'

'And trust me, he knows it,' I muttered behind the steering wheel. Praying Len was close by, we went to his regular hangouts downtown.

'Hope he's not on one of his walkabouts.' Rose peered out the passenger window for any chance of happening across our head barkeep.

'He'll be out for the night with his latest flame. Or if it's a breakup, then he'll be bingeing in the city and drowning his sorrows for at least a week.' I parked the car under the hue of streetlights. 'Right. Let's find him.'

Hand in hand, we peeked through the windows of the smaller cocktail lounges and pubs that ranged from the sombre one man and his dog in the corner watching soap operas, to the thunderous headbangers in mosh pits.

'Nothing here. That leaves the Blue Lagoon.'

'We might as well make a night out of it,' Rose said, then released my hand to answer her phone. 'Hi Gary. I'm sorry, no luck as yet. We're still out looking for him.' She rolled her eyes. 'You will? Thank you so much. We'll make it up to you, Gary. No, don't worry, we'll be there later to lock up. See you then. Bye,' Rose switched off her mobile and smiled up at me. 'We'll kill two birds with one stone. Find Len and party.'

'But, but…' I had no excuse or reason not to go along for the ride. Rose loved the nightlife, and I adored seeing her happy.

The Blue Lagoon sign danced and flickered above the doorway, at odds with the sleepy town of Germiston – and the community to boot. I took a deep breath, dreading the next hour or three. The love of my life and I entered the building. *Why deny her a rare night out?*

Inside was as ostentatious as the signage outside declared. Lavish carpeting, drapes, and décor matched by the piano man playing in the corner. Everyone wore smocks, tuxedos, and an array of matching boas, hats, shoes and jewellery, which I had never seen before. Colour and festivity flourished.

'Wow. Posh place, Rose. Can we afford it?'

'Posh?' Rose gave me a quizzical look, then grinned to herself. 'Oh, right? Don't worry, it's expensive, but whatever. Let's enjoy.'

I shrugged. 'Looks like some of our caricatures are here, too. There's Kugel 1, Kugel 2…'

'Just behave.' Rose nudged me in the ribs, trying to ignore me.

'A spot for you good people?' A tall lady in a sequined dress seated us at a crowded table towards the back. 'Remember folks, it's a two-drink minimum per person unless you're eating.'

'A couple of lagers with shots of tequila, please.' Rose pretended to touch my cheek, instead closing my gaping jaw.

'Absolutely, my dear. I'll run a tab for you. It's so nice to have you guys from Cobblers here. Have a blast.'

'Thank you.' Rose noticed my attention on the lady who'd served us, now ramp-walking her way back to the entrance to welcome more clients. 'Rory? Just relax and enjoy.'

I looked into the kind eyes of my Rose, smiled, and nodded. 'You are right. Here's to us.' I took Rose's hand and gave a gentle squeeze. 'Nice of them to acknowledge that we are from Cobblers.'

'Ooh, you guys celebrating. Have a lovely evening.' The same server squeezed my shoulder as she took small, delicate steps past us that did not look comfortable.

The people in this place were beyond my social realization. *Must be the money. Hope I can live up to Rose's expectations.*

'I think you can remove that gobsmacked expression, Rory Wilde.' Rose said to me behind her hand. 'Not your best look.'

'That woman's makeup is so over the top,' I answered, looking around. 'Mind you, seems to be the fashion these days.'

'That's what it is, Rory. Each to their own,' Rose said, caressing my hand.

'True. Who are we to judge? Just feel a little underdressed.'

A trumpet fanfare interrupted our chitchat from across the room, followed by the opening of red velvet curtains.

'I didn't know there was a theatre here. Must be a show on tonight.' I moved my chair next to Rose and ordered another round of drinks. *Chill, Rorke Wilde. Enjoy. Rose is showing you an aspect of life you never knew existed. Posh restaurant and entertainment, mind you. Very nice.* My paranoia about losing Rose playing its part once more.

The piano man leapt on stage in his Elton John gear, including oversized spectacles, and seized the microphone. 'Good evening, folks. Welcome to Saturday Showtime at the incredible, awe-inspiring, trend-setting Blue Lagoon.' He lifted his arms above his head and waited for the whooping and clapping to die down.

'Ladies and gentlefolk. Fill your glasses. Empty your bladders. The extravaganza begins in five minutes.' He jumped down onto his piano and played *Sisters Are Doin' It for Themselves* to roars from the audience, who got to their feet and danced at their tables.

'Sounds great. I'm headed for the gents' room before the show starts.' I kissed Rose's head and ducked away to find the toilets.

Aware that time was short, I checked for a free stall or urinal to avoid obstructing others from watching or missing the show's start. None were available. The bathroom attendant smiled and offered me a choice of cologne.

'I'm all good, thanks,' I refused, then noticed women standing in front of the mirrors, brushing their hair and refreshing their makeup.

'Oh, shit, I'm sorry, ladies.' On exiting the restroom, I double-checked the genre signs.

You've had too much to drink, dumbass. I scolded myself and hurried to the other entrance, thinking they were the correct ablutions. Screams and laughter chased me out of that washroom, too. Both had women in them. The urge gone; I headed back to Rose at the table.

'What happened? Looks like you've seen a ghost.'

'Nothing. Just can't find the loo.'

'What do you mean? They're over there.'

I related my experience to an ever-reddening Rose, who did her best not to fall on the ground in hysterics. 'Rory,' she said, composing herself, 'look around and think about it. What do you see?'

My lightbulb moment coincided with the opening of the curtains and the emcee announcing, 'Please welcome this year's Miss Germiston competition.'

A parade of pretty girls mixed with men dressed in drag filled the stage with shrieking and applause.

'You, all right?' Rose asked.

'Sure. It just took me unawares.'

'That's okay, Rorke Wilde. Enjoy the ride.'

'Oh, I intend to. You open my eyes in so many ways, and for that I thank you.'

'I love you.' Rose hugged me.

'Loved you first.'

I watched the show and learnt the nuances between hilarity and seriousness. I observed the crowd and discovered no right or wrong, just different. That night, my Rose taught me humility and acceptance.

She signalled for a server.

'Please send Miss Germiston a drink of her choice and our congratulations.'

'How kind, thank you, guys.' The server swished away in her evening gown.

My eyes broadened. I stifled a choke on my drink when I realised what was happening.

Miss Germiston made her way over to our table. 'Thanks for the beverage, both of you.'

'You're welcome. You look amazing.' Rose pulled a chair for her.

'Are you sure? I don't want to intrude.'

'Not at all. This is my partner, Rory.'

A small 'Hi' was all my brain allowed.

'How cute. You two are straight.'

Rose nodded, looking at me.

Miss Germiston placed a hand on my forearm. 'Don't beat yourself up, darling. We're also human.'

'He'll be fine once he gets his head around it. Socialising isn't his strong point. No matter the circumstance.' Rose shared my recent toilet incident.

'Poor thing. Rory, it's okay to use the gents. They are just men dressed as women. So, all good. Drag queens, my dear.' Miss Germiston and Rose chatted amongst themselves. I excused myself and darted for the toilets, my bladder bursting at the seams.

'Come on, mister, there's a line of people waiting after you.'

I stood at the urinal, unable to pee with an audience behind me and the incomprehensible banter. All too much for a simple country boy.

'Oh, leave the poor guy alone. Is it your first time here, love?'

I nodded over my shoulder.

'Are you a friend of Dorothy?'

'Don't know a Dorothy.'

'He's a breeder, bless him.' The restroom filled with sounds of endearment and pity. 'Good on you for joining us, brother.'

'Thanks,' I said, still only capable of single words, and with that I relieved myself in more ways than one.

With a wink, the bathroom attendant gave me a towel after I washed my hands.

The lady next to me, wearing an exaggerated headpiece, asked, 'So, what brings you here tonight?'

'We're looking for our barman, Len.'

'We?' He raised deep-turquoise eyelids.

'My wife and me,' I said, a little uncomfortably. 'He didn't show for work, so we're worried about him.'

'Are you guys from Cobblers?' he asked as the restroom broke out in squeals of delight. 'Well, you never know. You might just find him here buried beneath some outfit or other.' The drag artist whooshed a dramatic exit from the room.

'Hello, Len. Fancy seeing you here.' I opened my palms on returning to the table. *Bloody hell. That lot knew all about this. Made me look like a dork.* I didn't listen to Len's response.

'Isn't it just?' Rose said, beaming back at me. 'He turned up after you went to the men's room.'

I pulled a face at her innuendo and finger punctuation, teasing me.

'Sorry, guys. I've met a new man, and I lost track of time.'

'Come on, Len, that's an old card to play.' I gave him a sceptical look.

'I'm fast becoming old, too. Turn fifty next month, you know?' Len sank forward over his glass of beer.

'Now is not the time to feel low. No harm done. Gary is covering your shift,' Rose consoled him whilst eyeing me not to push the issue further. 'So, who is the lucky new man?'

'Oh, my God. He's delicious.' Len perked up.

I zoned out as the two discussed the latest love of Len's life and listened to the piano man in the corner playing the blues.

Eventually Rose poured Len into a taxi. 'Go home and sleep it off. I'll see you at work tomorrow.' She gave his shoulder a tap. 'Len, I mean it. Be at work tomorrow. I need you to be reliable.'

'Okay.' Len peered out of his bottle-thick glasses, his lined face revealing his age. 'I really like this guy, you know? He may be the one.'

'I can see you do. We'll chat at work. We open at ten-thirty but be there at ten o'clock. Sleep tight.' Rose tapped the taxi's roof; its wheels crunched the stones as it pulled away. 'I hope Gary's been coping on his own.'

We climbed into the car and headed towards Cobblers Bar & Grill; thankful we drank alcohol-free beer that evening. Running an establishment with a liquor license requires attention to every detail and at any time of day, or it can turn into a disaster.

The bar was quiet, apart from a few stragglers.

Rose waved hello to Gary, who did not respond, remaining

transfixed in the same spot, leaning on the bar top with his hands. His eyes stared at the varnished wood surface.

A dull lad, lacking drive or ambition, Gary drank too much and suffered from poor self-awareness. His half-hooded eyes, woolly blonde hair and blank expression did little to help. He served tables and helped behind the bar when we were busy. With no interest in the job, he struggled with the idea that his work ethic –, or lack of it – reflected on himself. He was there for the money so he could drink and looked forward to nothing but his next day off. Sober, he was a kind soul without so much as a gripe. One too many beverages and he transformed.

'Hello, Gary. Are you all right?' Rose touched his shoulder.

'Oh, you guys are back.' He'd jumped at our appearance. 'It wasn't fun, you know?' He looked us up and down.

I watched a realisation cross his face.

'You owe me a drink. I'll have a large brandy and cola, thank you.' He turned to fix himself a drink.

'I don't think so, Gary,' Rose told him. 'We'll pay you for your time at work and it was a quiet evening.'

Gary continued reaching for the cognac bottle.

'Listen to Rose. No more alcohol for you. Time to head home. We'll discuss you drinking during work hours on your next shift.' I supported my wife.

Gary clutched the bar.

'Relax.' I reassured him, but he refused to let go. 'Gary, this is not helping. Let's not make a scene.'

He shook his head, his eyes glazed.

We said our goodbyes to customers who were leaving, then returned to our stubborn mule.

'Gary? Time for home. Relax your grip and we'll drop you off at your house,' Rose offered.

Another shake of the head.

'If you don't, Rory will carry you out.'

Nothing.

I lifted him over my shoulder and put him out on the doorstep.

No reaction.

Rose showed me the whites of her eyes in disbelief.

We locked up and convinced him to ride in the back of the car. We'd have to go five kilometres out of our way to drop him off but needed to be sure he got there.

'Sorry, Aunty Rose,' he slurred, slumped in the rear seat.

'Do not start all that, Gary. Now's not the time and I'm not your aunty.'

'I don't know what got into me.'

'Shut up. Gary. Enough is enough.' Rose slapped her thigh.

He stopped slurring and tried to focus his crossed eyes on Rose, but to no avail.

'Will your mom be home?' Rose asked as I parked the car.

He didn't answer, so she pulled him out by his collar and knocked on the door. A frail lady with thinning grey hair and large glasses opened it, light spilling out. Only their silhouettes on the porch were visible, but Rose's communication was clear.

The door closed and darkness returned, along with my wife. She swung the door open, slid into the front seat beside me, and sighed. 'Thank goodness that's over. Quite a night, hey, Rory?'

Both of us broke down laughing, though we were unsure why.

'I feel sorry for Gary,' Rose said as we drove home.

'Why is that?'

'His dad walked out on him when he was young, and his mom is not the most dynamic person.' Rose paused for a while, then continued. 'The same lack of initiative and enthusiasm caused his underperformance in school.'

'How do you know that?' I asked.

'He was at school with James but left when he was sixteen. I think this is the only job he's had. Poor kid.'

'That's a shame. He just needs to change his attitude and understand that life doesn't owe him anything.'

'That's harsh, Rory. I reckon we can help him if we are patient and positive.'

'I suppose. Happy to give it a go.'

'I'll have a chat with him on his next shift.'

'Morning, Gary.' Rose was waiting just inside the pub the following morning.

'Hello,' he answered, his eyes darting around the room to establish what he might have done wrong. He picked the sleep from his eyes, then pulled a dirty handkerchief from his jeans pocket and blew into it, waiting for Rose to continue.

'Let's talk.' Rose led him to a private table in the restaurant's corner.

'What have I done? Are you firing me?' he asked Rose, then looked at me sitting opposite him. The lightness of his eyebrows gave the illusion of their absence.

'You're not in trouble,' Rose said. 'We're interested in helping you to grow so you can work your way up through the hospitality industry. If that's something you want to do.'

He gave us a suspicious look, followed by the shrug. 'Why would you do that for me?'

'Several reasons.' Rose said. 'Upskilling you would benefit both you and our business. What I don't want, Gary, is a half-hearted attempt. It won't be easy at first, but it will be worthwhile. Rory and I have done this with many individuals in our careers.' Rose smiled at the lad and leaned back. 'So, what do you say?'

Gary rubbed his hands on his jeans, staring at the floor. 'I'll need time to think about it.'

Rose's face said it all. 'This is what I'm talking about, Gary. That's not the response employers are looking for.' She shook her head. 'But I'll give you until your shift tomorrow to decide. Is that okay?'

Gary nodded, staring up at the ceiling and avoiding any eye contact.

'All right. Get to work. We'll catch up again tomorrow.' Rose waited for Gary to leave, then rolled her eyes at me. 'For goodness' sake. He's going to be a big job. That poor boy hasn't got a clue.'

I hugged Rose. 'There is only so much we can do. The rest is up to him.'

'I know. But let's see how we can help him, Rory. It's the least we can do, and heaven knows we need a backup for Len and his antics.'

Gary slipped into the pub unnoticed on his next shift until Rose found him donning his apron ready for opening time. 'Morning, Gary. Forget we had a meeting first thing, did you?'

He gave a sheepish grin but did not reply.

'Come on, Gary, don't be shy. Let's talk about it.' Rose took his arm and sat him at the bar. 'So, did you give our suggestion some thought?'

'Yeah.' He paused, as if deciding which answer to give. 'I don't mind trying it.'

From my vantage point I saw Rose struggling to maintain composure. 'Well, that's good. Perhaps the first thing we'll work on Gary is energy. What do you say?'

He shrugged then blew up his cheeks, letting the air blow out through his lips.

I stepped in before he triggered Rose. Not an advisable start on his part. 'Gary, Rose is right - we'll take small steps. But you need to be more aware of how you project yourself.'

'Huh.' He screwed up his face and slumped backwards onto the bar.

'Never mind. We can work on that.' Rose forced a positive face. 'I want us to talk about goals before your first shift of the week and again at your last.' Rose waited. 'I'm asking you, Gary, which means I need you to respond.'

I wasn't sure if Gary's sitting upright was a coincidence or he read Rose's demeanour, but it counted for something. He looked at her and nodded. 'We can give it a go. Why not?'

'Great.' Rose said, the strain of self-control showing in her eyes. 'So, for this week I want you to do one additional thing while you are working.' She paused. Nothing. 'I would like you to look at others for clues about what they may think or feel about you and the service you offer.' She hesitated again. 'Can you sense I'm waiting for an answer, Gary?'

'Do you want me to start now?' He avoided eye contact.

'Yes, Gary, and always. It will help you read the room and avoid embarrassing situations.'

'I'm all up for that.' Gary's show of enthusiasm surprised the two of us.

'Great. Look forward to it,' Rose said, holding her hand to seal the deal.

It was to be a long journey, as it was with many in our time there.

Chapter Eleven

Sheila considered herself to be a chef, though not everyone else did. Her cooking was renowned throughout the village for the wrong reasons, but her intentions were honourable. Her lack of training was the reason, rather than her inability. A no-nonsense single mother of two, she travelled by minivan taxi from the outlying township, hailing from the apartheid era.

'Hi, Sheila. We have all been working together for a while, and Rory and I have been enjoying your food for a few months now.'

'Hello, madam. Thank you.' Sheila curtsied, one hand clutching her elbow, the other offering to shake hands.

'Call me Rose, please,' she said, uncomfortable with titles, especially when not earned. 'I want you to show me around the kitchen and tell me how I can make your job easier.'

'Oh, Mrs Rose, I'm so happy you have taken over Cobblers. It needs a woman to help sort it out.' She threw me a look. Or was it a challenge?

'Isn't that the case for everything?'

The ladies nodded in agreement.

Rose continued, 'In order to improve things, changes are necessary.' She dropped her face and looked into Sheila's eyes. 'Some of it won't be easy.'

'I agree.' she said, nodding at the obvious message from the new owner of Cobblers Bar and Grill.

'But first let's have a coffee. I want to hear more about you.' Rose pulled two chairs from the dining area, pouring the water from a jug on the table and offering one to Sheila, who hesitated, unsure of the new boss's intention. Word had got out about the two employees that had left. 'Relax, Sheila. We're just two mothers getting to know each other.' She patted the seat next to her.

Sheila took the hot drink and sat on the edge. 'Thank you.'

'You're welcome. You can ask me anything you want to.' Rose broke the uncomfortable silence. 'Personal, business, whatever. We've worked together a bit of late, but let's get to know each other better.' Hoping to reassure Sheila, Rose began telling her about the family, where we had worked before, what made us happy and what we hoped for with the business. 'Now, how about you?'

'I have two young girls, both under ten years old. Their *gogo* (grandmother) looks after them while I'm at work.' Sheila smiled when she mentioned her family. 'We are a house full of girls as my husband left one night, and we never heard from him again. That was five years ago.'

'I'm sorry.' Rose held Sheila's hand.

I tidied up the stockroom as I listened in to the conversation. They started with small talk about their families and South Africa, then discussed the challenges of running a kitchen in a pub and restaurant. While they talked, I cleared out old furniture, cleaning supplies, and cooking utensils, and organised the backrooms where we stored the beer.

'You will not believe what I've just found,' I said as much to myself as the other two.

'What've you got?' Rose peered from out of the kitchen. 'Wow. They're stunning.' She wiped the levered keys on one of several mechanical tills. 'Wonder how old they are.'

'Ancient.' I pushed one of the large buttons causing the number two to flip up in the narrow window at the top of the casing. 'These are so cool.'

'Let me see.' Rose pushed another then pulled the lever on the side. The machine whirled then rang out followed by the cash drawer opening. 'We've got to use them at the front of the house, Rory.'

'Agreed. They will add to the character of the place. Gary? Help me lift these things.'

We replaced the electronic machines in the pub with the antiquated manual models alongside the credit card zip-zapper.

Rose stood in the middle of the bar, her eyes flicking from the tills to the furniture and décor. 'Gosh, she needs a makeover and soon, Rory.'

'She?'

'The pub. I know I've said it before.'

'Still a lot of work,' I answered.

'We have no better options and must be trendy if we're going to appeal to the youth.'

'Then let's do it.'

'It will be fun, you'll see.' Rose took my arm in hers and placed her head on my shoulder. 'It's ours, Rory. We're publicans. A fresh start.'

Gary coughed, pulling a face in disgust at our excitement as he cleaned the antique tills.

'Right. Open the doors. Trading time,' Rose called, embarrassed.

The rest of the day passed without issues and the next shift was due.

'Sheila, I reckon that's about it for now. Must be time to catch your taxi. Thanks so much for all your help today.'

'You are welcome, Mrs Rose.' Sheila collected her bag, waving goodbye as she made to leave the building.

'We will discuss new menus and standards in the kitchen at your next shift.'

'Okay. I have left a list of stuff we need for the cooking area and toilets,' she said. 'Bye!'

'Have a safe trip home,' Rose answered. 'Rory, are you ready to call it a day?'

'Yeah. Let's get out of here.'

'Hold on. I just want to get Sheila's list from the kitchen.' She spun around and darted back to where she came from, then called to me, 'Oh, my word. Rory, come and see this. That is so sweet.' Rose pointed to a piece of paper pinned to the noticeboard above the sink. 'I like Sheila. She has a good heart and a great work ethic. We just need to get her some help with the cooking. Read this, Rory. So cute.'

Hello Rose.
Please add these to the Cobblers food list.
Lettuce. It has gone vrot. Her use of Afrikaans to say the lettuce was off.

Onions
Potatoes
Red pepper
Green pepper
Toilet pepper
Dish wash
Fresh melk (milk)
Chef Sheila

The next morning, I drove into town armed with shopping lists from Sheila and Rose, an order for the brewery, and instructions to collect change from the bank.

On my return to the car after running errands, I pulled a bunch of pamphlets tucked behind my windscreen wipers, as was the norm. People had to try to eke a living in a society unable or unwilling to support the needy.

I tipped the car guard, and because the traffic was busy, I stayed in my carpark, sifting through the adverts in my hand. Retailers offering specials, butcher promoting deals, donations needed for charities, clearance items at a shoe shop. Then the last pamphlet caught my eye. Bright pink and typed in italics.

MAMMA HOPE & DR. KIDDU
PENIS EXPERT – MONEY BACK GUARENTEE
I have your last solution try me
Try my new steaming method - (Biocell herb Method)
No Pills needed just bring your penis to me
I will work on your penis and you will leave with surprise,
INCLUDING -:
1. Power of weak penis stronger and harder
2. Gives feeling for sex-mentally
3. Stops quick ejaculation – quick sperming
4. Power for having long sex – many rounds
5. Size expansion tall or larger
CALL 072 ....
N.B. can work on *bad work* lost lover* business.

Turning it over, I read the other side of the poster.

MAMMA HOPE & DR.KIDDU
SOLUTION TO LADIES PROBLEMS – CHEAPEST
& CURES RELATIONSHIPS
Is your husband having an affair you suspect
Is he weak in bed
Is he stinge with money
Is there somebody jealous with your relationship
Body Illness
Do you have bad period pains, lots of blood or no blood
at all
Do you have vagina problems
Do you have any stomach pains plus all old people
Sickness like legs, back joint, chest

I could not wrap my head around the concept and pondered. A mix of sadness and fascination overcame me, but the style of the marketing intrigued me. This was a well-planned blurb for a specific market, not a last-minute sales pitch.

What wonderful names - Mamma Hope and Dr. Kiddu. Were they the same person? My mind whirled. *Perhaps they brought about Hope? I Kiddu not.* I smiled at my pathetic dad joke. The joy of Africa and her diversity. So special.

The attendant coughed at my open window, holding out his hand with a look on his face that I vacate the space, leaving me in no doubt he believed I was unwell.

'Oops, sorry, buddy.' I tipped him another two rand and drove off, deep in thought.

This is what it's all about. Starting over. Experiences outside of my comfort zone. Different people, cultures and beliefs. I wondered where Themba was and if he was okay.

Next stop was the local bottle store in town. Inside the dingy shop the prim and proper owner greeted me. 'How is business, Mr Wilde?' His immaculate black hair and olive complexion suggested this was not what his dream was. His family, though, had an ominous reputation of retribution should you not pay your bills on time.

'Getting there, my friend.' I handed over a wad of fifty-rand notes to cover my order of drinks and cigarettes. 'See you next week.'

'Not if I can help it, Mr Wilde. Just joking.' His smile did not reach his eyes.

I packed the drinks into my car boot and walked a block down the road to a shop labelled Germiston Wishy Washy – We wash your troubles away.

I found the manager's windowless office amidst the laundry machines and steam in the far corner of the building.

'Morning.' I greeted the large man sitting at an untidy desk with paperwork strewn all over it.

'Well, hello Rory,' he said, replacing his reading glasses with another pair from on top of his head. 'What can I do for you?'

'Here to pay the rent,' I said.

'What, already Mr Cobblers? A day early?' He beamed.

'While we had it, we thought we'd pass it on.'

'I knew you two were worth the risk. Well done.' He lifted a cash box from beneath his desk and opened it with a bunch of keys around his neck, rubbing his fingers together as I counted out the seven hundred rand in bills. 'Why, thank you, young sir.' With careful attention he arranged the bills and then wrote out a receipt using a carbon book, tearing my copy from it.

I said goodbye to him and went back to the car, feeling somewhat intrigued by the sleaze of an underworld I had not experienced before. Hardly, but it sure felt that way.

Next, I headed out of town to the industrial areas of Germiston, where the national South African Breweries had a depot. It was a shining icon of industry compared to the other businesses and factories in the area. Immaculate gardens surrounded buildings that featured brands such as Castle Lager, Lion Lager, Hansa Pilsener, and Carling Black Label. All promised a life most could not dream of. Well-dressed security officers stopped each car and denied access unless there was a booked appointment.

Inside the office, reps, and customers sat in a waiting room most hospitals would be envious of, listening for our number to be called.

'Hello, Cobblers. What can we do for you this week?' A woman dressed in a grey business suit invited me to sit opposite her.

I handed over the order and paid the bill upfront.

'Delivery before Friday, okay?' she asked.

'Perfect, thank you.'

'Great. I'll read your order out to make sure we have it right. Twelve cases of Castle, five cases Black Label, three cases of Lion, three kegs of Guinness, two kegs of Kilkenny and two kegs of Scrumpy Jack cider.' She looked at me and smiled.

'Thank you.' I took the receipt she had wrapped in advertising pamphlets and left the building down a flight of white steps. The experience was far less pleasant than from the two enterprises I had visited earlier in town. The sense of condescension struck deep with this one.

A visit to the greengrocer and supermarket came next, and then Len helped me unload it all. 'Apart from Philemon, the place is empty.' He waved his jazz hands at the desolate bar.

'You pack the stuff away and I'll serve if anyone turns up,' I said, passing Len the last box of vegetables. 'Leave these in the kitchen, Sheila will be in soon.'

Len gave me a look of horror at being asked but changed it to a smile of capitulation and disappeared.

'Aha. I see the new owner is very busy.' Philemon shuffled past on his way to the bathroom.

'Morning. How are you?'

An awkward silence followed as my only customer of the day disappeared down the passage. *Nice work, Rorke Wilde. Great service,* I admonished myself as I wiped down the top of the bar.

'Don't be hard on yourself, young man.' Our author friend reappeared, startling me from myself. He stopped in front of me and offered out a hand in greeting. 'I'm Philemon Dlamini.'

'Yes, we know. You are our resident writer.' I smiled back, shaking his hand.

'Well, I don't know about that,' he answered. 'Not sure I'm a writer or a resident, but I appreciate the sentiment.' He hesitated for a moment, then asked, 'Mind if I join you? I'm in a bit of a bind with my writing, so I just need to step away for a bit.' He pulled out a bar stool and sat in front of me.

'Writer's block, hey?' I said, pleased to relate.

'Indeed. Not as dramatic as the industry or films suggest, but frustrating nonetheless.' His diction was amazing, as was his demeanour.

'Sorry, did I say something wrong?' He gave me a confused look.

I closed my mouth. 'Please excuse me. It took me aback, hearing you speak.'

'For a black man, you mean.' He pronounced each word distinctly.

'No, no, that's not what I meant,' I stuttered. 'Well, yes, but…but not in a derogatory way.' My face was red from embarrassment.

His laughter quietened me, and with a huge smile he lifted his hand to talk. 'I understand, Mr Wilde. I'm just winding you up.' His eyes brimmed with humour. 'I know I don't sound local for I spent many a year studying abroad. You should see how the Black folk here respond - the same way as all nationalities. Shock at someone not falling within an expected perception.' Philemon rubbed his hands together, then pointed to his corner. 'Anyway, time I returned to the grindstone; I have taken up enough of both our times.' He got up from his stool and moved away.

'Perhaps we can catch up when we're not so busy. I'd love to hear more about you and your writing and travels.'

He stopped and looked over his shoulder. 'Maybe.' Then continued on his way.

'Right, that's me done.' Len returned from the back just as a group of sales reps entered the pub. I extricated myself, my mind still on my meeting with Philemon Dlamini. Before returning for our night shift behind the bar, there would be time for a nap.

Rose, too, had completed her business and family chores. The household did not run itself, and the family also wanted quality time. *How does she do it? I'll never know.* I appreciate that women like Rose are where our superhero icons originate – the ones we see in comic books and on the screen. My failing was and still is that I do not pay enough homage to the fact; nor do I show my admiration and love for her as I should or want to. I try to help with menial jobs given to me without confidence. The shame is mine.

We collapsed on the bed and passed out, and within what seemed minutes, the alarm clock sounded, and the radio played.

'Come on, Rory. We don't want to be late.' Rose yawned, heading for the shower.

I stirred. Although I was always exhausted I was enjoying the change in our life. Sure, there were aspects of running the bar and grill that did not sit well, but the freedom and making calls for our own good was exhilarating.

'Quit your daydreaming, mister. Hop into that bathroom.' Rose sat in front of the dresser, blow drying her hair. 'I want to focus on Gary today, see how he's getting on with his assignment of assessing people and situations.'

'Sounds like fun.'

'Rory? Unnecessary.' Rose shot me a look.

'He just drives me crazy. I can't handle –'

'I know. I know. Laziness and stupidity.' Rose interrupted. 'Not everyone is clever.'

'Stupid has nothing to do with intelligence. Quite the opposite. I've come across more idiots with master's degrees who are as dumb as shit,' I said, heading for the bathroom. 'That and the lack of gut feel are a lethal combo.'

Rose sighed at me riding on my white horse. 'That's your boarding school upbringing coming through.' She changed the subject. 'We must watch our corporate-speak because it can intimidate people. If they even understand it.'

Without drawing attention, Rose and I spent the day observing Gary as he went about his work.

Sheila stopped Rose around lunchtime with a concerned look, her hands were on her hips. 'Is Gary all right?' she asked. 'He's acting strange today.' She pursed her lips in distaste.

'In what way?' Rose gave me a sideways glance.

'He keeps staring at me and making faces. *Eish*. I don't know why.' Sheila laughed. 'Silly boy.' She rubbed her hands against together and bustled off, muttering to herself.

'I know what she means.'

'Me too,' Rose said with a sigh. 'We'll have a word with him.'

'So how are you finding the task we gave you, Gary?' Rose asked at the end of his shift.

'It doesn't make much sense to me, to be honest.' He gave another of his classic shrugs. 'Everyone has a different face, so I can't tell what they're thinking, and I don't really want to.'

The awkwardness between the three of us was almost palatable.

'How does this situation we're in now feel?' Rose asked.

'Okay.' he responded, but we could see there was nothing on offer from his end.

'Why don't we keep going with it until the end of the week and take another look at it then?' Rose suggested.

'I don't see the point.' Gary had raised his voice but brought it back down. 'It's all mumbo jumbo. Do you think I'm a clown or something?' His anger reappeared in the colour of his face. 'Or a dog and you're trying to teach me new tricks?'

'Gary,' Rose said, 'it's nothing of the kind. We spoke about this last week.'

'Yeah, well, it just makes no sense. If I wanted to do more than I'm doing now, I sure as hell wouldn't stay in this shithole.' He looked at us both, then said, 'Okay, so now I feel the room,' and giggled, which turned into fractious laughter.

'Oooh, boy.' I looked at Rose.

'Not now, Rory.' She turned to Gary. 'Have you quite finished? You're not funny. We'll end our chat here and catch up again next week.'

'No need to chat. Just let me carry on as I have been. Not much to ask.'

'We'll determine that next week, shall we? Thanks for your time. Have a good day.' Rose stood and left to open the bar. I joined her.

Gary left the room.

'Wow, that was hard work. You know my thoughts about a leopard and its spots,' I teased Rose.

'Hope I will not hear this all day, Rorke Wilde.' Rose pretended to be cross but hid a smile. 'I'll tell you what, Rory, I just don't want to worry years down the line that we could've done more.'

'I hear you,' I answered. 'But my gut is screaming in protest.'

'Mine too, Rory. Mine too.'

Chapter Twelve

'We have a pretty good understanding about how Cobblers runs now, Rory. What's even clearer is the need for entertainment,' Rose pondered. 'But I've got an idea, Rory. Tomorrow we're heading for the city to find a few live bands and maybe some karaoke.'

'Sounds good to me.' Her joy and beauty lifted my spirits. *Who am I to argue?* My heart pumped with love despite my reservations about visiting clubs in the city.

'What we need is a decent cover band for Friday nights that does chart-topping songs well. Mixed with the classics from the nineties so we can broaden our customer base.'

'Last of the Boomers? Can't help you there. I'm a die-hard Pink Floyd fan.'

Rose huffed at me with slitted eyes. 'Tell me about it. Talk about stuck in the seventies and eighties.' She changed track - no pun intended. 'Saturday nights we should have a more mellow vibe. Like a guitarist or someone playing a piano in the corner. A singer crooning in the background.' She sat in silence each of us in our own thoughts. 'Karaoke Tuesdays?'

'That works but karaoke? Really?' I screwed up my face.

'Some people find it fun and are true fanatics of singalongs. It never goes out of fashion, and it seems to be making a comeback of late, so it's worth a try.' She looked at me for support.

'It's so embarrassing standing in front of people singing. Especially with a voice like mine.'

'Don't tell me. *Tone deaf Wilde* they call you,' Rose spoke in monotone to reiterate the point.

'Thanks, Rose.'

'My pleasure.' She gave me a pat on the head. 'So that's settled. Tomorrow night, we're off to Joburg in search of talented individuals for this place.'

'It's a date.'

'Not a date, Rory. Work. But if you behave we can have some fun.' Rose looked over her shoulder at me.

'See you later,' I said after her, picking up the car keys. I was standing in for Gary, who had called in sick. He preferred to avoid Rose rather than face the consequences of not finishing his project commitment.

Sunette and Len were going to look after Cobblers while we prepared to explore Johannesburg's nightlife. Len would be in charge and loving it.

We soon realised in our search that the well-known musicians were too expensive and could perform nowhere near us because of their contracts with other venues. So, we changed our plans and sought the smaller bars and restaurants on the outskirts, leaving the nightclubs alone. What followed was a distressing ordeal of exploring grimy neighbourhoods with sketchy characters loitering around questionable dives. If we spotted promise in a band or singer, we would pretend to be fans, approach them on their break, and slip them our business card.

'This lot is hopeless and boring.' Rose finished her drink and climbed off the stool after the eighth or ninth nightspot in just a few hours. 'I've seen and heard enough. We're out of here. This is not what we're looking for.'

'At last. Now you're talking.' I followed her, leaving the fake Joe Cocker grinding to a depressed collection of down and outs in a seedy tavern.

We crossed the street, jay walking to avoid the shifty clusters of people selling their wares on the corners. The smell of marijuana filled the night sky. Flashing lights of a cop car and neon signs highlighted the dour buildings of the inner city.

'Right. Last one. Then we'll have got to choose from what we've found so far.' Rose pulled me into a small cocktail lounge.

'Great. I'm over this shit,' I said. 'If I never see another spittoon, smell another funny cigarette or have to dodge any more shiny poles it will be too soon.'

'Thanks, Rory. You've been an angel. Very patient.'

I contemplated whether her words were genuine or laced with sarcasm. Deciding on the former, I kissed her cheek, slipped into the booth and ordered alcohol-free beers for us both. The night was taking its toll.

A man in a tuxedo walked up to the stage, grabbed the microphone, and said, 'Good evening, everyone, for another evening of entertainment. The irrepressible Breathe will play in about fifteen minutes, but first, I want to introduce you to a new band. Please give a big hand in welcoming The Coverettes.'

A trio of two guitar-clutching guys and a woman took the stage, greeted by indifferent applause. Nerves were dancing behind all their stage smiles. The presenter wiped his brow with his sleeve, shaking his head at the lack of response.

'Hi,' the bandleader jumped in but we lost the rest of what she was saying because the speakers went silent. She acknowledged the small crowd seated at the tables after an eternity of sound checks. Finally, the speakers kicked in. 'Evening, everyone. We are The Coverettes and here is our latest cover. You should all know it. OMC's *How Bizarre.'*

'Not that bloody song again. It's everywhere,' I mumbled to Rose. She put a hand on my arm and shushed me.

Ooh, baby (Ooh, baby)
It's making me crazy (It's making me crazy)
Everytime I look around
Everytime I look around (Everytime I look around)
Everytime I look around
It's in my face

We waited to hear more songs until they thanked the crowd, who managed a reluctant gesture of light clapping and made way for the main act.

Rose got up off her chair and strode to the singer, giving her a business card, and returned without a word. The vocalist glanced at it and stuck it in the opening of her blouse, gave Rose a thumbs up from across the room and continued to help the group pack up their gear.

'The band?' I asked.

'Too fucking right.'

'Rose?' I gave her a fake look of shock.

We laughed at her choice of language, relieved to have found what it was we'd been looking for.

Rose invited them over by sending them a round of drinks. They responded by approaching us with thanks. Not one for wasting time, Rose suggested they do a trial run at Cobblers Bar & Grill the next weekend if they were available.

'We'd love to,' the singer said, bouncing up and down with excitement, still wearing her stage makeup. 'Right, boys?' The lads mumbled in agreement, looking ill at ease.

'Germiston beware. Things are going to get hot around here.' Rose lifted her glass. She and the singer chatted about the details while I watched the next performance.

The vocalist was the epitome of everything I feared. *How do they do it?* The same question ran through my mind whenever I watched, listened to, or saw a fledgeling composer. A cocktail of pity and admiration stirred in me. In a room of apathetic listeners, an artist sang covers and their own songs, looking for a break. Hoping that one day the world would hear their voice through the songs they wrote. I related to the misery I noticed in this one's eyes and downtrodden body language – it was why I had stopped dreaming of becoming a writer. There can be nothing more awful than to bare your soul to others and risk being ridiculed or, worse still, ignored.

Here I was doing the very thing I despise-judging artists. My conscience and spirit waged a battle in my mind. *Original artists should only perform their songs. Least of all this middle-aged man singing 'Money' from Dark Side of the Moon. Copying Pink Floyd is sacrilege and should be a social offence.* I shook my head at my own embarrassment. *Oh, shut up, Wilde, you should know better.* I scolded myself.

'All right, guys, see you next week,' Rose farewelled our new signing. 'One down, two to go.' She showed me on her fingers.

'The same to you,' I answered in jest.

She turned her hand around to show a peace sign and pulled a face.

'Sorry,' I said. 'What now?'

'Karaoke.' Rose's eyes lightened. 'I want to hire a gig that relates to our customers.'

'Are you serious? I thought you were joking about that.'

'The Coverettes will bring in the kids and the young at heart. Our karaoke night must appeal to our middle-aged and older generation yet not exclude any of them.'

'Tough call.'

'I know, but each of the entertainment evenings must attract a different crowd. That way we will appeal to a broader cross-section of the community.'

'Good point. Where do we start?' I asked.

'Pub crawling.' Rose gave me a smirk.

'Now that's what I'm talking about. What more can a man ask for? Not.'

Rose slapped my knee, and we finished our drinks. 'Less of the contempt, thank you. We might find our Saturday singer there as well.' She stood, pulling at my hand. 'But we've had enough for one night. Let's head home. I'm buggered.'

With the same team managing the bar the following week, we set out to find our artists, this time with better preparation. Customer suggestions on places and people supplemented our research.

We found our karaoke gig within the hour. Karaoke, Okes, *Oke* being South African slang for guys, was the perfect fit for our intended crowd. A middle-aged brother-and-sister act whose choice of music was wide enough to cater for most of the generations. Their sense of humour helped to overcome shyness and promote sociability. Rose offered the same deal of a trial run on Tuesday evenings to see if both parties were happy.

Nevertheless, that was the end of our success that evening. Despite encountering many solo performances through the adjoining suburbs, we did not find anybody suitable. All were talented in what they did but were geared towards a particular target audience. Greek,

Portuguese, spiritual, religious, Afrikaans, Zulu, to name a few of the cultures we encountered. A marvellous diversity of lifestyles makes up Johannesburg and its plethora of clubs, bars, restaurants, and dives. There too we met our seven Brothers Grimm characters, more prevalent in some bars than others, but all present.

'We'll just have to keep our eyes and ears open.' Rose said on our return home. 'I don't want to get the wrong entertainer – the Cobbler's lot won't ever let us forget if we do.'

Once home, we settled into bed with a hot drink and watched a silly movie on the TV, cutting ourselves off from the rest of the outside world if only for a while.

In an advert break I turned to Rose. 'This is a lot tougher than I thought.'

She smiled and rubbed my forearm. 'It's hospitality, baby - nothing harder.' She faked an American twang.

'I mean tonight was bloody awful.' I put my mug on the side table and lay down.

'It doesn't get any easier, Rory.'

'You could have told me before we bought the place?' I gave her a sideward look.

'Don't start with me.' She played along.

'It's been quite a night, all right.' I said, grinning.

Rose looked at me and laughed. 'That's some mouthful of rhyming words, Rorke Wilde.' She switched off the TV. 'Way past your bedtime, methinks.'

'You can say that again and if I don't hear another folksong, I'm fine with that.' I said.

'At least you have a sleep-in tomorrow morning. All we need to do is open the pub at ten o'clock. Everything else is ready.' Rose kissed my forehead. 'Night, Rory.'

'Goodnight.' I mumbled, almost asleep.

Chapter Thirteen

It was time for the hard slog – notifying the residents who our entertainers were and when they would perform. We advertised in the local rag and trudged through the suburbs, stuffing leaflets into post-boxes, inviting punters to the bar with the hook of live music. Rose designed and costed the re-fit. All that we had and dreamt of depended on the business's success. Every cent and spare moment at our disposal rested on appealing to a broad base within the community.

'Rose? Are you ready?' I asked.

'As I'll ever be.' Her nerves were apparent.

We drove to our tavern just a kilometre away, where we planned to stay until dawn.

The afternoon regulars were finishing their drinks and bidding farewell to mates and acquaintances. Newcomers were securing evening spots at the dining tables.

'Looks promising.' Rose looked at the patrons and waved at those she recognised.

'Sure does. The word is out.' I ducked beneath the bar flap, checking the fridges were full and backup bottles of spirits were on hand.

Rose acknowledged Len. 'So, what have we got today?'

'A solid mix,' Len answered, scanning the room. 'Joker and Weirdo are in the corner telling smutty jokes. Doom's watching the news on the telly.' He pointed each of our caricatures out. 'Sloth has left Truther, searching for a place to sleep. Haven't seen Kugel or Balsak. But it's early days.' Len gave us a wide grin. 'It will be a busy night. Everyone in Germiston is talking about the live band.'

'Hope you're right. A lot depends on tonight. The team is already to go?' Rose smiled at him.

'Yup. All except Gary, who hasn't arrived yet.'

Rose rolled her eyes. 'If he doesn't arrive in ten minutes, send him a text. If half an hour passes and still no response, I'll call him.'

'Right, guys,' I told the team. 'The Coverettes set up at seven o'clock and start playing half an hour later.' I chatted with the team of supplementary servers and bartenders. 'Don't be nervous, just do your best. Any issues, speak to me or Rose. Remember, the money is in the shooters. When customers order a round, recommend a quick shot to accompany it. Anyone too drunk or offensive, let us know. Don't get involved or escalate anything. Good luck and enjoy.'

At that point Gary finally appeared.

'Glad you could make it.' Rose gave him a sarcastic smile, which he didn't read.

'You're welcome.' He joined the rest of the team, offering no explanation.

Dressed in their Irish-emerald aprons, the servers began taking orders for food and drinks. Cobblers Bar & Grill was filling at a rate I had never seen, even before we owned it. With limited room at the counter, the patrons stood behind the first row, thrusting money through the bodies in front of them at the bartenders and placing their drink orders. The old-fashioned tills' ka-ching harmonised with the drawers' mechanical clatter slamming shut.

Sweet music to our ears. The punters were three rows deep at the bar, and every chair and table were taken. Young adults occupied windowsills and the steps to the toilets and leaned on walls.

The band completed their final sound checks, then introduced themselves.

'Good evening, Germiston.'

The crowd's cheer was a little sarcastic.

'Welcome to Cobblers Bar & Grill.'

The horde was less vocal.

'My thanks and best of luck to the new owners, Rose and Rory. Come up here, you two. The town's folk wants to meet you.' Wolf whistles and generous applause ensued. 'These two are rocking Germiston with Cobblers. The go-to venue in town and you ain't seen nothing yet.' Her voice surged and sped up with excitement. 'Enjoy, folks.' The singer waved and danced to the music of the guitarist and keyboard player.

Drinks flowed with the melody. The bar remained three deep, with people clawing and pleading for service, chit-chatting and laughing as they waited.

'Four lagers, two white wines, a brandy and Coke, and two whiskeys on the rocks, please, *boetie* (young brother)?' a client called out. 'Oh, and while I'm here, nine springbok shots.' These were mint liqueurs topped with a cream-based one.

'Coming up.' Len repeated the request to Gary, who oversaw mixing the cocktails.

'Might as well add the same number of tequilas, my friend.' The customer added to his order. 'Saves me queuing up again.'

Trays of drinks and empty glasses shuttled between the bar and kitchen as we shared the washing up to keep pace.

Thick swirls of cigarette smoke defiled the dance floor before the band, where customers jiggled and cavorted to the beat. Raucous laughter and giggles filled the band's breaks between songs. People spilled onto the sidewalk, the doors wide open to ease the heat of the African summer night. The walls were glowing in a disco-esque fashion due to the flash of headlights from passing traffic.

'Who needs mirror balls?' I said to Rose, taking a moment to connect with her. 'It's like a friggin' nightclub in here.'

She smiled and disappeared, serving another round of drinks.

'All good, Len?' I called across as we poured drinks at the bar.

'Perfect,' a sweaty Len answered. 'This is amazing.' He didn't break his flow. 'Best pub in Germiston after this. The word is spreading like wildfire. Woo-hoo!' He pirouetted behind the bar to a loud applause by those waiting for their drinks.

The band played until midnight, then stayed for a while and mingled, pleased with their reception and the nicer location. At three o'clock the remaining staff departed. The rest of the diehards disappeared around an hour later. The sweetest sounds were the front gates clicking closed for the last time. All who remained were Rose and me.

'That was fantastic.' Rose hugged me in the middle of the littered dance floor. 'Just look at the place. Like a bomb has gone off.'

We laughed as much from exhaustion as relief. A trouble-free evening to boot. The behaviour of our seven caricatures followed the expected norms, but the team managed them with a professional aplomb. We cleaned up the mess, put the garbage bags out, filled the empty crates with beer bottles, and packed them in the shed behind the building.

'What say you we go home, Rose?' I put my arm around my exhausted but still stunning partner, who rested her head on my shoulder.

'Sounds wonderful.'

We checked all the equipment, turned off the lights and chained the security gates. Sunrise was lighting the horizon in gold and oranges, and birds were chirping in the trees to welcome the morning. We drove home in silence. Satisfied with a job well done and looking forward to a rest.

I stripped off my clothes and took a shower; the water massaging the back of my neck, my chin on my chest as I relaxed. I hated every moment of what we did. It was way beyond my comfort zone. I returned to the bedroom, where Rose sat in the middle of the bed with a pile of cash, wearing a broad grin.

'We're rich.' She threw the money into the air, for it to cascade over her head.

'What a great night. Not sure about rich, though.' I picked up another handful of notes and tossed it to the ceiling.

I had never seen so much cash. A mountain of fifty-rand bills. One was enough to buy us a decent meal in a quality restaurant. Rose sorted the money into thousand-rand bundles wrapped in elastic bands, put the wad into a cloth bank bag, and placed it under the bed. I turned off the television and climbed under the sheet, resting my head on the pillow beside my gorgeous wife. A sense of peace and contentment overcoming me. Despite my negative feelings, I knew I was growing from the experience, and it would stand me in good stead for the rest of my life.

'Wonder how long we can keep this up,' Rose murmured in the darkness.

'Don't know, but it sure isn't for the fainthearted.'

'No more than two years, Rory.' Rose turned on her side. 'Let's set that as a goal.'

'I'm with you.'

We slipped into the peace of sleep.

Every week after that, our Friday night event became bigger, so we had to keep track of the number of people inside. This did not prevent the revellers dancing on the pavement outside, much to the local police's and nearby homes irritation. Rose's shower after the first night turned into luxurious saunas of cash.

Our reputation as the trendy place to be forced competing hospitality locations in the area to follow suit. The difference was in the entertainment's quality. Strangers would approach us in public to express gratitude for the wonderful moments. Despite our objections, restaurants would gift Rose and me extras and discount prices when we ate out. It was an uncomfortable sense of popularity that Rose and I shied from, although I noticed her enjoying it occasionally. And why not? The work was challenging by any standard.

The reputation came at a cost, though. Most of the team worked hard and needed longer periods to recover from the rowdy evenings. Besides The Coverettes on Fridays, karaoke was also becoming popular.

One Friday evening after a heavy night before, Rose and I called into Cobblers to see how everybody was doing, including the entertainment. Since it wasn't busy, we dropped by an hour before closing.

'That's funny. The gate's locked.' Rose pulled again, then used her keys to unlock it.

'Shouldn't be,' I said, taking my time to open the gate should there be any danger within. 'That's strange. It's quiet too.'

'Careful, Rory.' She held my hand, which I used to try to stop her from entering the building with me.

I reached for my .38 Special revolver from my jeans front pocket and peered around the wooden screen separating the rooms from the outside doors. Dim lights, no sign of anyone.

'What the hell was that?' Rose asked in my ear after a light giggle sounded from the restaurant corner booth.

'Not sure.' I answered in a low tone. 'Gary's bicycle is still out front.'

'Don't rush, Rory.' We inched along the curtains to avoid being targets.

'I recognise that smell.' Rose inhaled again. A sweet musky odour wafted our way, followed by a puff of smoke. 'If that is Gary, I'm going to kick his arse.' Rose stepped forward. 'Gary, what do you think you are doing?' Rose's voice grew to a yell.

He and a girl sat in their underwear smoking a joint. On the table in front of them was a bottle of our finest Bushmills single malt Irish whiskey and two shot glasses, and empty packets of salted chips, nuts, and biltong were strewn around them.

'Chill, Mamma Wilde.' He smiled with wasted eyes, even less able to read the room. The friend giggled, then staggered towards the toilets, clutching her clothes.

'Don't you speak to me like that, Gary.' Rose lifted a finger at him. 'Get yourself dressed and go home. We'll talk about this at a later date.'

'Why are you always so uptight? The singer had a sore throat, so she left early. The crowd didn't hang around either. Take a chill pill,' Gary grumbled, using an arm on the table to steady himself. 'I feel sorry for James.'

'Just get out and take your friend with you.' Rose slammed the gates closed after they left and turned up the lights in the bar. 'What are we going to do with that boy?'

'Not so much of a lad. He's old enough to know better and understand consequences,' I answered.

Rose looked at me and shook her head in disappointment at Gary's behaviour. 'At least we tried.'

'That we did. Let's get out of here. He's ruined the sales for today.' I offered Rose my hand.

'I'll give him what for the next time I see him.' Rose took my offer. 'See if I don't.'

'I bet, but don't stress over it. He's not worth it.' I knew Rose would do anything to help someone, but you crossed her kindness at your jeopardy.

Chapter Fourteen

Our entertainment rollout continued unabashed. Despite exhaustion, stress, long hours and challenging individuals, we pushed forward.

Dez and Lez, a middle-aged couple, ran Karaoke Okes. We booked them for a midweek slot on Tuesday evenings. This was the perfect place for the customer who enjoyed listening to newcomers or singing their favourite songs from a specific era.

Jokers were in their element, at peace with their own company. The rest of the Grimm-like crew? Not so much.

Dez and Lez started their evening with a rendition from Sonny and Cher, followed by The Carpenters. Usually by then the audience would have made enough requests to keep the show going.

Shy singers pretended to be alone by avoiding eye contact and staring at the big screen on the wooden entertainment stand. They'd be turning every shade of red, the sweat exposing their fear, yet there they were facing their terror – kudos to them. Most sang solo, focusing on the lyrics, while the more serious competitors danced and interacted with the guests. Karaoke triumphed, despite the absence of talented performers.

Disliking every moment, I still felt revitalised after each session. Folk left in an improved frame of mind, humanity benefitting from the pastime. What fascinated me was watching people's behaviours.

Doom accompanied the fearful. Some were so shy they burbled through their chosen song. Again, I asked myself. *What made them do it?* Week after week in some bizarre ceremony, hoping one day it would transport them to the mystical world of the paid performer.

Some hesitated before the mic but transformed into seasoned

entertainers after the first bar. Perhaps these were shy ones who were in the process of meta morphing.

Kugel, Balsak and Truther fell within this zone. Their self-awareness was harnessed by illusion, infused by alcohol, and bolstered by conceit, ego and bravado or a combination thereof. Bemused, if not perplexed, I observed each of them just as I had done in the seedy bars, my question still unanswered. *Why? What drives them to put themselves under such duress?*

I had always viewed Hans Christian Anderson's folktale, *The Emperor's New Clothes* with scepticism as a child. My young logic fumed about his lack of awareness that he was parading around in his underwear in public. At Cobblers Bar and Grill, evidence showed that people believed in what best suited them. Despite what was clear to others. How prevalent is it today in world politics and the blind lemmings who follow because of an ingrained fear of standing out from a perceived norm?

Occasionally, a natural talent would step up and sing a popular song but with their own take. Oblivious of its cruel impact on those without the gift, their confident humility converted a doubting audience who waited in anticipation for the break in the voice or for the nerves to take over.

Rose also favoured watching instead of participating, but if convinced, preferred a singing clique for safety in numbers.

Sloth succumbed to the crooners, unable to cope with the tribal ambience of banter, encouragement and competition. Preferring to nod off in a corner or with head slumped upon the bar top in abject oblivion.

It was the busiest night of the week aside from Friday, making it very profitable since the fees they charged were so much less than The Coverettes. It was like a social club where people from other hospitality establishments visited for a karaoke competition, similar to a quiz night. The close-knit group discouraged misbehaviour and isolated those who hindered the performance.

Rose's brother Jess became a regular and, after one too many jars, would send in a handful of song requests. Even consuming beer did not dull his embarrassment, and he would call for backup.

'Rory Wilde,' he spoke into the mic. Then: 'Rory Wilde' a little louder. When he spotted me, he waved me towards the stage. 'Come on, Rory. This one's for us.'

I pooh-poohed his attention, but to no avail. Joe Cocker's *You Can Leave Your Hat On* chords belted through the pub.

The audience cheered as he and I sang.

> *Baby, take off your coat*
> *Real slow*
> *And take off your shoes*

They threw the odd object in our direction in jest while taunting our group with wolf whistles and mocking howls. I still struggle to understand why people find it funny when they persuade the owner or boss to take part.

Another busy evening passed by without significant incident.

'Okay, Rose, we're on our way,' the brother from Karaoke Okes, said, winding up the last of the cables from his machinery.

Before we could respond, his sister interjected, 'Nice action on the stage tonight, Rory.' Her coy tease did not go unnoticed by a lone figure in the far corner of the room who snorted in delight.

'Is that you, Philemon?' I asked, peering in the dim light, unsure, for we had never seen him attend any of the entertainment nights.

He howled with laughter, holding his hand to cover his mouth. 'Forgive me.' he gave a playful trot towards us, his tear-filled eyes from the mirth glistening in the bright lights of the stage. 'I'm doing some research on this sort of scene, so thought Cobbler's karaoke night would be ideal.' He sipped the last of the beer in his glass and placed it with care on the bar top. 'Bless my soul, I've had a blast tonight, I am telling you.'

'It's great that you came, Philemon. Awesome to see you here.' Rose took his elbow, and the two sauntered back to his corner.

The *Okes*, Len, Philemon, Rose and I remained, and all were in fits of laughter. Not just by my embarrassing effort at performing, but because Philemon was an absolute delight, and I am sticking to that surmise. Rose had another less complimentary version.

'Anyhow, I must go,' Philemon eventually said, picking up his backpack and waving a takeaway bag in our direction. 'Sheila fed me a wonderful meal earlier and I have leftovers for tomorrow.' He pushed his glasses back on his nose and gave us all a wave as he left the building.

'Goodnight,' Rose said, closing the gate after him, then gave me a puzzled stare. 'Mr Dlamini and Sheila?' She smiled and widened her eyes. 'Well, I never. Philemon getting special treatment, hey? The real reason he was here tonight.'

'Don't get ahead of yourself.'

'Oh, Rory. Didn't you see the look on his face when he mentioned her?' Rose asked. 'That is so sweet. I can't wait until tomorrow when I chat to her.'

We saw the Karaoke Okes duo out, did a quick tidy, then headed home. Rose still enthusing about what she saw as a fledging relationship.

Standup comedy was a short-lived effort. Humour was an unquantifiable apparition with too many variables even for an individual, let alone a crowd under the influence of liquor.

We knew ourselves that we found something funny one day, but on another occasion wouldn't even break into a grin. I cannot explain for certainty why this is the case other than being in awe of the fickle art and the successful comedian.

We found none in Germiston or Johannesburg on our searches, all being just plain boring or an embarrassment. Bum clenches, as we called them, because when humour fails, nothing is more painful.

If there ever existed a way to deter people from drinking, failed satire could do the job. Is there anything worse than performing before an unresponsive crowd because the clown could not read the room? There was nowhere to hide.

We spent many evenings searching clubs and theatres throughout the city, on occasions venturing further afield.

Finding an act that could please everyone posed a challenge, since most shows were geared towards specific groups or caused uncomfortable situations, accentuated by the changes happening in our beloved country and its people. Political correctness and intolerance curtailed once popular performers and topics. We have all watched comedy shows our parents thought hilarious whereas we feel only alarm at the prejudice and slapstick approach.

Those comedians who had the talent to become inclusive became household names and hence were unavailable.

After-parties were the highlight of our entertainment evenings – private moments after the revellers had left, leaving only a few close friends, relatives and the band members to relax behind closed doors. These were a welcome downtime for us after dealing with the pressure of managing people in confined areas who drank too much. Contrary to what many think, it was the older singles, not the young people, who were the most problematic. They were desperate to make up for lost time or endeavouring to try something new.

We grew close to the crew in The Coverettes, who would always stay behind in the evening for a chat and a few beers. We would relax, have a proper drink, and play the fool to release the stress of a busy Friday night. Although it was in the wee hours of the morning, it was our recreation time.

Our favourite amusement was taking turns running out from the kitchen to the barroom and performing scenes from movies, musicals, or famous singers in silence. Charades. The rest then would try to guess who or what it was from our actions. It doesn't seem entertaining, but we would spend hours playing and fall about in tears of laughter. No doubt liquor played its role. Swapping out the alcohol-free beers for authentic Irish stouts was indescribable. I was pitiful, Rose funnier and more believable. They were special times with friends and family whom we are still in contact with decades later. Oh, the memories.

Many of our fonder recollections of running the bar and grill were precious moments like these and meeting people from all walks of life. I'd been unaware of the nocturnal lifestyle, but Cobblers introduced me to it. My childhood and private boarding school were designed to do the opposite. Discos in my teen years held little attraction, and nor did socialising in pubs of an evening. My social inadequacies perhaps had a part to blame.

Rose signed Karaoke Okes for every Tuesday at the end of their first gig. They had brought with them followers, which helped pay the bills. We opted out of them running the evening as a competition, instead choosing participation by encouraging the reserved and inexperienced. Contests and alcohol were a lethal cocktail, often bringing out the worst in people, something we were keen to avoid. Too much drama could destroy a public house's reputation.

Peculiar to such evenings was the propensity for serial sleepers of every age. The energetic gigs often resulted in someone dozing off at the bar or in a chair, sometimes even ending up prostate on the floor. Disturbing them was unpleasant because they could awaken startled, unsure where they were. No doubt a dubious mix of medicine, drugs or alcohol was to blame.

Sloth was in the house one such karaoke evening and remained at the bitter end. Rose shook the middle-aged woman on the shoulder, whispering, 'Hello. How are you?'

Sloth roused, resettled, and snored out loud.

'Wake up. Time for you to go home.' Rose tried her utmost not to snigger.

The lady opened her eyes and looked through the glazed confusion etched in her pale face.

'It's Rose from Cobblers. Think you took a little nap.'

She sat upright, scanning the empty bar, and got up off the stool. 'I'm sorry. I didn't mean to. It's been a tough week.' She ducked into the toilets to freshen up, then with a sheepish gaze said goodnight and bolted out the door, leaving us to clean up.

Dez and Lez stayed for a coffee afterward, but that was their lot and fair enough. They devoted themselves to their craft, being kind-hearted and reliable individuals who were older than Rose and me. Professional in every way, they understood the industry, and this was something we often leveraged off. Goodness knows we needed an impartial sounding board.

'Well, look at that. Seems like Philemon is here again.' Rose nudged me, pointing with her eyes.

His focus was not on his computer but on Sheila, whose body language was coy and engaging as she stood next to his table with her serving tray under one arm.

'Shit, he's here late.' I murmured. 'Did you speak to her?'

'I meant to, but it's been hectic this week.' Rose put a hand to my chest not to follow and headed for the two. 'Well, well. What do we have here?' she teased.

Sheila held her hands to her face to hide her wide smile.

Philemon shuffled in his seat, greeting Rose. 'Evening. Another great night, don't you reckon?'

'More research, is it?' Rose couldn't resist.

Philemon showed the palms of his hands but didn't utter a word.

Rose was not leaving it there. 'You've missed your taxi, Sheila. I think the last one left a couple of hours ago.'

Philemon made his move. 'Actually, Rose, Sheila will stay over at my place. Walking distance from here,' he said, barely audible and ever so uncomfortable. 'We were meaning to tell you, but Sheila was worried you would not approve.'

'Oh, Sheila. That is wonderful news.' Rose grabbed her by the shoulders. 'Why wouldn't I approve? Not that it's any of my business what you get up to in your private life.'

Sheila hugged her back and sobbed. 'It's hard to get over the past here, and how previous employers were mean to us people.'

'I know, my sweetheart, but that doesn't happen anymore, even if it's still happening elsewhere.'

Philemon wiped a tear and stood, holding Rose's shoulders in friendship. 'You are good people, Mrs Wilde.'

'No, we're just everyday folk,' Rose answered. 'Congratulations, you two.'

'Sounds like a champagne moment,' Len chirped, his face alight from the excitement and, as always, on point.

'Now you're talking, Len. Drinks all around.' Rose waved her arms at the handful of people remaining in the pub. 'Come on, peeps, celebratory sip before we all leave for home.' She held her glass high. 'To the loveliest couple whose presence is always a delight,' Rose toasted, looking at Sheila, who squirmed at the attention.

The Karaoke Okes finished their sparkling wine and bid everyone goodnight. Len joined them so they could drop him off at home, which was on their way. Rose and I tidied as we did after each night of entertainment, leaving the new couple with some privacy in Philemon's corner.

A light cough distracted us from our chores. 'Excuse me, Mr and

Mrs Wilde.' Sheila approached, holding Philemon's hand. 'I just want to say thank you.' Her voice was a whisper, her eyes avoiding ours. 'I assure you; it won't alter things here at work.'

Philemon nodded in agreement, stroking at his thin beard with the other hand.

Rose walked across with her palms out in front of her. 'Of course it won't, Sheila. If anything, it will make it better.' She took both Sheila's hands. 'And you know what will happen if it doesn't?' Rose said, showing a fake angry scowl, then changing into a cheeky smile. 'You enjoy your day off together tomorrow. Any plans?'

'Sheila's and my children are meeting for lunch at my place.' Philemon responded, his voice beaming with delight. 'It will be a family day.'

'Sounds amazing,' Rose said while opening the outside security gate to let them out. 'Enjoy.'

'How sweet is that, Rory?' she gushed, hugging me. 'Oh, my word, I've seen it all now.'

'Philemon's quite the player,' I agreed.

'Oh, Rory, you're so full of kak.' *Shit*.

Chapter Fifteen

Two years in, we were even more desperate to change the decor of our Irish-styled pub. The loud, paisley-style carpet in the dining section haunted us and was enough to induce retching. It was not just its awful design but an indescribable odour that worsened should anyone spill liquid on it. The wet dog effect. Regardless of how much vacuuming we did, it made no difference, and we were too scared to have it washed in fear it would unleash all that it held in its grip.

Certain walls had embedded drips running down the paint that even the strongest detergent could not remove. What caused this was a mystery. An answer none of us wanted to find. The old-fashioned wall lights covered with dirty cloth shades gave off a creepy vibe, like a scene from a horror movie or a rundown funeral home.

The once-polished cement floor surrounding the bar and making up part of the dancefloor begged for a decent covering. The toilets were beyond mention – caked in human and animal excrement so not even the flies dared to enter. As for the kitchen, that was a losing battleground against the cooking oil monster. No amounts of soap, lemon juice or even industrial-strength degreasers could cut through the all-engulfing film upon every surface. A tad melodramatic, but you get my drift. We'd raised the funds so decided now was the time.

'All right. Are you ready for the grand reveal? I know it's been a while, but we're ready to start.' Rose shook an A4 folder at the Cobbler's team before opening time one day. 'Exciting times, hey, Gary?'

He looked as if he had missed something, then raised his shoulders.

'Haven't seen nothing yet.'

'Well, you're about to. Focus. I want everybody's honest feedback, please. Drum roll, Rory.'

'Yeah, right.' I smiled.

Rose opened her folder with a flourish. 'Have a look, everyone. The plan removes the seating from the restaurant section, and we'll serve only Irish tavern grub, but the pub remains unchanged. See here?' Rose pointed to the dining space. 'Instead of tables and chairs, we install booths with tartan padded benches and backrests. Similar to an American diner. They all line the walls, so everyone can access the bar and entertainment floor.' She paused for the team to digest this, then moved to the next area. 'In place of the dark wood and Irish green colours running through the pub, we use teal.'

'What's teal?' Gary asked.

'You're such a pleb.' Sunette gave him a withering look. 'A light blue-green colour.' She scowled at him, her forehead exposed from wearing her brown hair in a pony.

'Concentrate on what Rose is saying. What is wrong with you two?' Sheila weighed in. 'Spoilt, that's what. I think it looks great.'

'Teachers' pet,' Gary reacted, and everyone ended up talking at once.

'Okay, guys, focus.' I brought the team back to order.

'Thoughts?' Rose asked.

'It's okay.'

'Thanks, Gary.' High praise indeed.

'I like it too. It will spruce the place up,' Len said, squinting at Sheila in a dare to say otherwise, who laughed.

'But then it won't be an Irish pub.' Gary offered.

'Good point.' Rose lifted a finger. 'More a modern version of the traditional Irish tavern.'

Gary shrugged.

'Right.' Rose rallied the team. 'I'll be searching for DIY volunteers to help with the refurbishment and redecorating. I don't need your answer straight away. Of course, you will be paid, but I'm looking for what you prefer doing. Painting, building, etc.' Rose paused, assessing the team in front of her, then said. 'Okay, we'll leave it there. Back to work, guys. Sheila, can we have a chat, please?'

'Oooh, you are in the shit.' Gary flicked his fingers and disappeared before anyone could respond, Rose shaking her head in disbelief.

'Now, Sheila, I don't want you to think we're closing the kitchen or that your job is in jeopardy. As I have said before, we are looking to simplifying the menu, so we'll have less wastage.'

'I get that,' she responded, showing the whites of her eyes. 'A basic menu means work is easier for me and I'm all for that.'

'Another benefit is leaving earlier in the evenings. Better for your home life.' Rose indexed the words with her fingers in an air quote.

I listened in to the conversation whilst busy with reordering stocks. My presence had been requested; my input - not. Decorating was not my forte like it was Rose's. She had an uncanny eye for turning the blandest offering into tasteful bling.

'When I ask Rory's opinion on colours he can't tell the difference between the various shades,' Rose said, laughing. 'Yellow is yellow, red is red. Nothing in between.'

'Hilarious, Mrs Rose.' Sheila smiled, loving the insinuation. 'You know, Philemon is concerned about losing his corner now that he is back to his writing.'

'I wondered why we hadn't seen him at karaoke of late,' Rose said, holding her chin. 'Well, he needn't worry. We'll make sure it is to his liking.'

'Thank you. He will be happy with that. I'm here to help in any way I can.' Sheila stood, ready to return to the kitchen.

When Rose stopped her. 'On second thoughts.' She gave Sheila a sly look. 'Maybe he can help us with the booths, so he has no excuse.'

'Ay. I like that. Good thinking, missus.' Sheila clapped her hands and almost skipped out of the bar area.

'Poor bugger.'

'Don't you start, Rorke Wilde.' Rose punched my arm and walked off, drawing on her pad.

Like most do-it-yourself projects there were challenges, along with plenty of fun and bonding. As expected, the same group of customers who didn't like previous changes were expressing their thoughts.

'Feels way too modern in here.' *Ballie*, now nothing more than a painful customer, piped out aloud to his drinking mates for all to hear.

'No issue with it as it was, young man. Why the alterations?' another asked.

'Change for the sake of change, I say,' *Ballie* said, taking strength from his buddies.

'I preferred all the traditional stuff. Made it feel like home. Oh, man, I miss Belfast,' a brogue Irish accent joined in.

'They're trying to be trendy to attract all the kids.' The last of the Doom mob had to say his piece.

'Too young. They have no idea,' *Ballie* snorted, putting his arms around his mates in support.

However, the dropping of comments became less frequent, and was now in the minority. Most embraced the new look, and some even contributed their expertise or donated product.

'Just ignore the idiots,' an older lady with long grey hair told Rose. 'If they don't behave, I'll let their wives know at Bingo.' She looked at the band of *Last of the Summer Wine* characters, who pretended not to have heard her but uttered no further remarks.

'Thank you.' Rose touched her hand.

'It's the least I could do, and it is I who should thank you for giving me the contract to supply all your new curtains.'

'You're welcome. The sooner these velvet nightmares are out of here, the better.'

The pressure of attempting to please everyone was taking its toll on the entire team. Rose and I were trying to appease disapproving stalwarts while looking to tempt a wider clientele.

On a quiet weekday evening, when I was running the pub on my own, Philemon approached from his usual corner. 'You are looking a tad down there, Mr Wilde?' He handed me his depleted tankard for a refill.

'Over the refit, to be honest.' I gave an empty smile. 'Nothing serious, but there's no pleasing everyone, so we're doing what we feel is best.'

'That is true, especially those who, until now, were used to a privileged life.' Philemon took his jug and had a swig, wiping the froth from his top lip. 'Remember, it takes time for self-entitlement to disappear. Something the country is struggling with today.'

'An interesting point,' I said, mulling over his words. 'Times are tough at the moment.'

'I suspect that trend will continue for at least a while, if not longer.' Philemon raised his drink in thanks and made his way back to his writing.

Two months later, a short write-up and photographs appeared in the local newspaper.

The Germiston City News.

Exciting news for Germiston. Make your way to Cobblers Bar & Grill. Rose and Rory have breathed new life into the establishment. Great atmosphere, amazing decor, and good pub grub. Live entertainment is making Cobblers the place to be. Come to the party, Germistonians. See you all there.

The approaching new millennium promised to change the world.

The cost of KY2 paranoia was in the billions as businesses safeguarded their computer systems.

Europe united behind the Euro currency.

NATO bombed Yugoslavia.

The USA developed their Missile Defence Systems.

Pokémon took the world by storm.

Mbeki was the new president.

The Springboks failed to defend their world rugby championship status.

And sadly, violence was on the up.

We noticed this spilling into the Cobblers Bar & Grill culture, too. People's patience waned faster, and their acceptance faded. They did not limit this to just race, but also nationalities and cultures. Personal sidearms were more noticeable within the white communities. Secure fencing and security alarms in businesses and homes were widespread. Paranoia and self-preservation were more tangible, and when this was mixed with alcohol, it all became a powder keg of emotion and fear for us. Growing unease stemmed from public unrest, business disruption due to the internet, corruption, and uncertainty.

We would often have to intervene in spats between disagreeing parties. Most, if not all, were historical concerns that happened long before most of the grumblers were born, but that was where we were. The men's violence would spill over and spoil yet another evening. Cobblers, like most bars, dealt with family arguments, domestic abuse, loneliness and drug issues.

Rose and I lived on edge, observing the growing chaos and disruption of life in South Africa. We didn't always discuss it, but every so often we would make comments or vent our frustrations.

Chapter Sixteen

1999 saw South Africa's second election and the end of Nelson Mandela's presidency, replaced by Thabo Mbeki. The Truth and Reconciliation Commission's report on past human rights abuses was overdue. Political aggression persisted, as did widespread xenophobia.

Violence was part of the country's way of life. Centuries of exclusion, wars, tribalism, colonialism, apartheid, and corruption shaped the inevitable outcome. Via politics and greed, hatred filtered through to every enclave of a nation that had the potential to become a superpower, blessed as it was with an abundance of minerals and other resources and a diversity of people and entrepreneurial endeavour not seen elsewhere.

In Cobblers, a minor trigger could cause fisticuffs between males, though sometimes the cause was an ongoing rivalry or an intolerance of others based on the usual issues of race, belief or gender. It could be as small as someone looking the wrong way, bumping into somebody, or someone not liking someone else's appearance.

We eased situations by eliminating the troublemakers, either separating rivals or outright banning them. Most disputes dissipated as quickly as they broke out, but a few left a lasting impression. One impacted us so much that it changed the direction Rose and I were heading in life.

A young man was unresponsive to repeated warnings from us to stop drinking or leave the bar. His determination to add fuel to the inferno of growing public violence in the country matched his infamous reputation as a troublemaker. We'd had several encounters with him over the years, where he misbehaved, got drunk, and vomited in different places. After a three-month ban, he promised that inappropriate days would be behind him. He was the ultimate Balsak, brutal and bullying.

After a week of decent behaviour, he went off the rails again.

'Hey, listen up. Your conduct makes others in here feel uneasy,' I said, 'The ladies do not appreciate your actions, and less so the men. You need to tone it down. We've been over this before. Let's not go there again.'

'I am not fucking doing anything wrong. Piss off. I'm just having a blast.'

'That will do, my friend. Your language is not appropriate. If you don't behave, you'll have to leave.'

He looked at me with dilated pupils and nodded, raising his beer bottle in my direction.

'That's better. Now relax and have a good evening. Keep the noise down and respect other people's space.' I cleared the table of empty bottles and glasses while monitoring him. Still wary, I sat where I could watch from a distance.

In a matter of minutes, the intoxicated agitator started again by bumping into and provoking others, throwing insults and teasing all in his path. While doing so, he knocked into Rose, causing her to fall as he stumbled. The bar fell into a collective hush, anticipating what would happen next.

Brad, our nephew, used his two metres of height and one-hundred-and-twenty-kilogram weight to throw the drunkard out into the street.

'*Gaan huis toe snotneus,*' someone yelled after him, suggesting the young offender go home. The more aggressive members of the group threatened his wellbeing if he did not leave.

'Fuck off,' other onlookers taunted. With a collective ovation and further threats for him not to return, the crowd returned to their amiable state.

'Thanks, Brad. I'll handle it from here.'

My nephew returned inside while the troublemaker climbed into his car, but not before swearing and gesturing. 'You'll be sorry, you dick,' he yelled from his window as he sped past.

I checked on Rose, who had her friends around her. She was

shaken but okay and preferred not to attract further attention.

'He didn't do it on purpose, Rory. He tripped on something and lost his balance.'

'That boy is not bright,' I muttered. 'He doesn't understand his limits. Good news is he's gone now, and there are only a few hours left until the night ends.'

'Can't wait,' Rose said, and returned to her chores. It was the first time Rose had expressed her unhappiness about her job at the pub to me.

Twenty minutes later, the same drunken fool returned, barging into the pub with a loaded handgun. 'None of you even know who I am!' He raised his voice, addressing the crowd. 'No one gets away with treating me like that.' He pointed the gun towards the bar, but at no one in particular.

At the exact moment, Brad and I collided with him. Brad held the revolver with one hand, clasping his wrist with the other, lifting him to the ceiling before throwing him onto the pavement.

In the scuffle, the pain-in-the-arse dropped the weapon, which I kicked away, then chased after it. Brad grabbed the delinquent's pants and jacket, and like a swing repeatedly slammed his head on the Stop sign outside the bar.

I convinced Brad to release him, unloaded the bullets, returned his gun, and let him go. The man jumped into his vehicle and screeched away, swearing out of the open window. 'Do you know who I am?' He waved a fist. 'I'll be back with my brothers. You'll see.'

'Not the first time we've heard that,' I said to Brad, thanking him for his help.

Down the main road, we witnessed a police car with blue lights stopping him for a breathalyser.

'Do you think we should tell them?' Brad asked.

'No, he's an idiot. It's not worth the trouble. Let's go back inside and try to enjoy what's left of the night.' I thanked him again.

'You're welcome, Rory. We're family.' My nephew, with his enormous build, gave my shoulder a beefy pat. We joined the crowd who had returned to their evening, unperturbed by the incident. An acceptance of lawlessness being the norm I just could never get my head around.

The night was almost over. Stragglers propped the bar up, and the state of the place reflected the night we'd just had.

'Last drinks, folks. We close in half an hour,' I called, thankful the evening was ending.

The remaining customers lingered over their drinks until four o'clock.

'Come on, you lot. Five minutes left. Drink up, please.'

'Don't worry, we will take them with us,' one suggested.

'Regrettably, you can't do that. My license is at risk if I let you out with alcohol. Please, just finish what you have and leave the empties.'

'Piss off. We'll leave when we're ready.'

'There's no need for that language, guys. Do as I ask and move on,' I said, trying to stay composed.

'I doubt you even have a liquor license for this shithole,' another chirped.

'Where is your licence anyway, old man?' a third joined in.

This, my first experience with ageism, occurred when I was only thirty-three years of age.

Rose noticed the mounting tension and approached to ease the situation. 'Time, guys. We're locking up. Take care out there.'

'Here comes back-up for Grandad now,' the loud-mouthed slurred with suggestive undertones.

'I'd give her one,' another leered.

The stress of working at Cobblers Bar & Grill and the quality of life declining in South Africa caused me to lose my shit. 'Get out now,' I said through clenched teeth.

Mouthy leaped forward, coming so close I could smell the brandy cola. 'Or what, old man?'

'Or I'll make you leave,' I hissed.

'You or your bitch?'

'Rory? Rory? Let him go.' Rose yelling was the next thing I remembered.

I had lifted this Balsak off the ground and pinned him to the wall. His feet dangling.

'Sorry, sir. I apologise if I upset you.' The once arrogant idiot's bloodshot eyes were filled with tears, and his complexion had paled. When I released him, he vanished with his friends in their car.

'Sorry about that,' I said to Rose and kissed her. 'I should know better.'

'Not to worry, Rory. It won't be the last time, either. Not in this industry.'

Once more that night, Rose expressed negativity towards the business.

'Let's lock up and get out of here,' I said. We studied the dark streets, making sure were clear before we hurried to the car, jumped in and took off, relieved another shift was over.

Before going to bed we sat on the front lawn, winding down from the fraught evening. The tranquillity of dawn breaking embraced us, our arms interlocked. The events of the previous night played in our minds.

'I feel so guilty.'

'Oh, Rory. The imbecile provoked you, and you simply held him against the wall. Violence isn't in your nature. Never has been.'

'I still regret stooping to his level.'

'I know, my darling. I know. Everyone has triggers, and that's what they wanted.' She chuckled. 'And boy, did they find them!'

We listened to the birds' morning serenade in complete silence.

'Rose?'

'Rory?' she whispered back.

'Is it time?' I asked.

'It is time.'

Exchanging no further words, we both stood up and went inside. We were at peace with our decision to sell up in the new millennium – we couldn't do it any earlier without losing our investment in the business. In our third year of owning and running Cobblers Bar and Grill, we had decided in principle that was enough.

Chapter Seventeen

The pub mirrored the growing distrust in the country caused by narrow-mindedness. There were the day-to-day social issues of inappropriateness towards men and women, young and old, that we had to deal with. The bullying of children by parents and vice versa. Intolerant people often attacked those who did not follow societal norms like skin colour, sexual orientation, religion, gender identity and political beliefs. Alcohol had no effect in easing these fears, despite the hopes and wishes of the consumer. Quite the opposite, for booze did nothing but lower or eradicate civil boundaries, thus exacerbating the situation.

Harder and more stressful to regulate were the groups of Balsak bullies, who got a kick out of disrupting folk and challenging those in charge. They showed a total lack of respect for businesses or people. To this day, Rose and I cringe at some incidents we witnessed. Allow me to share a few with you.

A particular pair of Balsak brothers were notorious for causing fights and altercations on a whim. That day, as well as the two brothers, a Truther and a couple of Neanderthals were present.

'Hey, lady? Get me another beer.' Balsak 1, a large oaf with piggy features, called out to Rose, looking at his cronies with smug delight. 'Make it snappy. I don't have all day.' He flashed a sarcastic smile that did not reach his small pig eyes, his shoulders bouncing as he joked with his band of cohorts.

'Come on, sweetheart, move that lovely tush and hit us with another round,' his skinny mate the Truther cackled. His slouched posture reminded me of a hyena.

Bloody hell, it's like Animal Farm in here – George Orwell's going to walk in any moment, flashed through my mind before I stepped in and placed a beer in front of him. 'Any of you other gents ready for a refill?' I asked.

'Was I speaking to you, *snotneus* (snotty nose)?' Balsak *2* stared at me with the same aggression as his brother, the nostrils on his snout flaring.

'Were you talking to anybody?' I asked, ignoring his insult to me.

'Don't get smart, *lightie.* (young child). We'll tear this place apart for the fun of it if we want to,' Balsak 1 said.

'I'm sure you will try.' I looked at him and smiled, not wishing to intensify the situation.

He pondered my remark, uncertain whether it was a compliment or a challenge. Instead, he got distracted and joined in with his friends, who stood in a circle discussing politics, Doom egging the morons on.

'Swine at a feeding trough.' I whispered under my breath,

'I will not put up with their shit,' Rose said to me in the storeroom a few minutes later. 'I don't want them here at all, never mind drinking on top of it. They are nothing but trouble wherever they go.'

'Let's see how it goes, and if they get too much, we'll ask them to leave. Might be less drama if we don't escalate the matter. That's what they're aiming for.'

'Okay, but another insult and they're out.'

I smiled, aware that Rose tolerated nobody's nonsense, least of all bully boys. *This is going to get interesting.*

The evening party crowd replaced the sombre afternoon tradespeople and pensioners.

Doom had left the building. His partner had turned up and dragged him by the collar to the car. 'Come on, dipshit,' she said. 'You never know when to stop. Leave these lovely people alone so they can enjoy themselves.' His flip-flops swished on the concrete floor. She flashed me a smile and mouthed an apology. Her droopy, bloodshot eyes reflected a glimpse of a once pretty woman.

Joker remained with Weirdo and the Balsak brothers for the festivities.

The Coverettes were in place and tuning their equipment.

'Look at the arse on her,' the twat who'd insulted Rose shouted across the barroom at the singer. The gang, now down to just four members because Weirdo had distanced himself, laughed and sought approval for their jokes. However, it was all becoming too much for Joker, who sought a more responsive audience to his jocularity. Gloom, too, disappeared – probably aware that if he'd stayed, he'd have ended up the butt of the Balsak brothers' teasing.

'This place is half asleep. No one appreciates any fun around here.' The other Balsak – a neanderthal boar with a shaved pumpkin head – said.

'Time to liven this joint up, *boetie* (brother),' the first one suggested.

'Don't you dare.' Rose stepped in front of the two before they could reach the dance floor.

'What you going to do about it, *meisiekind*?'

'Ja, little girl, what you gonna do?' the second repeated and reached out for her.

Rose stepped aside with ease, not flinching from their physicality. 'It's time for you two to leave.'

'You and whose army, *skat* (treasure)?' They both snorted with chests pushed outward, rocking on their heels. Challenging anyone within earshot.

'Anyway. What's a girl like you doing in a nice place like this?'

I joined Rose to help diffuse the situation. 'Come on, now. This isn't worth it. Behave yourselves.' I looked them in the eyes again, hoping they could not see the pulse throbbing in my throat. Rage and fear becoming one.

'Fuck off. Who do you think you are, wanker? I'm talking to the chick.' His eyes narrowed as his brother took a step closer to me. 'She needs a real man,' he smirked with twisted lips of anger.

'You boys need to leave now,' a gruff voice from the crowd said before I could respond.

The hog-like individuals scanned the bar, uncertain of the source of the statement. They looked at me, Rose, then glanced around at the now silent customers and tried to find who was challenging them. Nothing.

Perturbed by the change in atmosphere and unable to assess their adversary, they gulped down their drinks.

A different voice threatened, 'Get lost, *skomgat*,' naming them as the rubbish they were, followed by another saying, 'Piss off back under your rock.' The Cobbler crowd, losing their buoyant mood, now closed in on the disruptors.

'We'll be back. See if we won't.' They left their table and slunk out of the building, snorting and grunting at the patrons, who were clapping and cheering their departure.

'Wow. Great work, Germiston,' The Coverettes' singer said into the mic. 'That's how you take care of each other. Impressive.' She applauded. 'I reckon it's party time. What say you, Cobblers?'

The band broke into Queen's *Another One Bites the Dust*, altering the atmosphere to one of joy and relief as folks spilled onto the floor in dance and merriment.

'Did you see what our customers did, Rory? Amazing.'

'That was a lesson in not messing with people's drinking time or space,' I agreed.

'Doubt they'll be back in a hurry,' Rose said with a smile.

I wasn't so sure. My days at an all-boys boarding school had taught me that bullies didn't relinquish their hold on others unless their fear of reprisal was greater. Since that hadn't happened enough tonight, I suspected they would return at a time that better suited their agenda.

The problem with bullies occurred on the quieter nights when they felt they had more control and were unlikely to be challenged by the loyal locals. As with most of the Balsaks, they were cowards.

One such incident occurred on a Sunday winter's evening when Rose and I worked behind the bar since our staff were absent because of leave and illness. Sheila was there till ten, but then left to catch the last taxi to spend time with her family.

Trade was slow apart from a small group of ladies sipping sherry and discussing books.

Two guys sipped on beers, talking in hushed voices. I kept my eyes on them, unsure of the demeanour. Their body language suggested all was not well, but that was none of my business if they behaved. Youngsters were playing a game of darts. A couple sat in the corner whispering sweet nothings to one another.

Jess, Rose's brother, had turned up for a chat when we noticed the suspicious two having an argument.

'No. Fuck you.' The shorter one pushed the bigger lad in the chest. 'I'm out of here. You're not *lekker* (good), my friend.' and walked out the pub, his drink unfinished. The person remaining glanced at us, then resumed drinking.

'Keep an eye on that one,' Jess said as he was leaving. 'He's getting more and more crazy as he drinks.'

'Thanks, Jess. Yeah, I've been watching. We've called last rounds, so he should go soon too,' I said, walking Jess to the door.

'Let's sit behind the bar,' I said to Rose. 'Just in case.'

'He's a bit of a Weirdo,' Rose agreed.

We watched him talking to himself, noting the twitches of his face. On several occasions, he stared at Rose then jumped off his stool and strode to the bathroom. Each time on his return his eyes were mere slits and his forehead perspiring. Indecisive, he prowled the bar, clearly contemplating his next move.

Rose and I stood and watched in silence, not wanting to provoke him. It was when he stooped down and picked up a brick that was holding the door open that I opened the drawer under the till and put my .38 Special in the front pocket of my jeans. He stared at the revolver and walked up and down a few more times, glancing from the brick in his hand to the gun in my pocket. With the appearance of snapping out of a dream, he stopped and looked around. He gave us a sheepish grimace, said goodnight, and left the bar. I followed him out to shut the door, but he was already driving off in his car.

'Wow, now that was one scary shit,' Rose said, grabbing the cash. 'Rory let's lock up and leave before he changes his mind. Glad you had your gun.'

'You bet. What a Weirdo. I've seen him around before, hanging out with that dodgy lot who used to come here when we first took over.' I slammed and bolted the front gate after checking the carpark and down the street. 'We're out of here.'

'Is it just me, Rory, or is it getting out of control? All this madness and abuse?' Rose asked in the dark as we climbed into bed.

'You're spot on and it's why the xenophobia troubles are getting out of hand. People are scared and they are blaming others for it.'

'Is this a place we want to be if it carries on?' she asked.

'Cobblers or South Africa?' I held my breath, wondering if my best friend and love of my life was having the same thoughts.

'Both,' she whispered.

I held her hand as I heard her sob into her pillow. Soon we would have to decide. We could not carry on like this. The inclination was to sell and depart the country.

The obvious in-your-face bully was not the only one engaging in aggression and harassment. Often it came from people you'd least expect it. The infamous South African Kugel caricature raised her evil face regularly, accosting our staff for no other reason but her own ego. She desired material possessions and used her seductive behaviour to gain acceptance among the wealthy. A self-entitled, puffy-haired cougar bedecked in jewellery who preyed on our young, insecure staff.

'I ordered a Coke, dummy. Not this watered-down, vile shit,' referring to the on-tap machines. 'You know I'm doing you a favour frequenting this dive.'

Then there were the men who spoke in grunts and used vulgar language for no other reason than because they could.

And the perverts who pinched bottoms and rubbed themselves up against staff and customers on busy nights, making lewd suggestions with their words and eyes. Many a fracas started this way from offended partners or friends.

Likewise, the racist was ever present as a person or a group. Not just in colour, but in every genre imaginable. Provoking crowds and justifying their prejudices that were fuelled by xenophobia.

Arguments between people of the same race and different races were common at the bar, though interference usually prevented them from escalating. Not a great recipe when mixed in with drink and personal firearms.

Despite some troublemakers, good people from various walks of life filled Cobblers. Something I still see in today's troubled times. The power of the balanced and good-willed always conquers extremists and conspiracy theorists, even if the progress is slow. The focus on wellbeing and social consciousness weakened those who relied on chaos and on controlling others with anarchy. They know fear well, for it dwells within them, making them the lowlifes that they are.

Do not get me started on domestic quarrels, blowing up for all to see. A niggle at first that intensifies with each unit of alcohol until all their dirty washing is on display and – worse still – being wiped in everybody's faces. Hair pulling, face scratching, tears strewn and even wrestling on the bar top. Bottles broken on heads; the glass used as a weapon. Imagine how we behaved before we civilised ourselves, or is it because we are still not there yet?

Cobblers was often the secret rendezvous of couples cheating on their partners, sneaking in for an intimate twosome in a darkened corner. We noticed the constant glancing over of shoulders when someone entered the bar, and the clandestine phone calls when one of them headed for the restrooms. Why they thought we wouldn't recognise them beggars' belief – as does their assumption that we wouldn't spread the word or even inform the aggrieved partner of their companion's behaviour.

Worse still were the racial and cultural interactions. Customers often brought friends who shared their interests, and sometimes two noisy groups would clash after drinking one too many. Whether it was the Celts or English at variance with Afrikaans speakers, conflict was always present. On occasion it would be light-hearted banter, other times full of fisticuffs and drawn firearms.

Oh, how delightful it was to see humanity's true nature emerge when alcohol eroded the thinnest veneer of civility.

James was in his last year in school and Cobblers was not the right influence for him either, so this was another reason for selling. It was hard enough for young men in the new South Africa without normalising the consumption of alcohol and other social drugs.

Unbeknownst to Rose and me, James organised for his leaving school matric farewell mates to head for Cobblers Bar and Grill after the dance. In that awkward stage between childhood and adulthood, he believed it would be simpler for him and his underage friends to gain entry into our pub. It was a Friday night in November and our live band, The Coverettes, had just completed their gig. Patrons were on their way home while the team busied themselves with table clearing and tidying up.

Rose noticed a set of headlights flash across the room as a car pulled into the carpark. 'Looks like a latecomer,' she said to Len behind the bar. Further headlights shone, then another and another. 'Rory, see what's going on out there? We don't want any riffraff gatecrashing at this time of night. It's after one o'clock anyway.'

We'd dealt with our fair share of troublemakers who showed up after being kicked out of other establishments, often drunk and causing problems. I walked over to the front gates and slid them closed, then stood watching to see what was happening. The new arrivals filled the carpark with cars revving, music blaring and people fooling around in the headlights.

'What's going on?' Rose asked, coming up beside me.

'Not sure,' I said, not taking my eyes off the partygoers. 'They're youngsters.'

'James said the schools were all having their matric parties this week.' Rose peered through the bars of the security gates, trying to see if she could recognise the kids.

'Hi, Mom.' James, red-faced with excitement, appeared a few inches from our faces.

'What the hell are you up to? I hope you're not driving.' Rose looked our son up and down with a squint of disapproval. 'Looks like you've already had a skinful.'

James glanced around at his mates, hoping they hadn't heard the admonishment from his mother. 'No, I'm not. We all have designated drivers.'

'So, what are you doing here?' Her voice made it clear she hadn't believed a word.

'I've brought you guys a whole lot of customers,' he said with a proud expression. 'They're all my school friends. We're coming for a nightcap.'

'The hell you are. Stay right there, mister,' Rose said to James and the growing crowd standing behind him. 'Give these lovely people room to leave.' She opened the gate to allow patrons out of the building. 'Good night. Thanks for coming. Drive safe.' Rose's face transformed from an annoyed mother to a gracious host, then returned to the former. 'I'll tell you one thing, James Wilde. You and your cronies aren't coming in here, that is for sure.' She waved a finger at them. 'So, the lot of you can clear off and I suggest you all go home. It's getting late.'

Groans filled the air as students left for their cars. 'But Mom, it's just for one drink. I thought you guys would appreciate the extra cash.'

'Don't go there, James Wilde. You're just here to show off,' Rose said, not backing down. 'How did you get here?'

James tapped his friend standing alongside him, knowing he was in trouble when his mother used his full name.

Rose opened the gate and pulled the two lads inside, saying, 'Well, you're not going out there with the rest of those hooligans. Find yourself a table and I'll get you both a cup of coffee.' The boys did as they were told. Rose disappeared into the kitchen, mumbling about underage drinking and how males never grow up.

As a young boy I loved to go to the movies and watch rugged Westerns, stirring war films and the suave James Bonds. All faded into obscurity as I witnessed the bravery of my African Rose, who handled these Cobblers days with aplomb. A class act of a courage I have never seen equalled, even during the civil war years I lived through when Rhodesia became Zimbabwe. She had to consider the safety of her family in a country growing more perilous to live in, during a time when women faced inequality compared to men. Has much changed nowadays? I hear the talk, I see the token gestures, but I smell a rat.

Chapter Eighteen

For some time after that we didn't discuss leaving, whether it be the business or the country. Instead, we focussed on our plans for a celebration of the new millennium. The dawn of the twenty-first century provided everyone with a perfect alibi to forget the fundamentals of everyday living, though industry was on tenterhooks in the fear that the change of dates to 2000 might cause havoc with the digital world.

'How did the visit go?' I asked Rose as she entered the pub on a quiet afternoon a month after our unnerving incident with the disturbed man and the brick.

'Good thanks, Rory.'

'You are looking great. Enjoying the winter's day?' I kissed my wife.

'I am.'

'What are you hiding?' I gave Rose a sly grin, recognising she was up to something.

'Nothing.' She blushed.

I opened my hands to show there was no one at the bar apart from our resident writer, who was scribbling away and muttering to himself. We both knew that when Philemon Dlamini was writing he was oblivious to all about him. The only other customer was a gambler on the other side of the pub, mesmerised by horse racing on the television, and I didn't foresee anyone else turning up.

Rose looked both ways and teared up.

'Hey? What's up?' I came out from behind the bar.

'I've got some news for you.' She wiped her nose on a paper napkin. Her expression said it all.

'Really?' I said, the information sinking in.

'Yup.' She broke into a smile.

'Are you sure?'

Rose nodded, inspecting my reaction.

We hugged in the centre of the bar.

'That's the best news ever,' I whispered in her ear.

All she could do was nod in agreement, her head on my shoulder.

'I believe congratulations are in order.' The race pundit climbed off his stool and shook both our hands.

'Thanks, but we want to keep it quiet for a while.'

'Your secret is safe with me.' He beamed and showed me his empty beer glass. 'Ready for another, though?'

I poured a pint and placed it in front of him. He looked away from his racing card and thanked me.

'It's on me.'

'Why, thank you. A celebration drink it is.' He raised it above his shoulder.

'Yup, and a bribe of silence.'

We laughed.

'My name is Roger.' The suave, white-haired man said with a slight English public-school accent.

We shook hands.

He sat for a while distracted from his racing on the television, staring at his beer. 'I'll tell you what.' He looked up at us where we were stocktaking behind the bar. 'Are you considering selling because of the good news? Because if you are, I'm your man.' He winked and resumed his TAB betting.

Rose burst into tears and rushed to the restroom.

'I didn't mean to upset her,' he said with a crossed brow of concern.

'That's okay.' I showed him the palm of my hand. 'It's an emotional time for us right now.'

'I understand, young man, but I am serious.' He gripped my elbow. 'Let me know if you decide to sell this place.'

'That's very kind. I will, thank you.'

'Nothing to do with kindness.' Roger peered at me over the bar.

'This is my second home. There's nothing else like it here, and I'd welcome the challenge.'

'You'll be the first to know once we've decided.'

Sheila returned with her arms around Rose, consoling her with ahs and oohs. Rose patted her nose with a tissue and apologised as I clarified what Roger was trying to say and agreed that he would be the first we contacted.

'That's a deal. You two have done a great job, make no mistake.' Roger pulled his car keys from his pocket and settled his bill. 'See you guys later.'

Wiping the top of the counter with renewed vigour, I sensed a weight lift from my shoulders. *Karma comes home to roost.*

Rose brought coffee and biscuits on a tray, then sat across from me at the bar.

'I'm so proud of you, Miss Rose. You've made me so happy.' I said, reaching out for her hand.

'Me too, Rory.' She blushed.

We sat in an awkward silence, unsure of what the news meant to each other, until Rose spoke. 'Another fork in the road, Rory?'

'I know. Another one and so soon,' I answered. 'But that's a good thing, right?'

Rose nodded. 'It's the only way we're going to get where we want to be. By making the right choices - for us.'

'You're so right. You go first.'

'Nice try, Rory Wilde. Tell me what you're thinking.'

I stammered, unsure how to express myself, when Rose interrupted. 'I tell you what, Rory. Go see if our writer friend wants another drink, then come and share your thoughts.'

She knew me so well. Relieved, I took a moment to think. Walking over, I found Mr. Dlamini engrossed in his laptop.

'Can I get you another drink or a coffee?' I asked.

The author glanced at me and smiled. 'No, thank you, my friend. I think I will call it a night. You and your wife have a lot of thinking to do and you don't need an old fool like me hanging around.' He got to his feet, collected his belongings and called out to Sheila, 'I'll meet you outside when you are ready, my dear,' and then bid us a good night.

He waited for a response and after receiving none he rested his hand on Rose's shoulder. 'Congratulations. See you all later.' The sound of the security gate clanging behind him reverberated through the deserted barroom.

Rose and I finally stood alone, looking at each other, until Rose broke into laughter, ran over to me and jumped into my arms. 'We're going to have a baby. I'm so excited.'

'You and me both.' I hugged my wife for all I was worth.

We sipped on our decaffeinated coffee and enjoyed the moment. The bar's closure granted us precious private time away from life and the world. Rose changed the television to the music channel.

Destination unknown, as we pull in for some gas
A freshly pasted poster reveals a smile from the past.

'It's that *OMC* song *How Bizarre* again.' Rose giggled. 'It's following us.'

'Maybe it's *our* song?'

'Perhaps you're right, Rory.' Rose pondered the idea while listening to the music and watching the video. Another New Zealand influence passed us unawares.

Sheila startled us as she emerged from the kitchen in her civvies and did a little jig to the melody, then gave Rose a hug. I could see she thought about doing the same to me but chickened out at the last minute. 'Congrats, Wilde family plus one. See you tomorrow.' She waved and slammed the gate after her.

'With a baby on its way, Rose,' I began in a whisper. 'We may need to change our lifestyle again.'

'I'm listening.' Rose looked at me with large eyes over her coffee.

'The country is changing fast, to add to the mix.'

'Get on with it, Mr Wilde.' Rose gave me a slight grin.

'Sell Cobblers and look for something to do with better social hours.' I stopped to wait for Rose's response.

'Go on. Like what?' was all Rose said.

'Another business, or I find a job that will pay the bills.'

'I agree. Come here,' she smiled, putting her arms out to me.

After we hugged, I pulled back to gaze into her eyes and said,

'Perhaps we should consider moving abroad. The question is whether this place is right for our family.'

'I've been thinking the same,' Rose answered. 'Let's do it in stages and reassess as we go along. That way it doesn't put too much pressure on us straight away.'

'Nice. I like it. Leaving the country is not a popular decision here in South Africa, so let's wait until we're completely sure.'

Rose nodded. 'Okay then, first things first. Cobblers up for sale?'

'Nah.' I shook my head. 'First up, we share with the world that you're pregnant. That reminds me – we must celebrate.' I pulled a bottle of sparkling wine from the fridge and popped the cork.

'I can't, Rory.' Rose put a hand on her stomach.

'Alcohol free.' I filled two glasses and toasted. 'To us.'

Rose sipped, then raised her glass. 'To us…. and our baby.'

After a long chat about our plans, we locked up and headed home exhausted but somehow content.

On breaking the news to the family and receiving a wonderful reaction from them, we announced it to the team at Cobblers.

'Does that mean you guys will give up Cobblers?' Pretending ignorance, Sheila embraced Rose.

'We're still deciding,' Rose answered. 'You all will be the first to know of any decision.'

'Oh, please don't sell.' Len pressed his hands together in front of his face. 'You are amazing owners. The customers think you are great. So do they.' He pointed to the Cobbler's team.

'Thanks Len.' I patted his shoulder.

'It's true. Cobblers is the place to go in Germiston. You guys are famous.'

'Don't know about that,' Rose said, pulling a face.

'When is the baby due?' Sheila interjected.

'In March.'

'Oooh. Boy or girl?' Sheila asked.

'Not sure. Will find out at the birth.'

'So happy for you, Miss Rose.'

'Thank you, Sheila, and don't worry. Whatever we decide to do, we will make sure we look after the team, and that you have jobs.'

The day revolved around the pregnancy and its anticipated changes, but most of the staff remained in good spirits, although the underlying concern was understandable.

After several negotiation meetings with Roger to buy Cobblers Bar and Grill, he had set up a dinner at a restaurant to sign the deal with a final payment later to complete ownership. Rose, not feeling too well, excused herself. The very idea of food and drink did not agree with her.

'Evening, Roger,' I said, shaking his hand. 'Apologies from Rose.'

'Understandable.' Roger smiled. 'I've brought my daughter for moral support. This is Angie.'

'Looks like you've got the upper hand this time,' I joked.

Roger laughed, causing other diners to look around. 'Oops, sorry, just my nerves.' He put a finger to his mouth. 'It will be the first time I have the advantage. That wife of yours is sharp as a pin.'

'That she is. Trust me, I've felt the sharpness.'

While we were having drinks and dinner, we discussed the latest news of our town, social issues and national problems before getting down to business.

'Here are the contracts with all our signatures verified. One copy for you, the other for us,' I said, placing two laminated copies in the middle of the table.

'Don't touch them, Dad.' Angie restrained her father's outstretched hand.

Roger and I looked at her, aghast.

'What's the matter, angel?' Roger's voice gravelled from the shock.

She burst out laughing. 'I need to get a video of this occasion. You've waited so long for this.' The chuckles that followed were more from relief than humour. Angie placed the camcorder to her eye and filmed her father picking up his contract and pulling a cheque from his breast pocket. 'For you, Mr Wilde.'

'Why, thank you, kind sir,' I answered accepting his deposit for the business.

Angie captured the ham acting for prosperity.

The months passed with the usual behavioural issues and social inadequacies reflected in the country. We downgraded the millennial celebrations for two reasons - we couldn't compete with the big corporations who were organising vast projects with celebrities on multiple days, but also our hearts were just not in it. Rose, in her second trimester, was uncomfortable with long hours on her feet.

Our discussions with Roger continued in the strictest of confidence and were proving fruitful with an agreement of what was to be the final sum owing to us. The sales agreement just needed to run its course and then we'd notify the team. We waited until after the Christmas and New Year celebrations so as not to dampen anybody's spirits over the holiday period.

Businesses had Christmas parties on different nights than entertainment evenings, some paying extra for live music and lavish buffets. Sumptuous by Cobblers Bar and Grill standards anyhow. Exhausted, we welcomed in the millennium with nothing more than with the bar being open, and offering free nuts, crisps and cheese boards scattered on tables and the bar.

It provided a haven for those who sought company without the pizzaz and commercial hullabaloo. To enjoy some companionship in an ambience of calm and reflection. Outside, fireworks launched a foray of noise and flashes, syncing with the countdown of the television to the new year. Few generations get to welcome in a millennium. The previous one may have gone unnoticed or even ignored. The sombre gathering wished a happy new year to everyone with a handshake or a brief hug. Rose and I bought the room a round of shooters.

'Cheers.' Philemon sat next to me as Sheila pecked him on the cheek and joined Rose looking out the window at the sky bursting with lights, fire and bangs, echoed by excited voices.

Cheers.' I clinked his beer and shook my head, breathing out heavily.

'You can say that again, my friend.' Philemon patted me on the back. 'Who knows where all this will lead and how it will affect our lives? Fear not, as we writers have been chosen to guide future generations into the twenty-first century.'

'Deep. Mr Dlamini, but either way I look at it, the future is as scary as hell, with technology leading the way,' I answered. 'Not to mention having a baby.' We sat in silence, watching our partners joke about something with a client.

'Worth it though.' Philemon flicked me with the back of his hand. 'I wouldn't have it any other way.'

'Too right.' I swallowed the last of my beer. 'Another?' I held up my empty glass.

'Why not?' He swigged his down and handed me the glass. 'This is going to be one hell of a year for everybody.'

'Why do you say that?' I asked, placing two fresh amber filled lager glasses on the bar.

With a sip from his glass, Philemon signalled for me to wait, his gaze fixed on me. 'Worldwide, it is the fear of a change from the norm, of not knowing what is in store. Hyped up by governing bodies and industry.'

I snorted. 'Damn right – it's all anybody's talking about. Everything digitally unable to go from 1900 to 2000.'

'And then there is South Africa.' Philemon refocussed my attention. 'For those of us who live here, we have decisions to make.' He paused for effect. 'Things will get a lot worse before they improve.' Silence and another sip of beer, the ladies dancing together in the background.

'What do you mean?' I asked, unnerved.

'Mr Wilde, we have both lived and experienced most of what Southern Africa offers. Political parties must unite to prevent South Africa from suffering like its northern neighbours.'

'Fat chance,' I blurted, more by reflex than thought. 'I'm sorry. I just miss the thrill and hope of the Rainbow Nation days.'

'No need to apologise, my friend. It is how you feel and that is the closest most of us will ever get to the truth.'

'Must say, it's not looking great at the moment.'

'That is an understatement, Rory.' Philemon raised his eyebrows in sync with his glass, a look of pain deep in his eyes. 'From what I see, there is less and less spending on infrastructure at a time we need it most for housing, education and health.' He wiped the foam from his top lip. 'From what I hear, corruption and greed are taking hold. The stench of xenophobia is growing, and I dare not share with you what

I feel, young man.' He looked aghast, when I gave a quick chuckle and demanded, 'You think I joke or that the situation is amusing?'

'Not at all, Mr Dlamini. Quite the opposite, in fact.' I placed a hand on his wrist. He returned with his own, then shrugged at what I found funny.

'You reminded me of an old and dear friend of mine I haven't seen in twenty years.'

'I do? Pray tell me who.'

My stomach churned. *How I missed my childhood mentor. If only he were here now.* 'Themba Dube.'

'Tell me about Mr Dube. Where is he now?'

I repositioned myself on the bar stool and said, 'I don't know. I knew him from a child. He was our domestic worker in Zimbabwe. We became very close. So much so that he grew into my mentor and helped me through many a tough time. We lost touch when he returned home to Zambia and I to England.'

'He sounds a remarkable man. You were both lucky to have each other.'

'Thank you, Philemon. That means a lot,' I said.

'I didn't realise you lived in the UK. Whereabouts?' Philemon changed the subject.

'I was there as a youngster in the mid-eighties. Wiltshire and Gloucestershire.'

'Get out of here.' My friend raised his voice in excitement. 'My parents sent me to Cheltenham College in the hope I would go on to study at university.'

'Oh, wow. What a small world.' I whistled through my teeth. 'Posh - a private school in England. I wondered where you got your accent from.'

'Indeed. The annual fee is, or was, higher than the average person's salary for a year.' Philemon could not hold back his emotions and wiped his face with his hands. 'Truth is, it was closer to double that income.' He dabbed his eyes after pretending to wipe the sweat from his brow. 'I didn't go to university. I decided to attend the Cirencester Agriculture College up the road from the university. Much to my parents' disgust.'

'I know it well. I spent a lot of time there with friends who attended the college.'

'Many white farmers in Zimbabwe sent their eldest sons to the agricultural college so they could return to run their parents' farms,' Philemon confirmed. 'It was why my father was so angry at me for doing the same.'

'I guess so.' I contemplated the scenario.

'And that was exactly why I wanted to go. So that we local Africans could run commercial farms and reduce the monopoly of it being a white person's occupation.' Philemon looked down at his feet, obviously reliving the family conflict.

'Never thought of that,' I admitted.

He looked up at me and smiled. 'It's not a good idea to replace business-oriented farmers with subsistence farmers who struggle to feed themselves.

'No, it is not, Philemon. Not to mention the repercussions it will have on the country. Another contribution to the existing hatred.' Staring at the bottom of my glass, avoiding eye contact, I said, 'Can I ask you something, Mr Dlamini, that has bothered me most of my life?'

'What is it, young man?' He waited a moment. 'Free yourself by asking what bothers you. Fear not, I will take no offence.'

I looked up at Philemon's warm smile and all-knowing eyes. 'I'm just confused.'

'In what way, pray tell.'

'I was born in Africa. Having left once to live in England, I hated being away, but when I am here it feels like I am not welcome.' I shook my head and continued in a low tone, 'I just don't know what people expect from me, what I need to do to be a part of the country, a continent that is connected to me.'

Philemon put his hand on my shoulder. 'What you feel, my friend, is what every African feels, irrespective of colour. A history plagues us that won't let go and a present that ignores our future.' He placed his empty glass on the bar with deliberate intent and said, 'That makes you an African. It is time for me to go. Goodnight. Happy New Year and all the best for the next millennia.' He joined Sheila at the door waiting for him.

I remember that evening with fond memories of a bygone era.

Chapter Nineteen

Skinner - the Afrikaans slang word for gossip. Excuse my feeble attempt at translating a language known for its vibrant descriptions.

Skinder, skinner, chitchat, call it what you may. It is the heart of any pub. No less so than Cobblers Bar and Grill, aided by Len, who could never resist the latest scandal.

Len knew a lot about what was going on in Germiston. He listened to people sharing their challenges and failures during quiet evenings at the bar and eavesdropped on customers venting. From couples and relatives arguing after a few toots to someone sharing the latest slander at work events and private parties, Len heard it all.

'I tell you, Rory, if I were younger and knew what I know now I would have made a fortune being a counsellor.' Len held a glass to the light and gave it a rub with a dishtowel.

'I bet. Rose and I thought we knew most of what goes on in this town until we took over here.' I shook my head.

'Truth is that people need a place to vent. And where better than in a pub? Talk about a captive audience. The barman can't walk away.'

'You okay?' I asked.

'Yup. I'm often struck by the irony of places like this.' He looked around the room. 'Empty, she looks sad, even forlorn.' Len wiped at a tear rolling down his cheek. 'A bit like me,' he whispered.

'Your turn at being deep today.' I noticed Philemon raise his head from his writing and listen.

'Just my age,' he answered with a smile. 'It has a way of telling you the clock is ticking.'

'In what way?' I asked.

'Pubs are habitats where sad people come for a good time, even if they can't admit it to themselves. They're in search of relief and companionship.' Len paused, rearranging glassware, then continued. 'Alcohol has the opposite effect on them, whether they're drunk or hungover.' He had a long drag on his cigarette and only a little of the inhaled smoke emerged when he breathed out. 'I tell you; I've seen a lot in my days. I'm already in my fifties.' He looked at me for a reaction. 'Twenty years older than you.'

'Not quite.'

Len smiled but continued. 'This town has changed. While South Africa has made progress in accepting others, it has also regressed in some areas.'

'That's why Rose and I struggle sometimes with owning Cobblers. It is an emotional rollercoaster that is draining.' I pulled a stool for Philemon.

Len nodded and gave me a brief hug. 'Welcome to the dark side.'

'Or is it just humanity?' I asked.

'I guess it is just people in various stages of their lives.' Len hung his keys on his belt, adjusted the cloth he always carried to dust off glasses before filling them, and clapped his hands. 'Right, we're ready to open. Gosh, I hate these Monday mornings. We don't see a soul until lunchtime.' He slid back the doors to bright sunlight and returned behind the bar.

'One Buck's Fizz for you, Mr Rorke Wilde. My treat.' Len placed two glasses filled with orange juice and champagne. Well, sparkling wine, but it had the same effect. 'I know it's early and we're both working, but I had to celebrate the news of you and Rose having a baby. Cheers.' He slurped half of it in one go.

'Cheers, Len. Just one though.' I said, taking a sip. 'Appreciate it. Thank you. What about Philemon?'

'You don't drink the stuff, do you, Phil?'

'I do not. Foul substance.' Philemon said, pulling a face. 'If I want fruit, I will eat the damn junk, not drink it.'

We laughed at his refusal of the extract rather than the alcohol.

'It's something I will never have – children – but I know how precious my niece and nephew are to me. Having your own must add a whole new level of pressure to a person's life.' Len looked at me, serious once more.

'It does in some ways, especially around providing the basics. Health, safe home, education, prospects.'

'Sounds all too much to me. It's bad enough taking care of myself.' Len laughed, trying to hide behind the humour.

'It can be daunting, I must admit,' I agreed.

'So, what are you guys going to do now that you're selling up, what with the baby and all?' Len asked.

'Try to find a job, if there are any out there for white, male South Africans these days. Otherwise, start another business with better and more social hours.'

Len nodded. 'Not sure if I'll stay after you've gone. Might look for something else.'

'Like what?'

'Oh, I don't know. It will have to be in the hospitality industry. That's all I know...' Len started to cough and splutter. He put his cigarette out and took a swig of water.

Philemon reached over with a couple of serviettes from the bar top and gave them to Len.

'That cough's getting worse,' I said. 'Best you stop all that smoking.'

'I know. Got an appointment with the doctor next week but you know how expensive they are.'

'You'd better. Anyway, I've got to be going. Thanks for the drink and chat, Len. I'll see you before the end of your shift. Gary's taking over, right?'

'Yup. Appreciate you listening, Rory. Something that hasn't happened around here of late.'

'Any time. We're all in this together.' I looked across at Philemon. 'Are you, okay? You haven't been your chatty self today.'

'I'm fine, thank you. A big part of what I do is listen to people. To contribute would be to influence what is said. In doing so, I'd fail in my endeavour to hear,' Philemon said, smiling. 'It's what actual authors do. Write what they perceive others feel.'

'All right then. I'll see you guys around.'

Len followed me to the door, taking in the sunny morning. Life going about its business – birds singing, vehicles rushing up and down, a dog taking their owner for a walk. He breathed in the air, 'Aah the stories I could tell,' then turned back inside. 'Take care.'

Len's cough worsened, and a few Mondays later, when we were opening the pub together for the last time, he looked at me with a gaunt face and said, 'I know you guys' hand over to Roger at the end of this week, but I just wanted you to know I went and saw the doctor about my cough.' Len recomposed himself. 'He's sending me for further tests. He thinks it might be throat cancer.'

I didn't know what to say other than give him a bro hug and say that I was sorry.

'I'm really going to miss you two,' Len snuffled.

'And we you, Len. You've been our saving grace.'

'Oh, I don't know about that.' He shuffled his feet. 'Please don't tell the others about my throat.'

'I won't, but let me know how you get on, even after we've gone. You've got my contact details,' I said. 'I'm sure it will work out just fine.'

We popped into Cobblers a month after we sold to tie up loose ends and see how Roger was getting on. Rose also wanted to catch up with Len and Sheila.

An unfamiliar face greeted us behind the counter. 'Morning, guys. What can I get you?'

'Two coffees, please,' Rose ordered, looking around, then headed down the passageway to the kitchen. 'Back in a sec. Just want to say hello to Sheila.'

'Sure.' The barperson gave me a quizzical look and placed the coffee receipt on the order board.

'Well, hello there, Rory Wilde,' a voice sounded in the distance. Sure enough, in the same corner Philemon closed his laptop and beckoned me to join him.

'Great to see you again. Can I get you a drink?' I said, taking a seat.

'No, thank you, I am fine. How are you? How is life treating you?' Philemon's face showed genuine interest.

'All seems on track,' I answered. 'What about you two?'

'We are just fine.' Philemon paused, perturbed.

'What is it?'

'We're anxious about Len, Rory. He never comes to work and sounds terrible on the phone.' He held his throat.

'I'm sorry to hear that,' I said, looking over my shoulder. 'It's one of the reasons Rose came to see Sheila. To find out how he is.'

'Sheila isn't here.'

'Day off?' I asked, but before Philemon could answer, Rose returned, announcing Sheila had taken the day off to look for Len.

We all sat and discussed what we could do to help Len. Philemon would let us know how Sheila got on when she returned to Cobblers later that day.

Just as we were getting comfortable to watch TV after dinner, Rose's mobile phone rang with an old-fashioned telephone sound.

'Hello, Philemon.' Rose put the phone on speaker for me to hear.

'Hi, Rose,' a glum Philemon answered. 'Here's Sheila for you.'

'Are you there, Rose?' Her voice spluttered. 'Can you hear me? … How about now?'

'That's perfect.' Rose lifted her phone as if she could see.

'No luck with Len. He isn't answering his phone or responding to messages.'

'Well, that's not good,' Rose said.

'No, but it gets worse. I went to his flat today, and it was empty. I tried to ask the neighbours, but I think they thought I was up to no good, so they told me nothing.' Sheila stopped, only to take a breath. 'His parents do not know where he is and think he may have taken off with a boyfriend.'

'I don't think it's that.' Rose shook her head at me for confirmation of my thoughts.

We never heard from Len again. He disappeared without a word to anyone, as was his way. Sidelined because of his choices. Bullied for his preferences. I had a sense he could not afford the medical care required for his throat cancer. Instead, he chose to do what he had always done. Seize the day, consequences be damned. Withdrawing so he would not impart pain on or evoke sympathy from those he loved. Brave in so many ways, foolish in others. Is that the difference between the two?

A year after we sold Cobblers we were in a restaurant when one of our well-known karaoke singers from Cobblers greeted us at our table as she was taking hers. 'It's great to see you guys. Been a while, hey?'

Rose stood and gave her a hug and sat back down.

'Can't stop. Having dinner with the kids. Lucky me.' She bent over the table and said to Rose. 'So sad about Len.'

'Why? What happened?' Rose asked.

'Didn't you hear?' She held a hand to her heart. 'He passed away a few weeks ago. Cancer. Such a shame. He was quite ill, you know? Died alone in his room,' she whispered, and disappeared in a flurry to her table across the room.

Rose and I looked at each other, dumbfounded.

'Poor old Len. He was a sweetheart.' Rose raised her glass. 'To Len.'

We toasted the best barkeep in the town, our night spoilt by the sadness of the news.

'I wish we could have done more for him. He was such a lonely person,' Rose grieved. 'All he wanted was to be loved and have a partner he could grow old with.'

We spent the evening reliving Len's escapades. His wonderful wit and sorrowful lows. Never a dull moment, which is who he was.

Rest in peace Len. You lived your life according to your own rules. Faced hardships and loneliness because of others' ignorance and intolerance. You were a character. A person with enormous courage, never hiding who you were or caring what others thought. You have left a legacy of providing a place of comfort for those in need. Your ability to listen and not judge, to offer support and, above all, make people laugh.

You are an example of someone affecting other people's lives without being part of their world. I am one such person you influenced and amazed and am a better person because of it.

You showed us a life scorned and ridiculed, but that was only one issue plaguing the nation and our business.

Rose and I remember searching everywhere, including Johannesburg, when you didn't come for your shift. We could not stay mad at you. We tell stories about the gay bars you recommended to us for their entertainment and delicious food. Your legendary talent as a barman was matched only by your infamous tantrums. For someone who was in our lives for a short while, you left an indelible mark. We shall never forget about you.

Hamba kahle, Len - go well.

The colour of one's skin too was an issue we did not consider before we bought the business, but that was no surprise with hindsight. We were privileged white people living in the country that created apartheid. Apart from Nelson Mandela's brief period, the discrimination continued in the same manner, just in another direction.

The new government created affirmative action to readdress imbalances of the past, but this fanned the flames of suspicion and hatred. Discrimination of another kind, no matter the intention, heightened the prejudiced.

The married couple, Doom and Kugel, were at each other's throats.

Chapter Twenty

Roger signed the final stage of the sales agreement and handed the paperwork to his attorney, who sifted through the pages and passed the final cheque on to us.

'Well, that's that.' Roger said, clapping his hands together. 'Done and dusted.' He smiled at us, doubling down on his clichés, and shook our hands. 'I was thinking of celebrating in your honour at Cobblers on Friday, if that suits you both?'

'Sounds wonderful.' Rose answered. 'That is very kind.'

'Not at all. It's an opportunity to show our appreciation for all that you two have done and to celebrate your baby.' Roger followed us out of the lawyer's office.

'Do you need us to help in any way?' Rose asked.

'Just be there before seven o'clock.'

'Perfect. See you Friday.' Rose waved goodbye and climbed into the car. 'That is so sweet of him, Rory.'

I nodded and started the engine. We were heading back to Cobblers to pick up the last of our belongings. 'Feels like a weight has lifted. So glad that's over. Yes.' I pumped my fist. Some people would be missed, but the experience had exposed me to human intricacies. Not a pretty picture by all accounts.

'It wasn't all that bad,' Rose tutted at me.

'Speak for yourself,' I said with a smile. 'It ended up being a fucking nightmare.'

'Well, it's all over now.' Rose changed the subject. 'Looking forward to the party, though.'

'We won't stay too long, will we? I don't want you two overdoing it.' I rubbed Rose's swollen belly. 'Almost time.'

Rose grinned, putting her hand over mine. 'Not bloody soon enough, if you ask me.'

'It's six thirty,' I called out to Rose. 'You ready? They'll all be waiting for us.'

'Yup. One last trip to the loo and then we can go.'

'You look amazing.'

'Thank you, Rory. Not too shabby yourself.' Rose trotted in slow motion down the passage. 'Must pee.'

The team had decorated the bar with streamers and a colourful sign that read *Best of Luck*. The locals inside cheered and blew whistles as we walked into the pub and restaurant.

'Oh, this is beautiful. Thanks, guys.' Rose opened her arms at the sight before her. The staff were all dressed up in bling aprons and silly hats.

'Here you go.' Roger handed us champagne glasses filled with orange juice. 'Are you sure you don't want something stronger, Rory?'

'No, thanks.' I lifted the glass at him. 'We're both not drinking for the baby.'

Sheila grabbed Rose by the arm. 'Excuse me, Mr Rory, I am borrowing your wife for a moment,' she said, guiding Rose to a crowd of ladies in the restaurant, all clutching gifts.

Philemon laughed out aloud and slapped me on the shoulder. 'Well done, my friend. You did it.' He took a stool next to me. 'No mean feat these days to sell a business. Hope you did okay from the deal.'

'Cheers. Yes, we did fine. Can't say we earned a fortune, but I reckon we broke even.'

Philemon pulled a face, impressed. 'A tough three years for you guys in a failing economy and plunging international exchange rate. Good work.'

'Thanks. We made some great friends along the way.' I clinked his glass with mine.

'I'm honoured, thank you. Now you will have time to write.' Philemon gave me a wry smile. 'I'll be checking up on you, young man.'

Sheila slid across the dance floor, taking my and Philemon's hands. 'Come on, you two. Look at all the lovely presents Rose got for the baby today.'

The evening ended when Rose became uncomfortable with sitting and tired from standing.

'You ready?'

'I think so, Rory,' she answered, turning to the well-wishers. 'Thank you all so much for coming. A special mention to the Cobblers' staff for the pressies and for your help over the years. You have been amazing.' She lifted a gifted bottle of champagne and box of chocolates. 'Look forward to this one day soon.' She laughed aloud.

'Don't be a stranger,' a voice called out.

'We won't. We'll always be popping in here for a drink and catch up.' Rose took my hand.

'Please bring the baby with when you do,' Sheila asked, teary-eyed.

'You bet I will. Good night, all.' Rose gave her a long hug.

I shook hands with Roger, who was more than a little tipsy, and helped Rose into the car. 'You, okay?'

'Too much cake, I think.' Rose held her tummy.

'Come on. Let's get you two home.'

Goodbye Cobblers.

The next day Rose went to see the doctor, who advised her to rest and keep her feet up, hinting the baby was due soon. I was waiting for responses from my job applications, so took up Philemon's suggestion to get back to writing. Easier said than done since the craft was about rhythm for me. A little at the same time every day rather than screeds once a week.

'This is nice,' Rose said, changing the television channel while lying on our king-sized bed. I sat scribbling away on an examination pad with my knees drawn up. 'Good to see you writing, Rory.'

'Hope I can read my scrawl. It's been so long.'

Two days later, with Rose still battling, the doctor suggested we return to her. She sent us straight to the hospital where Rose was to stay until the baby was born. A day and a half later, with me sleeping in the chair next to Rose in her wardroom, the specialist decided on a caesarean.

'You don't have to be there at the birth if you don't want to, Rory.' Rose whispered to me out of breath as she lay waiting for the operation. 'I understand.'

I squeezed her hand. 'Nonsense. 'I'll be there. Wouldn't miss it for the world.'

'Are you sure?'

I nodded and kissed her sweaty forehead. 'I've never been more certain.'

'That's good to hear. Thank you.' Her face contorted in pain.

'Right, Mr Wilde, come with me,' a nurse in a green gown said. 'Let's get you ready for the operating room.'

'Just a sec.' I bent over and whispered to Rose, 'See you inside. You'll both be fine. I promise.' I kissed her, then followed the nurse. My mind a whirl of concern my stomach a knot of fear.

The theatre was a kaleidoscope of emotions, moving lights and whirring machinery. There is no greater sense of helplessness than watching a loved one's lifeless body being operated on. Yet the joy of seeing your child for the first time and hearing their initial breath is unparalleled. Through tears, I watched the birth of my daughter.

A nurse ushered me from the theatre and into a sanitised room where she brought my baby inside a heated incubator. 'Here you are, Mr Wilde.' She handed me a small tin of gel. 'Rub this over your baby. It will help her keep warm.'

I applied the gel through the hatch of the machine. The fresh minty smell of the rub reminded me of the wintergreen we used to heat our muscles in my rugby years at high school.

'Mrs Wilde is recovering well and is asking for you both.' A nurse wheeled our newborn from the room. 'Follow me.'

I watched mother and daughter bond in the split of a second and Rose turn from pasty to glowing. She put her hand out when she saw me. Neither of us had the words to talk or express how we felt. The three of us together said it all.

The rest of the week passed in a blur of visitors, doctors and family. Sleep was still not part of our agenda.

'Looking forward to getting home tomorrow,' Rose said, nursing

Chelsea, our beautiful daughter.

My stomach turned. *Oh, shit, I'd better tidy the place before Rose sees the mess.* 'Can't wait either.' I said, trying to stop the alarm from reaching my face.

We returned to our routine of lying on our bed, sharing the load of taking care of Chelsea. As we talked about our experiences, I continued to write, alternating between laughter and tears. Chelsea slept in her cot in one corner of our bedroom from the get-go. It made us reassess our priorities and aspirations. Despite many job applications, very few companies bothered to answer, let alone request an interview.

South Africa's demise or change, depending on one's perception and bias, went on. Affirmative action was making it tougher for me to be employed despite having experience. The infrastructure was in decline because of poor maintenance, and it needed to cater to a growing population. Farmers were being forcibly removed from their land, and the farms then given to the people, most of whom were not commercial producers. The brain drain was on, and those who could not find work emigrated to countries happy to take them on. Healthcare was under pressure, with enormous queues daily seeking help. Private medical companies charged high prices and seldom covered serious illnesses. The education system suffered the same way. Inflation continued to climb as we headed for the 2008 world recession. All these factors increased political violence, and organised crime at all levels of government and commerce was rampant.

The options available to us were to run our own business or leave the country. A government ruling made it more the first option even more difficult by mandating companies to buy from businesses with a Black South African shareholder. Emigrating was a big decision and would take time. Meanwhile we had little choice but to do something ourselves.

I had submitted a couple of short stories to local glossy magazines, and the one whose customer base was Zulu requested that I have an African nom de plume. Heaven forbids a white man should write a story about black people or vice versa. How long will it be before authors cannot write beyond their gender, or social, psychological, cultural or behavioural label? It'll be the beginning of the end for fiction, nonfiction having been lost well before.

'I think we should do something we know,' Rose said after putting Chelsea to sleep. 'Open a shop and find a range of products to import that we can sell to other outlets.'

'Interesting. What have you got in mind?' Seldom did Rose suggest anything unless she already had more than a good idea of all the details.

We planned and researched our next move. The tenants had just moved out of our rental house, so instead of incurring further costs we would run the company from there. The added advantage was that it was walking distance from home.

In the meantime, we contacted the supplier of a kids' interior wall decor range we intended to import and distribute throughout the country. Our previous business dealings held us in good stead, and after a brief phone call they agreed in principle to supply us. They insisted on a personal meeting in England, which was the only thing standing in our way.

'Doesn't look like we got much choice,' Rose said after finishing the call.

'You made it easier by convincing them to pay for one of our flights. Great work.'

'Thanks Rory. At least Chelsea is old enough to travel.'

'True that. I'll organise for her aunt in Wales to take care of her for a couple of hours while we're with the supplier.'

'That would be nice.' Rose smiled. 'Let's see if we can get a deal on our tickets, shall we?'

Neither of us comfortable using the funds from the sale of Cobblers and choosing to pay off outstanding debts over time.

After two weeks of searching and negotiating, we secured three tickets for the price of two, essentially paying for one flight. We landed in Heathrow Airport just outside London and took a black cab to the hotel our prospective suppliers had organised for us.

'Oh, my goodness.' Rose put her hand to her mouth, climbing out from the taxi in front of an ornate hotel entrance. 'Is this the right place?' she asked, paying the driver.

'You better *Adam and Eve* (believe) it, luv.' His Cockney accent was so thick it was difficult to understand him. 'Ta, Ta, *China plate* (mate).' He gave me a wave and disappeared into the never-ending traffic.

'What the hell did he just say?' I said as we stood with our luggage on the sidewalk.

Before Rose could answer, a man came out of the hotel, dressed in a top hat and an overcoat that reached his polished boots.

'Allow me, madam.' He loaded our suitcases onto a trolley and escorted us into the foyer of the hotel. 'May I ask your name, sir?' He gestured to me with white gloves.

'Rorke Wilde.'

'Mr and Mrs Wilde are with us,' he called across the room to a well-dressed woman behind the counter. He took us to the elevator, operated by a bellhop who took us to our floor. Waiting for us there was another porter who pushed our luggage to our room, making sure we were following.

'Enjoy your stay, madam, sir.' An awkward moment followed his words before he saw himself out.

'I think he was expecting a tip, Rory.' Rose cringed.

'Fat chance. He earns more than we do,' I said, helping Rose put Chelsea to bed after our long flight.

The following day we did all the popular tourist attractions, enjoying the vitality and diversity that is London. A pub dinner and warm beer finished our day and we retired early, still adjusting to the time difference. Chelsea's aunt would meet us in Bath City the next morning to sit with Chelsea as we headed for our supplier meeting. A metropolis rich in heritage, culture, and greenery, the city boasted Roman-built baths on the Avon River that had been created some two thousand years ago for enjoyment and relaxation. Bath's stunning Georgian architecture of honey-coloured limestone was reminiscent of a Jane Austen novel. It would be a two-hour trip in our hire vehicle, so we needed to be up early.

We met our supplier at a prearranged carpark in Bath. He turned out to be a charming man with greying hair and salt-and-pepper-speckled beard.

'Well, how are you folk?' he said with a slight West Country accent. He shook our hands, asking how we were and if we had recovered from the flight. 'We have a table booked inside.' He pointed to a sign that read The Pump Room. 'They do a wonderful afternoon tea.' He guided us into a luxurious Georgian hall with dramatic chandeliers. Diners sat at spacious tables bedecked with tiered china serving trays that were filled with cocktail sandwiches, scones and savouries. Each table was waited on by its own server.

We took our seat at our designated spot, taking in all around us.

'This is amazing.' Rose held her hands to her face in awe.

I was too dumbstruck to utter an opinion.

'It is rather special indeed.' he said, proud of the British pomp and regalia. 'See that fountain? That building across the road is the Grand Pump Room –' he pointed '– where they pump water from the Roman Baths' underground hot springs and it goes into the fountain.' He smiled and stood up, gesturing for us to follow. At the fountain, he dipped a crystal glass into the water and took a sip. 'Ah, delicious. Try it. It's very good for you.'

We followed suit, surprised at how pleasant it tasted, then returned to our table.

'It's all very regal,' I said. 'The food is amazing too.'

'Yes. Frequented by royalty and the famous, including Jane Austen and Charles Dickens.'

My interest piqued at the sound of my favourite author. *Maybe he even wrote a line or two here*, I thought to myself, absorbing the atmosphere. *I'm privileged to share a room with him. Must try to write a line here as well.*

'Don't worry,' Rose said to the prospective supplier. 'We will have lost him for a moment. Dickens is his hero.' She tapped my elbow.

'A man after my own heart.' Our host beamed. 'As I live and breathe, I think we can do some business together.' He shook our hands across the table. 'Now tell me, Rory, what's your favourite book by Charles?'

I caught Rose slumping into her seat in my peripheral vision and, no doubt, a slight eye roll. I smiled.

We had everything in place ready for the next move. Every minute in the back of our mind deliberated the concept of heading abroad.

When the moment was right. The new business provided time and opportunity for Chelsea's growth, settling our debts, and researching emigration.

'One day, Rory, we will make that call. Promise?' Rose said after another of our future planning chats.

'With all my heart,' I replied. 'We have seen and lived through what happened to Zimbabwe, and although South Africa may take longer, we may not be young enough to start over again.' I shook my head. 'So many pensioners trapped there who cannot afford to eat never mind leave. We cannot allow that to happen to our family.'

'Agreed,' Rose said. 'When we decide, we must try to convince all the family to move. I know it won't be a hit for some but if we can convince the kids, the others might follow.'

'Fair enough. It won't be easy but we're up for it.'

'We are, but it is so sad, Rory.'

'That it is.'

The decline of the economy resulted in families losing their life savings, falling into poverty, and there was a rise in violence and unrest. This had a devastating effect on the exchange rate, which affected inflation and assets.

We had seen it happen across the border. The Rhodesian, now Zimbabwean dollar, plummeted in comparison to the US dollar.

Rhodesian $500,000 had been worth the equivalent of US$250,000 in 1979 = 2:1 ratio.

Zimbabwean $500,000 was worth the equivalent of US$1,380 in 2016 = 362:1 ratio.

A loaf of bread cost more than people's pensions.

The South African rand was performing better, but its decline was a concern for the assets we had. Although at the time there was no way of knowing for sure, my experiences in Zimbabwe suggested South Africa would follow a similar trend. My premonition back then proved accurate.

R500,000 equalled US$125,000 in 1996.

30 years later that same asset depreciated to.

R500,000 equalled US$27,000 in 2025.

A 78% drop in value just because of where we lived. House prices were not rising, and the cost of living was exponential.

Many ignored these trends and now they had reached the age where reserves are crucial to a dignified retirement. The proverbial horse had already bolted. When older folk are living in a country that lacks a social security system, saved assets are what they survive on if they don't want to become a burden to the children.

I am not an ambitious person. I've never been interested in selling my soul in search of corporate adulation or accumulating wealth at any cost. We are told time is money, whereas the truth is that money is time, and it is time that we have a limited supply of. I am a determined man who loves what he does and who he loves. Rose is my all and is the centrepiece of everything I strive for. Nothing will make me deviate from her and my family's wellbeing.

Hence why leaving Africa now sat in the forefront of our minds. There was no choice. I left once before, then returned when I and the world saw hope with Nelson Mandela. I have never witnessed such anticipation, except when the people destroyed the Berlin Wall in 1989. But Southern Africa's dream was not meant to be.

I stopped writing, looked up from my pad and watched Chelsea asleep in her cot. Rose smiled up at me as she enjoyed the television, her red hair spread across the white pillowcase. 'Love you, Rory.'

'Love you more.' I turned off the lamp and settled alongside my African Rose. I had everything. Now I must give that to my family. Sleep overcame me but the questions ran rampant in my nightmares.

Chapter Twenty-one

On a bitter winter's evening Roger called Rose to say his barperson had let him down and he was unable to find a replacement. Did we know of anyone who might fill in. Out of ideas and hearing the angst in his voice because he had family commitments elsewhere, Rose volunteered my services. I didn't mind. It was a quiet night, and just for a few hours.

Trade at the pub was slow. We had not seen a customer in ages, and the remaining two punters were building up the courage to face the journey home.

I flipped through the television channels, but nothing sparked my interest.

Philemon raised his eyebrows at me and threw his arms up in a sign of frustration. From the far corner, he smiled, stood and stretched. 'Slow night, Rory?' He traipsed over and handed me his empty beer glass. 'Great to have you back. Like the good old days.'

'Afraid so, and I don't think we'll see anyone now, considering how late it is.'

Philemon looked at his watch. 'I'm having a bit of a mare, too. Got deadlines to reach but can't seem to put anything down on paper tonight.' He tapped his temple 'Writer's block.'

I shrugged. 'Perhaps another beer will help?'

'Go on then, twist my arm. Do you mind if I pull up a stool?'

'Not at all.' I indicated to the empty places in front of me.

We sat in silence until he sighed and said aloud, 'Migratory patterns of a lame duck.'

'I'm sorry.' I gave him a confused look.

Philemon turned towards the bar stools filling the room, stood up, and addressed the emptiness before him. 'Raise your hand if you are tired of hearing negative comparisons between South Africa and Zimbabwe,' he said, using air quotes. 'Don't be shy, folks.'

He beamed at me and raised his fist above his head in oration. 'Do not even get me started on the finger pointing South Africans who have already left and are now hiding behind the aprons of their newfound nanny states.'

'You go, *Meneer* (sir),' I applauded, and joined my writer friend on the other side of the bar. 'Brethren and comrades,' I called to the imaginary crowd. 'It is my honour to introduce you to Mr Philemon Dlamini.' I swore I heard their collective breaths and hoped one day they would not be able to justify their premature decisions to 'duck' - leave the country (pun intended). My hypocrisy and duplicity of doing quite the opposite of what I was preaching smarted within.

Philemon stood forward with dramatic elegance. His chest stuck out. 'I am all for freedom of speech. I admire those who stand on their virtual or real soapboxes and deliver passionate rhetoric.'

He paused for a moment, surveying his fictional audience we both could see, then continued. 'Censorship, whether imposed by the state or cloaked in political correctness, is unjustifiable. But if I hear another person say *That's the final straw, I am emigrating* because of an inconvenient power cut, or a player did not make the Springboks, I will *kak* (soil) myself.' He gave me a nervous glance, to which I clapped and motioned him to continue, enjoying the role play.

'Denouncing these instances is crucial with the right approach. We lost the validity of these causes when people bandied about threats like *I'll leave the country if you don't change it.*' He air-quoted again. 'Or tell everyone. *This place is going to the dogs because of the violent crime.*' Philemon dabbed a Louis Armstrong hanky to his eyes then shoved it into his pocket before getting back into his stride.

'Well, hello, those of short or selective memory. Did we not all arm ourselves to the teeth and train our children to kill on both sides? I would much rather today's criminal blew up ATMs than movie houses, restaurants and missions, as they did in the past. That doesn't make it acceptable, but it puts it into perspective.'

'No shit, Sherlock,' I interrupted, immediately regretting my outburst.

My friend smiled but did not miss a beat. 'Let me introduce you to author Rory Wilde.' He gestured towards me, inviting me to say a few words.

Ah, what the hell, it's a bit of fun, I thought, ignoring my inner conflict and jumped off my barstool, double-checking nobody else had turned up at the bar.

'We have to include the entire country this time. The authorities must prioritise education and the feeding of our kids over the wealthy buying luxury cars every year,' I said.

Philemon joined in from his seat. 'How many depart because of a perceived decline in living standards?'

'A good question, sir. Only to find themselves twelve months later residing in a shoebox in Wimbledon on Mud Island (England). Where African soapstone carvings, springbok ornaments and South African souvenirs adorn their interiors.' A car's headlights outside flashed through the bar. The front door rattled as it drove past.

I continued, 'They play Johnny Clegg music and Ladysmith Black Mambazo CDs when the family visit, and serve Castle lager that costs forty-five rand for a bottle. They admit to being unhappy after a couple of beers and switch slogans. *It's for the kids' sakes,* but one look into their children's glazed eyes, the healthy African glow long gone, suggests otherwise. Trust me I know I was one of them when I left Zimbabwe.'

'I suppose they can always treat themselves at the local chippy though?' my friend said to me, now standing by my side and turning to the imagined throng.

'People may live wherever they want without having to justify themselves. However, those who feel South Africa's demise justify their decision to leave and who choose to chirp to the detriment of our nation can then expect a response.'

Philemon patted me on the shoulder, and we fell about laughing at our childish make-believe. Returning behind the bar in case another customer turned up, I positioned one more beer in front of my cohort. An awkward silence descended as we contemplated – avoiding eye contact.

'That was fun but silly.' He thanked me and tipped the glass in my direction in salute. 'But you know what? That gives a premise for my next article.'

'From us fooling around? Really?'

'Hear me out, Mr Wilde.' Philemon wiped the froth from his moustache and addressed the ghost crowd once more. 'Enough is enough. As I mentioned earlier, the bleating and whining remind me of when I studied the migratory patterns of the Lame Duck.'

'Ducks.' I mimed the word.

Philemon held up a finger to me, continuing, 'Fortunately for me and the rest of the world, the likes of Steve Irwin burst upon the scene. My aim was to join the wildlife fraternity of Southern Africa through my observations of this lesser vulture. The name Lame Duck is misleading, as it is a scavenger and not related to the traditional duck family.'

I opened my hands and shrugged. 'What are you talking about? You've lost me, Mr Scribe.'

He pretended not to hear, instead holding up an index finger. 'It earned its title due to its foolish behaviour when in an uncomfortable or dangerous situation, such as pretending to be hurt or running away. The fowl's natural habitat stretches from the western tip of Britain to the eastern border of Greece. Being hypersensitive to its surroundings means it spends much of its life searching the globe for a dwelling.'

I sat down and listened as Philemon Dlamini's story and its relevance to the surge in emigration of late.

'The creature's quest for Eden will end in failure. When a male Lame Duck arrives in a new environment, it shows aggressive behaviour and is renowned for displacing other animals. The game ends when locals counter-challenge the Lame Duck. It resorts to a tedious display of umbrage in an attempt at self-preservation, before taking flight to the safety of its birthplace. Today the Lame Duck still flits here and there in search of paradise. Our ability to complain is a privilege. Let's not waste it on futile, selfish ideals, but for our communal betterment.'

'That's deep.' I said as I watched Philemon gather up his stationery from his favourite writing table.

'That is only the start. Have you the time to hear more?'

The clock showed nine-thirty. 'Sure – it's still too early to close, and I've heard nothing from Rose. What have you got?' I asked.

After placing his belongings by the till, he held up one of the writing pads and said in a subdued voice, 'This one is about the debasing anagrams being used here in South Africa. Like AA for Affirmative Action and BEE for Black Economic Empowerment. The flip side of the apartheid coin, so to speak.'

'Touchy subject, my friend. It has affected many.'

'It has, and it's what has contributed to the Lame Duck exodus of skilled people from our country,' Philemon answered.

'I'm listening.' I poured myself an alcohol-free beer and put out a bowl of salted peanuts for us to share.

'Suspend reality and imagine me without political bias. Hard, but humour me.' He gave a smile. 'Is it time to stop promoting one group over another? Decades later, shouldn't we allow natural forces to decide who is better suited to a job or position?'

I blew through pursed lips but listened, not disrupting him.

'I hear the vehement protests that some are still profiting from an unjust system. In a decade we have failed to resolve the problem. Does the government believe that a couple more years of this mismanagement will lead to more success? Isn't it time to take stock of these initiatives and decide whether they have helped or hindered our progress as a nation? South Africans know only too well how a community suffers when it's excluded from the rest.'

'Isn't that the truth? Is it fair for middle-aged white men to fight against AA and BEE if it harms them and thus their family?' I interjected, while Philemon wet his lips with his beer.

'Be my guest, Rory.' He invited me to carry on.

'Are we forcing their arm, creating unspoken codes of self-preservation so all they want to do is look after their own? These guys draw from the old pool of apartheid businesspeople who outwitted international sanctions. What chance do a few half-hearted programmes have? Encouraging them to be part of South Africa's leadership doesn't mean it absolves them from past injustices, but it may be a positive way in which they can make amends.'

'Why should we worry about these Jurassic entities?' My learned author took over answering his own question. 'We don't have to. We could label them as scapegoats and take pleasure in their discomfort. But what if we tried a different approach to solving the problem?'

We laughed again at our theatrics, took a comfort break and refilled our drinks. The pub's cologne filled my nostrils with a cocktail of alcohol permeating through the rooms, mixed with remnants of earlier clients' perfumes and bar meals. My complicity smarted.

'Is it possible that these guys have more to contribute than we realise or acknowledge?' I resumed to the imaginary audience. My falsity tearing me apart at Rose and my plan to leave the country.

'What if we included them in the transformation where they could offer their expertise and skills without charge?' he answered me.

'Take heed of the recent sport fiasco. Athletes strive to be the best and seek selection. Choosing them on any other basis would be insulting to them.'

Philemon nodded. 'Is this unique to sport? I think not. We hear about the brain drain that plagues our nation, yet what is being done about it? No one knows how much we have lost as they keep it confidential.' He paused, taking a sip to clear his throat while I continued.

'Those skills have not all emigrated. Many have moved into self-employment and small business to feel valued. It leaves the corporates short-staffed or worse still, incorrectly manned. An electrician quitting an Eskom job with twenty years of experience to buy a burger franchise is crazy. He cooks on gas to boot.'

'Very interesting point Rory Wilde. Despite our cynicism, most South Africans love to help one another and get involved, but don't push us around and force us into anything. Observe the good done from pure hearts. Perhaps if we rewarded those in business for taking on previously disadvantaged workers (not to forget school leavers) by offering real tax relief. Would skills transfer quicker? You bet.'

'In what way?' I asked, stifling a yawn.

'Two major driving forces for any businessperson (corporate or entrepreneurial) are reward and satisfaction. Teaching a new skill benefits both individual and country. Participation is optional. Pariahs serve as a yardstick in a free society.'

Philemon took a swig of his beer, then continued. 'There will be bastions of racially motivated businesses and communities, but very few. Money talks and customers walk. There is inevitably going to be a sport, or an ideal, supported by one race, colour, creed or gender. So what? Isn't that real independence?'

I knew his questions were rhetorical so didn't respond.

'We are not trying to reduce the diversity of South Africa into a single grey hybrid—or are we? We demand freedom of choice; therefore, must accept our differences. Coercion doesn't achieve good intentions. Cream rises when left well alone. Natural selection works overtime.'

'Getting a tad heavy again.' I squeezed in a word, copying a phrase Rose often used on me.

The man smiled, still unfinished. 'If we have different goals and rush the process to gain what others have, we might end up losing ourselves. Our neighbour removed commercial farmers without considering who would feed the people. We should speculate how diverse that country might be today if they had not fast-tracked for thirty years.'

'Are you done?' I gave him a sarcastic smile. 'Now I understand why you went to the agricultural college.'

'I'm sorry, Rory, but thanks to you my mind is alive again, which means my writer's block is on the way out. Thank you.'

'My pleasure.' Sirens wailed past Cobblers Bar and Grill, blue and red lighting the dimmed interior of the pub.

In the silence that followed, Philemon stated, 'Let us bleed every single South African dry of every skill and expertise they possess. Their continued contribution to the community will be an added benefit. The minute we show favour to one tribe, gender or race over another, we risk alienation and repercussions.'

'It's been a fascinating evening, my friend.' I hinted it was time to wrap up. 'Sheila will wonder where you got to.'

'She told me you were helping and, in fact, suggested I join you.' He returned to our debate. 'No doubt many will disagree with my sentiments. I am excited to read their responses. We look forward to hearing from those who have benefited from AA or BEE and used it for company and country improvement. Not to mention the inevitable diatribe from the dinosaurs in charge themselves.'

Philemon swallowed the last of his beer and headed for the restroom.

On his return, he fetched something out of his backpack and came back across to me wearing a broad grin. 'I don't know if you read much, but after our shenanigans tonight...' He pointed to the Irish emblems on the Cobblers' sign on the wall. 'Did you see what I did there?' He laughed at his own joke. 'Shenanigans... Irish?'

I rolled my eyes. 'Really?'

'Bad, I know. Anyhow you impressed me, Mr Wilde, with your knowledge and use of language so thought you might like this.' He handed me a paperback book.

'What's this?' I looked at the cover. *New Best Friends* by Philemon Dlamini. 'Your new book. Thank you.' I shook his hand.

'Here, let me sign it for you.'

'That would be great,' I said, and he scribbled away. 'I envy you, sir. I wish I had time to write. It has been a dream of mine most of my life.'

Philemon stood up and looked me hard in the eyes. 'Then why aren't you doing just that? Stop finding excuses as to why you can't make the time.' He held the book out to me, and for a moment we were both holding onto the novel. 'Write for yourself. Don't worry about what people think. You might choose never to reveal your words, but at least you are writing. One day when you are ready, you will share a sentence or two.' He let go of the novel.

'You know, I just may do that. I have several scribblings I have written in the past,' I said.

'Then you are already a writer. Revisit them and start over.'

'I might just do that. Thank you.'

'Goodnight, Rory.' Philemon shook my hand. 'I shall be back in my corner tomorrow, writing away.' He hesitated, lifting his index finger at me. 'A word of warning though. Don't expect those close to you to be fans of your work.'

'What do you mean?' I gave him a quizzical look.

'They will support you in just about every way other than actually reading your book.' He smiled. 'They're too close and see more than the public. Take care.'

'Go well, but remember, I won't be here. See you soon.' I let him out after walking him to the door. 'Thanks for the book. I appreciate it.' I waved it at him, locked the gate once he had driven off, and flicked through the pages. Inscribed on the first page were the words:

Rory
Your tenacity has earned you the honouree title of 'Zulu
Warrior'.
Philemon Dlamini a.k.a., the fool sitting in the corner.

My mind was in turmoil. I could understand both arguments Philemon raised. Neither was wrong, yet both were subjective, lacking empathy and acceptance. *Philemon spoke about some deep stuff.*

Where are you, *baba wami (*my father)? I need you, Themba. *Ngiyesaba* (I am scared.) *Kwenzakalani* (What is going on)?

My loneliness deepened, and my gut clenched as I tidied up and prepared to head back home. My old pub companions, urine and ammonia, filled the air.

I would be forever indebted to Philemon Dlamini for inspiring me to follow my dreams. To write and find a home for the family.

Chapter Twenty-two

Our distribution business was a challenge. Rose sourced ranges we knew would do well from our experiences before we purchased Cobblers, and with our contacts in the industry we secured outlets throughout the country before importing our goods. Along with a raft of independent shops, three major corporations bought the products – the country's largest grocery chain, a DIY warehouse company, and a retail paint brand.

The day I signed the final supplier documents after a hectic round of negotiations with executives and head buyers, I returned to the car and texted Rose.

> **We nailed it. I've got a copy of the contract in my hands :0) Damn we good.**

She replied: **You got that right mister. See you home in an hour?**

Celebrate tonight? I messaged back. **Somewhere quiet. Just the 2 of us - exhausted.**

> **Same here. Cobblers? Where it all started.**

> **Love it. See you later.**

Drive safe. I ended the chat and headed south, back to Germiston.

Motorway congestion doubled the commute home during rush hour. Taxis hooting and pushing in where not even a fly could fit.

Thought the annoying critters were sharing the car with me, orbiting my head, slaking their thirst from the sweat on my face.

'Tough drive?' Rose thought about welcoming me with a kiss and a hug, instead recoiling from the sight and no doubt body odour. 'Bloody hell, Rory.' She laughed. 'Straight into the shower for you. I'll fix you a drink and a bite to eat.'

'Thanks, but let's go to the pub. Dying for a cold beer.'

'Now you're talking. I'll get ready while you're in there.' She pointed to the bathroom, handing me a fresh towel. 'Always time for a freshen up.'

The initial beer didn't quench our thirst, so the barkeep brought additional lagers. We sat in the furthest corner of the bar – not that it was a busy evening, but we needed our privacy. For the first hour we chatted about nothing in particular, enjoying the ambience and our drinks.

'To us.' I toasted with my glass held up to Rose.

'To us.' She did the same. 'Didn't think we'd convert some of those big accounts, though.' Rose pursed her lips.

'Thanks to you.' I raised my drink again.

She smiled and rubbed my knee. 'Finances will be tight, supplying the major clients. The initial investment includes ordering the entire range and waiting for payment terms.'

'We knew it would be.' I offered.

'Hope we didn't discount too much to secure their patronage.'

'Don't doubt yourself now. That's just the nerves.'

Rose nodded and smiled. 'I guess so. We crunched those numbers, didn't we?'

'Sure did.' Butterflies in my stomach fluttered despite my reassurances.

With our import and distribution business set up and our daughter Chelsea growing up, time and cash were tight.

Socialising was a weekend *braai* with the family or a trip through the high street window shopping. Besides making sales calls in Johannesburg to get our products listed with buyers, I spent my day renovating our second home from top to bottom. The new business would operate from there, with storage and offices, eliminating the need to rent space. And when it was time to sell up, both the house and family would be ready.

Part of the upgrade was installing anti-trespasser equipment. The first line of defence was two-metre-high fencing topped off with barbed wire around the entire property. To deter ramming and improve identification, we put in meshed safety gates and a televised intercom. The windows had bars welded in place to prevent even the smallest intruder. Finally, we set up a surveillance system connected to an armed home security firm, who would respond any time of the day or night if the alarm sounded in their control room.

Before entering or leaving, it was customary to check the garden for ambushes and ensure the street was clear before getting in or out of the vehicle. This would protect those in the car while not exposing the home.

Out on the main road was a group of local men seeking manual labour jobs. At the rear of the throng of expectant workers I noticed a solitary, slim-built figure. Compared to the others, he appeared quiet and downtrodden, prompting me to call out to him. After a few shoves and swear words directed at him by the rowdier jobseekers, he stepped forward.

'Morning. Are you strong?' I asked.

'Yes, sir,' he said, peering down at his feet.

'I've got a big job I need help with, so I'm looking for a reliable person who is a quick learner.'

His skittish eyes disappeared with a boyish smile. 'That is me, boss.' He tapped his heart. 'I promise.' His face turned to hope.

'That's good to hear.' I smiled back at him and offered him my hand. 'Please don't call me anything except Rory. I'm not your boss, mister or sir. We will work together.'

He held on with both of his and gave a huge shake. 'My name is Joseph. When do we start?'

'Right now,' I replied. 'Jump in the car and I'll take you there. Along the way we can discuss pay, etcetera.'

He threw his battered backpack over his shoulder – raising dust from his tatty T-shirt and patched trousers, which ended above his ankles – and followed me.

Joseph excelled in repairing, repainting, with a speciality for working with wood. At the end of each day, I handed him his cash and bid him goodnight.

On the fifth day, a Friday, he did not take the wages I offered.

'Is something wrong Joseph?'

He reached and took the money, his eyes wanting to ask a question.

'What is it, my friend?'

'Are you able to pay me weekly on Mondays so I can save it for my wife and children? Carrying cash on the weekend is risky.'

My heart melted. 'Of course. We'll start next week, if that is okay?'

'Thank you.' He clapped his hands in appreciation.

'Where is your family?'

'In Mozambique.'

Like others in similar situations, this person was an undocumented worker trying to make a living to support their family – exploited by businesses and persecuted by local officeholders.

'So where do you stay?'

He looked at me, hesitant to say, his self-preservation instinct kicking in. He muttered something I could not understand and waved his arm in multiple directions.

'Well, jump in the car. I will drop you off on my way home. The weekend is here,' I said, looking more for his reaction than anything else.

To avoid offence, he agreed to my offer, and asked to be dropped off in town by the bus stop.

'Rest up on your days off, Joseph. We have plenty to do next week. Thank you for all your efforts.'

He waved, thanked me, and disappeared into the darkness.

Not convinced, I drove across the road to a supermarket carpark and watched him wander without conviction. He turned at the street's end, slunk back the way he came, and joined a group of homeless people by the railway lines. Cardboard walls erected around trees was their home. A fire flickered from a rusty steel drum. I left it there, returning to my plush abode, lavish food and loving family. I knew it would haunt me the rest of the weekend and, once again, my best friend and stalwart provided the logic and empathy I lacked.

'Well, there's not much we can do about it other than pay him for the work he does,' I said to Rose after sharing the day with her.

'Are you sure about that, Rorke Wilde?' She looked at me with one eye smaller than the other.

'I think so. I mean, we don't really know who he is.'

Rose turned her lips downwards in disagreement. 'Then why did you follow him if he didn't matter to you?' she asked. 'Why are we even having this conversation?'

'I… I…I do not know.'

'If I understand you – and trust me, I do – I reckon you're feeling guilty because there is actually something we could do for him,' Rose said, cutting to the chase.

'Like what?'

'Don't *wip jou gat* with me, mister.' Rose used a popular Afrikaans phrase that does not translate well but means throwing a tizzy. 'You tell me.'

I lolled down onto the couch and looked at the TV, not seeing what was on but contemplating what to do.

The rest of the evening we discussed and debated until Rose stood and, before leaving the room, turned to me. 'You know what to do, Rory,' she said. 'You don't need me to tell you.'

On Monday I picked up Joseph, who had wrapped himself in a tattered blanket to protect against the cold of the dawn.

'Morning Joesph. Ready for a busy week?'

Despite his smile, his bloodshot eyes revealed a night spent beside a smoky fire, his face ashen. A glimmer of hope was all that remained in his gaze.

When we arrived at the rental, he leapt out of the car and opened the gate, closing it after me as I drove up the driveway. Like before, we readied ourselves for the day by planning our activities.

'How about grabbing a coffee before we begin?' Joseph gave me a puzzled expression in response to my question, as I had not offered hot beverages before. Unsure what to say, he shrugged, waiting for direction from me.

'Follow me.' I placed a hand on his skeletal shoulder as we walked to a small cabin at the bottom of the backyard. 'Here.' I gave him a key.

Confused, he played along, suspicious of my motives. The door opened with a creak but the room was too dark for us to see what was in front of us.

'What are you looking for, boss... sorry, Rory,' he corrected himself, slipping into his subservient banter.

I flicked the light switch, where a bed greeted us in the corner, a couple of chairs, an electric fire, and a transistor radio on the windowsill. 'What is this?' Joseph asked, walking into the adjoining room with a shower and toilet.

He looked me in the eye, handing me back the key, which I pushed away, saying 'It's for you for as long as we work together.'

'I do not understand.' He shook his head. 'Why?'

'We don't want to leave the house empty with all the stock and computers inside.' I watched his reaction. There was nothing but a blank expression. 'Would you mind looking after it for us? Payment is free lodging and a cooked meal once a day. What do you say?'

Tears filled his eyes as he slapped my hand with joy. Unable to speak and not wanting me to see him emotional, he rushed off to get his belongings in town.

I carried on with the renovations, and when Joseph rejoined without a word we worked through to lunchtime. Rose arrived with sandwiches and a couple of cans of soda. We resumed until late afternoon, when I stopped for the day. Nothing spoken apart from the odd grunt, a gesture, or a cuss.

'Right, that's us done, my friend. We'll carry on in the morning,' I said, packing up and stowing the tools and equipment in the house. 'You sure you don't want your pay now?' I checked before leaving.

'Yes, I am,' Joseph said. He put a hand on my shoulder, jerking it away as if it burnt him. 'Sorry.' Uneasy at breaking my bubble.

'That's all right. Is there something bothering you?' I looked around, inviting him to talk.

He scrunched his face, placing a finger on his nose. 'Thank you, Rory. Please thank your wife too for her kindness.' His tone caught me in the chest. Never again have I heard such a purposeful voice. 'Not only do you keep me safe but also my family. Your food and shelter allow me to provide for my loved ones. I can never repay you.'

'You have already. More than you will ever know,' I replied.

We strolled down separate paths, empowered by the boundless potential of humanity, regardless of the prevailing forces of greed and political manoeuvring.

The following Monday we resumed as normal but were now comfortable with each other. We sat with our legs astride the apex of the roof, painting and repairing loose bolts. While discussing politics, cultures and assorted brands of beers, we laughed and enjoyed the clear African skies and the warmth of the sun. We dug holes and sweated until we almost fainted, setting new cement and cutting wood. Some afternoons, after a delightful lunch from Rose, we lounged beneath the shade of a jacaranda tree without as much as a word. But our families were the principal topic of conversation every day.

'Tell me more about your family in Mozambique.'

Every time he spoke of his family he lit up with joy and pride, which plunged when mentioning his country.

'We live in Beira. Do you know where that is?' he asked.

I nodded, to his utter amazement.

You do? How is that possible?'

'I am from Zimbabwe…'

'Ah,' he acknowledged. 'I understand. You're old enough to have visited there for holidays. No?'

'Yup.' I smiled back at him. 'How far is Beira from Johannesburg here?'

'One thousand five hundred kilometres.' He dropped his eyes to his lap. 'It takes fifty-two hours by train and bus.'

'Such a beautiful city,' I said, trying to keep the moment from becoming a downer.

'It is. Sitting on the Indian Ocean where the majestic Pungwe River flows into the sea.'

He spoke of his family, a time of hope in the past, and a present comprising poverty, cyclones and civil war. The events in neighbouring southern African countries were similar or the same.

'I'm sure you have a different story to tell.' Joseph gave me a wicked look, teasing me and my privileged heritage.

My memory of Beira comes from when I was ten years old. Zimbabweans – then known as Rhodesians – who couldn't afford to holiday in South Africa travelled to Beira. The wealthier families stayed in the illustrious Grande Hotel Beira with over one hundred rooms. The poorer households, mainly civil servants, hired the chalets along the beachfront – the barest of accommodation with concrete floors, plastic curtains, a shower, and a two-plate cooker in a stark kitchen. However, these were a far more exciting prospect for children who would slip away in the mornings to return just before dark as they did at home. Their days were spent exploring the kilometres of fine white-sand beaches, and swimming in the placid ocean where waves seldom reached a metre high.

The comforts of nature were compensation enough. Nights sleeping to the sound of the warm Indian Ocean through open windows. Days watching large ships glide into the country's largest port. We were oblivious of the civil war rebelling against four hundred years of Portuguese rule that had followed Vasco da Gama's arrival, ousting the Muslim traders and their trading posts along the Mozambique Channel and taking control of the opulent spice trade.

Chapter Twenty-three

We added the same protections to the home Rose, and I lived in. When the household slept, we secured the gate dividing the bedrooms from the house, setting the alarm in case of a break-in.

As I was repairing the front gates one day, two sleek German cars drove past the property and then came back to park in the driveway where I was working.

'Afternoon. How are you today?' A tall man sporting designer sunglasses and dressed in a dark suit and shiny matching shoes climbed out of the vehicle. He reminded me of a character from the movie *Men in Black*. The other driver peered at me from behind the wheel, also wearing shades.

'Hey, ma'gents,' I said, weighing up the situation and unable to make my escape. 'Doing what I can. No job. No money. What can I do?'

Removing his glasses, he peered at the garden and our car in the driveway. 'Is that why you are fixing your own gates?' he sneered with a slight grin.

'Why would I work in the sun if I had money?' I shrugged and continued repairing the gate as if unperturbed by their prying. Every muscle in my body was waiting for the next move, my mind racing with options. 'It's hard enough paying the rent on time.' I pointed to the house. 'You gents all right?' I asked.

'Ja, sure, *Kulungile umlungu* (okay, white person). Be careful sitting around with your gates open. Very dangerous.' I could see my reflection in the shine of his expensive leather dress shoes. He got back into his car. As the window rolled up, I saw him talking on his mobile phone. Both cars spun their wheels and drove away.

I sat recomposing myself, then went inside for a glass of water after locking the gates.

Joseph emerged from beneath a tarpaulin in the garage, his face filled with cobwebs and insects, terror in his eyes. 'I thought they were coming for me, Rory,'

'No, my friend,' I replied. 'They were looking to invade the property and steal what they could, including the BMW.' *Plus do whatever they decided to with people they encountered in the process.* But I kept that thought to myself, not wanting to share the possibility. 'I have no idea why they didn't try.' We composed ourselves but left what we were doing until the next day. The gates would hold until then.

'Are you, okay?' Rose asked in the kitchen. 'You look flushed.'

'Too much sun, I reckon.' It was all I could to collect myself and not let on what might have happened. My thoughts were spinning. *Bloody hell, that was close. They were some bad boys. They're not from around here. Big-time gangsters from the inner city.* Thankful that the years at Cobblers dealing with potential situations had paid off.

Unrest spread to the suburbs, with violent invasions occurring even when residents were home. Retribution, not just theft, motivated some. With it, xenophobia emerged, discriminating against African immigrants from neighbouring countries. Young men rampaged through squatter camps, destroying the belongings of undocumented migrants, maiming women and children, and beating men to death with sticks or stoning them. Politicians used anger towards foreigners to distract from their own failures and to make illegal money. Yet these immigrants were merely trying to eke a living that their homeland had failed to provide.

Churches, community halls and charities worked hard to provide shelter, food, and clothing for these wretched people. Rose and I put aside time to help where we could and, as I have described in my first memoir, *The Chameleon,* this was when I reunited with my child mentor, Themba Dube. In the book, I talked about my younger life of going to boarding school, of civil war and the birth of Zimbabwe – all under the watchful eye of Themba. A small positive amidst cruelty, inconsequential compared to that found in the twenty-first century. Who knows where that might lead? My emotions and thoughts are at odds regarding the outcome. My gut is keeping silent about it.

As a means of quality family time and normality, Chelsea loved visiting the bunny park in the neighbouring town of Boksburg. Rabbits, birds, and antelope roamed in a beautiful, natural parkland with a stream. Visitors could buy cupfuls of seed and fruit to feed them or take rides on the docile ponies.

Arriving one Sunday afternoon, we sought shelter from the warm sun under a straw-thatched umbrella. Chelsea took off and joined the other youngsters doting over the springbok, mesmerised by their large, doleful eyes. I opened our rug and spread it onto the grass, opening the chilly bin to see that the drinks and food had survived the road trip. Rose patted the ground next to where she sat, inviting me to join her as we enjoyed our daughter's frolic with nature and other children.

A couple of hours later, Rose washed the ice-cream bought from one of the mobile kiosks from Chelsea's face as I tidied up our little campsite and prepared to head home. Strange noises from an old water tank reached our ears as we walked to the car park.

'Wonder what that is?' Rose changed direction.

Peering over the side, we saw a mother pig with a multitude of newborn piglets. Horror gripped Rose. 'What the ...?' Chelsea's presence prevented her mom finishing her expletive. 'Oh, shame, those poor animals.' She said, looking around for an official. 'These conditions aren't suitable.'

'Not great. That's for sure.' I agreed. 'But it might just be temporary.' I tried to comfort my wife, knowing exactly where this was heading.

'Excuse me.' Rose ignored me, beckoning workers nearby. I picked up Chelsea and from a distance watched Rose finger pointing and the shake of their shoulders in response. From her facial expression on her return, she was not happy with the outcome. 'Well, I'll take them up on their offer.' Rose stormed past us, talking more to herself than anyone. She vaulted the reservoir, reappearing with a piglet no bigger than a hamster wrapped in her hat. 'They said if I didn't like where the pigs lived, I could take one home,' Rose responded to the look on my face and marched off. Chelsea squirmed out of my hold and bolted off to her mother, skipping in delight. I trudged on after them, weighed down by more than our possessions.

The girls mothered the baby, feeding it milk by syringe. We built a large pen in the backyard, which he seldom used, preferring to spend his nights in our bathroom. Within a few months, the piglet grew to the size of a couch weighing over three hundred kilograms.

'Wilbur. What have you done to the furniture?' Rose called out from the bathroom he slept in. Chelsea and I peered around the corner to find Wilbur had chewed away the door on the cupboard to make more space for himself.

Wilbur, as named by Chelsea after the movie Charlotte's Web, developed an amazing character. In love with one of our dogs, he protected his territory and barked as well as any of them. James's friends, when visiting, had to run a gauntlet as he chased them from their vehicles to his garden flat.

The love of his life was Chelsea, to which he was ever so gentle towards. A fourteen-kilo child controlling the third of a tonne mass of Wilbur by tickling him on the back. He would shake as his skin crawled, then crashed to the ground on his side. Chelsea, then laid on top of him, the two would nap under the trees in the garden. The look of content on both glorious.

The saddest sight was Chelsea bouncing on her trampoline in the garden. Behind all the security fencing, she waved to the domestic workers coming and going along the street. Her favourite person, Isabelle, passed the house daily.

'Hello, Chelsea,' she said out aloud, waving her arms. 'How are you today?' Her smile was the widest I had seen. 'I have something for you, my friend.' She handed Chelsea a wrapped Chappies bubble gum. 'See you later.' She waddled down the road, singing to the world. Chelsea beamed and waited for the same the next day and every day after that– a sight that haunted me, wakening me in the early hours of the morning.

Social injustices should never hem in any person, let alone a child. Her eyes were the darkest reflection of a nation losing its way.

This situation affected people from all walks of life. Even the puppeteers faced their demise if a country lacked a sustainable infrastructure. Those able to leave did so.

Despite the despair, there were the good times. Chelsea, at three years old, was full of energy and mischief. Her favourite pastimes were visiting the malls to shop and going to quiz night at a local club in Germiston. Something Cobblers Bar and Grill had never hosted.

'Chelsea's ready,' Rose called out to me.

'All righty then. Quiz evening, here we come.' I picked Chelsea up and strapped her into her car seat. 'You looking forward to dinner and the quiz, sweetheart?'

Chelsea nodded and clapped. She loved the array of lights and shadows on the street at night on the rare occasion we ventured out after dark.

I set the alarm, closed the security gate, and looked down the road to see all was clear, then pressed the unlock button on the car and joined Chelsea and Rose inside. 'Let's go, guys.'

Chelsea and Rose loved to dress up for quiz nights where we ate from a buffet, danced to a deejay between competitions and vied to win our quizzes. Chelsea would wander around the room, visiting each table and chatting. Most knew her, and those who didn't, would soon become acquainted. Quite the belle of the ball, socialising with young and old alike. Sitting at a table of adults discussing her likes and dislikes. Dancing with her Uncle Jess and family. Tucking into ice-creams and cakes ordered by friends old and new.

One such night, after the quiz had finished, Chelsea watched her brother and his buddies playing cards at the table. 'Minimum bet five cents,' James yelled out, dealing another hand.

She laughed at the drama and humour and was reluctant to leave the gamblers when Rose and I called time.

'Come on, sweetheart, it's getting late. We must go,' Rose said, lifting Chelsea to me.

I put her on my hip and kissed her cheek. 'Say goodbye to your brother and his friends.'

The table's occupants waved and said goodnight.

Chelsea paused, eyed them, then raised her hand and yelled, 'Goodnight, bitches.'

A quietness fell upon the once lively room for a few seconds. James's crowd howled with laughter, with two of them falling off their chairs in stitches. The rest of the audience followed suit. We beat a hasty retreat, out of breath by her audacity and unproven wit. Our love for who she was becoming overshadowed by our parental instincts to reprimand her for her language. Her brother could not be prouder.

'Oh, my word.' Rose held her hands to her face in the car. 'She's so naughty. Reminds me of the time in the supermarket carpark.' Rose shook her head in fake shock. 'She needs to tone it back a bit.'

'She does,' I said, laughing at the memory.

Less than a week earlier we had just parked the car, ready for our weekly grocery shop. I was lifting Chelsea from her seat when an older man walked by and helped himself to a free shopping trolley discarded close to us. Chelsea took umbrage to him taking what she thought was our cart, muttering under her breath, 'Asshole bitch,' just loud enough for our family to hear. They all scattered in embarrassment, doubling up in mirth as they ran.

'Where does she even get it from?' Rose asked, showing the palms of her hands in her confusion.

'The company she keeps?' I teased.

'Don't start with me, Rorke Wilde.' Rose gave me a light punch on the shoulder. 'It's good to be home.'

We packed the groceries away, then over a cup of coffee Rose scrolled through her messages while I tackled a short story I was writing for a glossy magazine.

'Ah shame,' Rose said to herself. 'Sheila says Philemon is missing your chats at the pub. Reckons he's back to sitting in the corner on his own.' She punched at the keyboard, responding to Sheila's message. 'You keen to join him on Monday? Sheila is doing stocktake at the supermarket on her day off to earn some extra cash.'

Rose looked up from the phone and read the hesitancy on my face. 'Come on, Rory. You enjoy it when you're there. It's a quiet night too.'

'Okay,' I sighed with reluctance.

'Sorted.' Rose turned back to her mobile, which beeped seconds after she sent her suggestion of the men getting together. 'Sheila's over the moon but asks we don't mention it to Philemon and make it seem a coincidence.'

I rolled my eyes and shrugged, not wanting to get involved. 'That's up to her. Tell her I'll be there around eight o'clock, after dinner.'

Monday came around all too soon,

'You look very nice, Rory.' Rose said, giving me a kiss goodbye. 'Enjoy yourself.'

'Feel guilty going without you.' I kissed her back.

'Don't be silly. It's a one-off and I really don't mind,' Rose tutted, handing me the keys. 'I'm looking forward to watching my romantic comedies anyway.' She pulled a tongue and locked the door after me.

The bar lady did not recognise me when I entered Cobblers Bar and Grill. I noticed Roger had changed some of the décor, and in fairness it looked fresh.

'Evening. What can I get you?' she asked with enthusiasm.

I glanced about the room, empty apart from Philemon in his usual spot. 'Hi. I'll have two Castle drafts please,' I said so only she could hear me. 'Make it a jug.'

'Sure thing.' She started the process of the beer pouring. 'Is there something else I can get for you? Snacks perhaps?'

'No, thanks. This will be just fine.'

'Fifteen rand, please.' I handed her a twenty. 'Enjoy,' she smiled at me. 'Shout if you need anything more or a refill.'

I pocketed the change taking the jug and two glasses over to Philemon, who carried on oblivious. 'As I live and breathe.' I said aloud, causing Philemon to jump in his seat.

'Rory Wilde. How the hell are you, young man?' He stood up to greet me. 'You scared the living daylights…' He didn't finish his sentence but shook my hand.

'Sit, my friend. Mind if I join you for a drink?' I showed him the jug of beer. 'I don't want to break your train of thought.'

'You bet and I haven't had one of those in weeks.' Philemon offered the chair across from him, moving his laptop out of the way.

I poured us a glass each as we engaged in the usual small talk of reconnecting after a while apart.

'You have made my day, sir.' Philemon beamed at me. 'Hope you have time to stay awhile?'

'That I do. Rose has thrown me out.'

A look of horror crossed his face, followed by a smile of realisation that I was talking nonsense.

'She is watching a chick flick and doesn't want me in the way.'

'Great. Sheila is…' Philemon stopped halfway through his sentence, then gave me a quizzical glance. 'She's stitched me up, hasn't she?'

'Only because she loves you, and to be honest I could do with your company,' I answered.

'Either way, I'm a winner,' he whooped, surprising the bar lady who I suspected had not seen this in him until now. 'Sorry.' He shot her an embarrassed look.

'No need to apologise, Phil.' She used the same condensed version of his name as Len used to. 'It's great to see friends catching up.' She tossed a bag of peanuts at us. 'On the house, gentlemen. Enjoy.' She turned away as two clients entering the pub diverted her attention.

'You've made my evening. Thank you.' He shook my hand again. 'Tell me how your writing is going.'

'I have to thank you.' I gave him a silent toast with my glass of lager. 'To be honest, the writing's not going too well. I just can't seem to get into it.' I paused, changing the subject. 'Am I right in assuming you're having another one of your writer's blocks?'

Philemon's face dropped a sadness in his eyes. 'I'm still struggling to write, Rory. Given the current state of affairs or lack thereof in our country.' He took a long swig on his beer.

'I hear you, my friend. Troubling times.'

'That they are,' he answered. 'But we cannot sit back and allow it to happen without writing about it.'

'I read your book, Philemon. Loved the humour highlighting the underlying decay and corruption.' I hesitated, looking for the right word. 'Impressive.'

'Why thank you, kind sir, but now I want to contribute to live debates on the radio, television and internet.'

'Ambitious, but if anyone can do it you can.'

Philemon looked around the room, then back at me. 'What say you and I form a pact?'

'I'm listening.'

'We write to make a difference. Meet regularly and support one another.' His kind, earnest face affected me.

'Can't think of anything I'd rather do more. You've got yourself a deal.' We sat in silence, unsure what to say or do next, taking awkward sips from our glasses.

'Actually, Philemon, that is not entirely true. We are thinking of emigrating.' I blurted the last word.

My friend broke into a wry smile. 'Who isn't, Rory?' We chuckled, aware of the irony.

'No matter how much I love Africa, my priority is looking after my family.' I said in a low tone – not that there was anybody close by. The barperson was conversing with the two customers as though they were friends.

'I understand Rory and I respect you for that. It makes my blood boil to hear it though. Until that moment arrives, can we stick to our agreement to write together?'

'It will take a while before we leave, if ever, but of course we can. There's nothing stopping us from doing so afterwards either,' I suggested.

'True. Words today are everywhere, whenever, in an instant. Such is the internet.' Using a drop of spilled beer on the polished tabletop, he drew an emoji, showing both a smile and a frown. 'Just be sure you don't take too long to decide, Rory. Your luck lies in a brief window to make the move. Many do not seize it and end up stuck in a country they do not wish to be in.'

'I know, and thank you,' I answered.

We whiled away the evening reminiscing, planning, and enjoying the moment until it was time for us to return to our homes. We swapped cell phone numbers, said our farewells, and left Cobblers Bar and Grill.

Chapter Twenty-four

Rose and I took a few days off to recharge and spend time together. Our hectic schedule of family life, trying to make ends meet and considering where our future lay was taking its toll. We stayed home and enjoyed a chill time, going nowhere and doing nothing. The first day we had a *braai* (barbecue) with friends and family. In the peacefulness, Rose offered snacks and cold drinks as we enjoyed the garden. We whiled away the afternoon, chatting about our youth – what we missed about it and aspects we were happy were no longer in our lives. Just shooting the breeze, until Rose asked, 'You never told me the complete story of you meeting up with your dad?'

'Wow. Where did that come from?'

Rose shrugged. 'It's been playing on my mind for a while now, that's all. You did mention you were writing about it?'

'Not much to tell. You know we don't get on. Have never seen eye to eye.'

'I realise that, but I would really like to hear it from you,' Rose persevered.

'Are you sure? I asked, trying to convince her otherwise. 'It's a long one and it's not pretty.'

'Please, Rory. I've always wondered, and I think it's important I understand.'

'Without the dramatics, Rory Wilde. Minus all the unnecessary chatter.' Rose gave a cheeky smile.

It all started when my father arrived in the country to visit my sister Cara. We hadn't spoken in years. He asked for a meeting in the East Rand Mall so we could iron out our differences.

My inner voices squabbled amongst the furore of alarm bells of self-preservation. *The family could let go of the past, just like the country. Okay, so we no longer have a Nelson Mandela, but we might try to emulate him. Are you mad? Nothing good will come from this. You're wasting your time.*

The radio mumbled in the background, and the world outside flashed past. Traffic was light because of Christmas break. I glanced into the rear-view mirror. Turning back was not an option. I had to do this. The motorway closed behind me.

We haven't spoken in over ten years. I wonder if he sees a difference in me. Will he have aged? At least my sister is coming.

A decade after my father's divorce, the wounds were still painful. 'Anger replaced sorrow as you and Chelsea popped into my head.' I looked across at Rose then continued sharing the memory.

'*Bastard hasn't acknowledged his latest granddaughter.* I wiped the sweat from my hands, not sure if it was nerves or the scorching summer sun pouring through the windscreen.

I reached the mall early, having planned to buy toys for the kids and gift for you. 'I stopped and pointed to Rose then continued.

The attendant greeted me, pointing out a parking space and holding out his hand for a tip. I filled an empty trolley with presents, hoping they would live up to everyone's expectation. With countless brands to choose from, remembering who already had what felt impossible.

The mall was bright and cheery despite tired decorations. Christmas lingered as shoppers continued their binge. I eventually decided on a voucher for my sister and a desk calendar of South African landscapes for Dad.

That ought to cheer up his office or flat in dreary old London. I found a table at a nearby coffee shop and ordered a soda. *I understood his decision to leave Zimbabwe, but why London?* He had options to go back to Ireland, where his brother and family were, or even South Africa, where his kids were.

I recalled the warmth of my Irish grandmother and the humour of my grandfather. Although we met but a few times, I missed them. The waiter served my drink, interrupting my thoughts with a grin. I took a sip and leant back, not relishing the rendezvous.

The mall visits during Easter, the last time the family was together, remained a cherished memory that brought a smile to my face. *What more could a man ask for? My love for my Rose and the children. It's hard to believe that they will soon be the age I was when I went to boarding school. What makes a father send his preteen son away?*

I'd never asked my dad about it, but for around thirty years I'd tried to fathom out why. People have given me countless excuses, but none of them satisfied me. The idea of exposing my children to constant bullying and fear is horrifying. *Should be fucking illegal. Parents go to jail for less.* Still, it could be worse, I suppose, if he and I'd been close. Though Mum reckoned we were until Cara was born.

Watching shoppers scurry back and forth, antlike, accumulating wares for consumption in the safety of their nests, I sipped my drink, grateful for the extra time before meeting my father.

We have all matured, I told myself, and a proper opportunity existed to patch up the past. *No doubt the bone of contention is the money I owed them, but we could mend all our issues.* I knew I should have repaid them by now and I shouldn't have used family shares to speculate with. I recalled when Dad lent me the cash to buy Cobblers Bar & Grill, telling me to repay him *"whenever possible",* I didn't expect it would take this long. *Must try to clear the debt. It's only fair.* I looked at my watch and headed for the rendezvous.

Five minutes later I imagined I saw them amongst the heaving crowd of shoppers but lost sight of them.

"Hi, Rory." Homing in on my sister's voice I was able to pick her out of the masses. *She is underweight,* was my first thought. Seeing her was a delight. Then I noticed a grey-haired man I didn't recognise hobbling beside her. *Shit, it's Dad.*

He and I shook hands and shared an awkward hug.

"Let's sit and have a coffee or something." Dad pointed to a quaint cafe emitting delicious aromas.

We chatted about life in London and Johannesburg, local politics, then caught up on general family issues. All the time I was studying my father's face. Sure, he had aged, and one tooth was missing, yet it was the same man. He still had a faint Irish accent fifty years after leaving the emerald isle. *This seems to be going all right. This is the first step to reconciliation and all he wants is to catch up,* I reassured myself.

I relaxed and enjoyed the company.

An hour later my cell phone vibrated, showing my next appointment. *"I've got to get going, guys. When are you flying back, Dad?"*

"Oh, about eleven pm on Sunday."

"Should I meet you lot at the airport for another coffee and chat?"

Dad looked across at Cara. *"Umm, that would be great. I'm sure we can make a plan,"* he answered.

My heart sank. *Ahh. And there is still more. How foolish of me.*

Dad glanced at me, then down at his hands, which he was now wringing with nerves. *"Well, Rory. I want to discuss the issues that divide this family before we leave."*

Okay, let's sort this nonsense out. Once and for all. I thought.

Father continued, avoiding any eye contact. *"It's unnecessary to go into details. We all know the background."*

We do...? Speak for yourself. This should be interesting. Apparently he has all the answers. I contemplated as he droned on.

"I am glad you contacted me because I felt it was your place to make the first move."

Is he serious? I can't imagine anything my kids could do for me not to stay in contact with them.

"It is time you repaid the money owing to me and Cara so we can put the issue behind us."

I nodded in disbelief; my father's voice fading into the background.

Cara brought me back again. *"Billy is very bitter about everything."*

If Billy Backwater took initiative he could make his own money instead of worrying about things that don't involve him. I swallowed the anger rising in my throat that turned to compassion when I realised my sister was distraught. *She deserves better than Billy.*

Father pushed on. *"You need to right your wrong. So what I propose is that you buy your mother a car with the money, and we will call it quits. That way everyone is happy."* He looked very pleased with himself.

Bloody hell, now he's brought Mum into it. A brief image of the three hatching the deal flashed in front of me, coupled with images of them on exotic vacations together while I remained at school. I dismissed the images, taking solace from her absence.

I got up from the desk and bid them all adieu. *"Okay, bye, Dad. See you, Cara. Catch up soon."* My sister was in tears so I put on a cheerful disposition to avoid adding further pain.

They will re-include me once I settle my debt.

My father glanced around, anxious that I might have made a fuss. His pursed lips told me he was furious. Not by the scene, but because he had no recourse. He lost that when I left home at eleven years old.

I wandered the mall in a daze, trying to make sense of it all. *Maybe I am the one at fault and it's my arrogance that prevents me from seeing what is obvious?* My head cleared. *I will pay back the money. He will not use it to hide behind for his past actions or inactions. That must prey on his conscience forever. If he has one, that is.*

I cancelled my appointment and headed home, turning up the news on the radio and catching the end of a political debate.

One politician was arguing for compensation and land restitution. Another interrupted, questioning the extent of historical reparations. The first replied with smug disdain, *"We go back as far as it suits us."*

I smiled at the irony, my thoughts returning to my father. He never called his parents in Ireland, never protected us, his immediate family, and he sent his only son away so he could pursue his career. His solution today, based on a monetary issue, says it all. Sad.

I felt pity for my sister too.

Forever making sacrifices, looking after Billy Backwater, and spoiling her family. There would be no thanks for it. Children begrudge excessive sacrifice because of the burden of watching their parents suffer because of it.

I had attempted to extract them from the towns Billy liked to hide in. I'd thought they were on the right track when they joined me in England and listened to my advice to buy a house across the street from us. But I suppose the lure of the brackish backwoods villages of Africa was too great.

Funny thing is, I don't remember any thanks when they sold up and pocketed the profit.

Just shows how long some hold a grudge compared to a good deed, and how no number of honourable actions ever seem to outweigh the grievance. Like politicians, people choose their restitution date to suit their own agenda.

Eighteen months later I got a text message from my father, which read:

> **Hope we can all meet mid 2007 in RSA b4 your sister moves 2 Aus and u make right yr wrong 2 them.** *So, they are emigrating to Australia. Good for them. Happy New Year to you too and trust you had a Merry Christmas, and yes, I had a great birthday. Thanks for not asking.'*

Rose leant over and held my forearm. 'I am so sorry. I know how hard this is for you.'

'Actually, it isn't.' I put my hand over hers. 'I've accepted being apart from family for my entire life. It just pisses me off sometimes,'

'You should write a book about it.' Then Rose shook her head. 'Never mind, it is all in the past now.'

'Damn right, and I am so happy, Rose. So lucky I found you. Perhaps I will write that book after all.'

Chapter Twenty-five

Twenty years on, it was time for me to reveal how that terse message and earlier mall meeting had a positive impact on me. I appreciate that wasn't my father's goal, but fate had an alternate plan.

His intent was for me to "right my wrong" to heal the family rift. After which he would re-include me in the inner sanctum. Instead, I realised I had left that circle too long ago ever to want to return – and instead I'd built a new, much more loving, sanctuary of my own.

I took Rose's advice, sat under my favourite tree at the bottom of our garden and started typing.

Let us reminisce, in each other's absence, of poignant times and ponder upon the question of forgiveness you spoke of, albeit one sided. Through your actions and, more to the point, your inactions, you have said your piece. Now it is my turn to share what I felt and why there was no love lost in your departing.

I forgave you at the age of four when you cut me off after Cara was born. I appreciated her importance and was aware of her frailty, but never quite understood why it was at my expense. Seldom did we interact again as we did before her appearance. Until then you were my everything, my hero.

I forgave your vicious demeanour whenever Cara screamed or threw a temper, because you assumed my teasing was the cause. Perhaps it was, but I was a child too. I still see glimpses of that same hate in your eyes hiding behind a thin smile and a stoic look, both in old photographs and new. How did no one else see that?

I forgave you for beating me when I found money in your bedside drawer and used it to treat my friends at the local corner shop. I was seven years old and bought nothing more than chocolate and mousetraps. I'm not sure why the mousetraps, but I suspect the contraptions intrigued us and I sought attention. There has been nothing more terrifying for me to this day than you wielding a weapon to inflict pain on me. Holding me face down on your double bed and beating me.

I forgave you when at eight years old you sent me sprawling across the bedroom with a slap to the back of my head, splitting my eye open on the corner of a table because Cara was throwing a tantrum to get into my room. Sometimes I needed quiet time on my own. The pain of the stitches was inconsequential to the assault, as was your façade of guilt at the hospital. I still bear the scar, and the sight of bloodstains on my pyjamas is ingrained in my memory.

I forgave you when the police force transferred you to another town every two years. The upheaval and anguish of leaving behind friends, schools and home and starting all over again was heartbreaking. It taught me how not to get involved, to remain aloof. I never put down roots anywhere, apart from during those seven years at a boys' boarding school, until I started a life on my own.

I forgave you for sending me to boarding school at the tender age of eleven where I endured bullying, beating, and long sleepless nights of homesickness that often resulted in me throwing up in the early hours of the morning. Though instead of wishing I was home with you, I missed Themba's reassurance. What drives a father to send a child away to boarding school? What makes a mother accept the notion, let alone embrace it?

I forgave you for selling my pony at thirteen without asking me whilst I was away at school. He was one of the rare highlights of the school holidays on my return. Him and Themba. On top of which, you kept the proceeds. No apology, and whenever I raised the subject you either ignored me or gave your usual glare of anger.

I forgave you for not wanting to kiss and hug me once I turned fourteen, despite my coming and going to school. A simple peck on the cheek or head rub of affection would have sufficed. Another of your lessons in how to shun emotion.

I forgave you for the days I waited in vain for a phone call or a letter from you while I was away at boarding school. Watching the other boys open their letters and tuckboxes. Three letters from you in seven years, none more than a page long and never a word of affection, let alone a dollar bill slipped inside. For some, it was a weekly occurrence.

I forgave you for arriving late on sports weekends. Sitting in the baking sun, hoping that each cloud of dust in the distance would be you. On one occasion I waited twelve hours without relief for fear of missing your arrival. Again, never an apology or explanation.

I forgave you for taking Mum and Cara on international holidays while I remained at school. Malawi, South Africa and who knows where else. Not a postcard, gift or explanation.

I forgave you for never bothering to watch me play sport or guiding me towards a career. I excelled in competitive games and found my way in life despite your lack of interest.

I forgave you for being at work every waking hour during the short-term breaks. A small welcome-home treat with the family or half an hour of your undivided attention would have meant so much.

I forgave you for causing me to miss my plane back to school when I was fifteen because you were too busy. I had to find my own way to the airport and spend a night alone in a motel. Not so much as a call to see how I was doing.

I forgave you for expecting me to lay down my life at sixteen for a cause that you believed in and for allowing me to sign up for the armed forces. There was never a discussion or justification from you. I recall cringing when waiting for you in the car at the police station where you were in charge. I'll never forget the derogatory words and racial slurs you used at the top of your voice or the tantrum you threw in front of your junior officers.

I forgave you when you wrestled a skinny seventeen-year-old boy to the floor because he dared challenge you. Outwitted, you turned to physical violence. It never happened again since you realised it had been a close battle. Another six months and the outcome would have been different.

I forgave you for the war memorabilia, dynamite, live rounds, shrapnel etc. you gave me to display on my headboard in my room. For teaching me to fire automatic weapons and arming me to the teeth when we visited the tribal lands together. I was frightened to death but it was worth it, just to be near to you.

I forgave you for flirting with women in front of my family and friends at social events when I was in my late teens. Your ego filled the room, your disrespect our hearts.

I forgave you for showing little concern for my mother's health and her wellbeing before and after the divorce. She never recovered. She spent the rest of her life alone in the hope you might change your mind.

I forgave you for leaving Mum and breaking up the family a few months after my return home from seven years at boarding school. Your excuse was that you had remained together for our sake, and now it was your turn.

I forgave you when Mum, Cara and I lived in rented dives to make ends meet once you left us. My relief. Mum's agony. Meanwhile you enjoyed a lavish lifestyle.

I forgave you for the time I spent in a prison cell at your station for being nothing other than your son. Apart from a brief appearance, your absence was significant. The officers who served under you showed more compassion.

I forgave you when I listened to your younger brother confiding in me as he wasted away. His concerns and worries of which none were about himself.

I forgave you for the pain in Gran's eyes when she asked how Mum and the family were coping after you had gone.

I forgave you for flaunting your new flame at my sister's wedding. Your arrogance was staggering. I do not have the words to express the grief you caused.

I forgave you for your self-indulgent speech at her reception that left her and Mum in tears. Neither forgave you but they found excuses instead.

I forgave you for your lack of contribution to our wedding. A tardy, silver-plated copper drinks tray summed up your disinterest. Cara, once again, was your focus.

I forgave you for not wishing me happy birthday on any of my birthdays over the last forty years. I cannot even guess at the last gift you gave me.

What I could never forgive you for was ignoring the existence of your grandchild, Chelsea. My blood boiled with a contempt I could taste - just as it does when I write these words.

Like you, I considered putting a value to these inequities, or at least to one of them. A pointless exercise, whether I assigned a single dollar or a million.

Recompense would be a scant reward for the hurt inflicted by one's own flesh and blood. I shudder just writing the words.

My thoughts turned to my own children as I wracked my brain for what it would take for me to ostracise them. At the risk of sounding melodramatic, I came to the conclusion that any of them could stab me in the back for my life insurance, and even though I'd feel fleeting internal disappointment I would kiss them with my last breath.

Cara lives in Australia. You and Mother followed her. I have accepted the reality that I will see none of you again. The fact that this doesn't concern me is a pitiful reflection of our non-existent family.

Two decades ago, I made a vow to not reimburse the money, since it held a significance beyond mere finances. I am more determined that I never shall, because it is not what destroyed the family.

Our last conversation occurred when you contacted me as a reference for your acceptance of Australian immigration. The phone rang, and you were the person I least expected. We had not spoken in years. You said hello and gave the reason for the call, and would I mind? A sugary sweet conversation that lasted five minutes so that you could change your life and live in a safe country near your daughter. Not once did you ask about my family or your granddaughter, whom you have never seen or spoken to. I did as you asked. That balanced the books. Neither of us owes the other anything.

Your grandson haunted you, for he is the very essence of me.

Your granddaughter disturbed you, for she reflects what I hide. She scared you, for she is everything you never knew about your only son.

I do, however, have one gratitude and perhaps it outweighs all the negatives. Thank you for not including me in the family from a young age. This has given me the freedom to be with the person I love and be where I am wanted. I am free from all that you were because I have the same failings.

I cannot forgive you for what you stand for.

I cannot forgive who you represent.

I cannot forgive the legacy you left.

I am not angry.

I am ashamed of failing to be better.

I see you within myself which haunts my very essence. That is my cross to bear in my wrongdoings and shortfalls. I have had my fair share and would make amends if at all possible.

I am not your son, just your offspring. The two could not be further apart.

Despite the years since boarding school, I have kept the ability to disconnect from emotions and conflicts. A capability that has remained with me, such was the impact upon a young boy. The effects of a flawed family have played their part, as did my own issues in my role as the odd one out.

Now that you have gone, it is your turn to ask for the ultimate forgiveness and stand accountable for your inaction. Your final act of exclusion was your estate that reflected the man you weren't.

I am confused by my sister and mother wanting to include you later in life. They either have a bigger heart than I or they approved of your behaviours. For that, I cannot condone the blinkers they wore and still wear. Cara chose to conform rather than face father's weaknesses and mother's subservience. She played the perfect sibling by enhancing the premise that I was the black sheep, the rebel, the tormentor. Her failure to become her true self prevented her from reaching her full potential.

Good riddance to you and your enablers.

My vulnerability was not in sharing my feelings but in holding onto them as I have done over the decades. My strength came not from myself, but from my loved ones. There was no shame but a sense of accomplishment in not just surviving but in flourishing, like my African Rose.

I closed my laptop and stared down at the brand emblem embossed on the lid. The whir of the machine matched my irregular breathing and the palpitations of my heart. A soft evening breeze from the open doors where Rose sat reading her novel cooled the sweat on my forehead.

'You want to share?' Rose asked without looking up.

'Not just yet. Maybe tomorrow.' I joined her on the patio, inhaling the smell of the African night. A sense of serenity ebbed through my veins. I drew on my Rose's strength of silence and unconditional love. *How lucky am I?*

'So peaceful.' Rose closed her book. 'Wonder what that is?' She pointed to a fluctuating orange glow on the horizon.

'Not sure. A bushfire or something,' I answered with a yawn.

'Bedtime?' Rose stood, taking me inside by the arm.

I followed her, as I have always done and will always continue to do.

Chapter Twenty-six

The sound of my mobile phone buzzing roused me from my sleep the following day. 'Who the…?' I stretched out my arm to see who was calling before it woke Rose. 'Fucking hell,' I whispered to myself. 'Philemon, it's six o'clock in the bloody morning.' The cell went dead, followed by the buzz of an incoming message.

Have you seen the news? Country has gone crazy. On TV. Regards Phil.

I sighed, got out of bed, closed the door, and went to the kitchen. I turned on the kettle for coffee and texted Philemon back while waiting for it to boil.

Having a look. Now that I'm awake. Cheers Rory.

His response was almost immediate. **Not a morning person then Mr Grumpy lol.**

I settled down in front of the television and flicked the remote. The newsreader's high-pitched voice and the savagery of the footage caught my attention.

People were being bludgeoned and stoned, homes were being ransacked, and villages were being razed to the ground. The coverage ended with promises to return with more news as the situation unfolded. Then the scheduled children's viewing returned, the screen erupting with colour and the chaos of cartoon characters chasing each other. I closed my mouth with my heart thumping in my ears as I drank the cold mug of coffee I'd brewed earlier.

What The F? I punched into my phone and sent to Philemon.

With no response, I carried on with my tasks, pondering the TV footage and the situation in South Africa. My emotions swelled with gratitude as I witnessed Chelsea and her mother sleeping. Rose would do her nut when she heard the news.

     We must talk, my brother. This is serious. Today.

I answered, **Agreed. 10 am. Usual place?**

His thumbs up concluded our chat.

Sirens wailed in the distance and sporadic gunshots punched the air as I paced on the patio outside, scrolling on my phone for more information.
    'What is it?' Rose asked from the doorway. The sight of her unkept hair and drowsy eyes in her pink dressing gown brought a tear to mine. So beautiful, no matter what.
    'Rory, what's going on?' Her eyes turned to the sound of ambulances and fire engines.
    'People are rioting. Attacking immigrants in the squatter camps and burning down businesses. Full-scale xenophobia like we've never seen before.'
    Rose turned in silence and made a cup of coffee in the kitchen, mumbling to herself, then gazed at our garden from the patio. 'How bad is it?' she asked, tears streaming down her cheeks.
    'Not sure yet but it doesn't look good,' I said in a low tone. 'That orange glow we saw last night was people burning down homes and businesses in Alexandra.'
    The township, situated close to the centre of Johannesburg city, was the country's most impoverished urban area, housing half a million people and containing over twenty thousand shanties. Wealthy suburbs surrounded the makeshift dwellings. The government declared it

an indigenous settlement in 1916, and later during apartheid the Department of Native Affairs took control of it.

'I'm meeting Philemon in a couple of hours to find out more.' I consoled Rose as best I could by rubbing her shoulder.

She nodded. 'What about Joseph? Is he okay?'

'I'll drive past the house on my way to catch up with Philemon.'

'Good call.' Rose said. 'He might have more detail.'

Sirens came and went, along with marked and unmarked cavalcades racing to the spreading riots.

'Right, I'm off, Rose. Keep Chelsea indoors until we know what is going on.' I called through the security gate on the front door, 'I'll lock the garden fence too.'

'Be careful, Rory.' Rose answered, watching a rerun of the news.

Eerie periods of silence between the wailing of emergency services lifted the hairs on the back of my neck. I hooted outside the gate of our second home, where Joseph was staying. The faded curtains Rose had put up for him twitched before he opened the door of his rooms and waved.

'You okay, Joseph?'

'*Yebo*,' he said with a thumbs up, distracted by the unusual mayhem of high-speed vehicles passing in a quiet suburb. 'This is not good, Rory.'

'No, it is not. The country has lost its collective mind.'

He gave me a quizzical look, not fully understanding what I had said. 'Sometimes I wonder if I am doing the right thing,' he said, looking at the sun rising over the horizon. 'Do I want to bring my family to South Africa?'

'I hear you, Joseph.'

'The choice is between starving, sickness and no education, or hatred and death.' He rubbed his eyes with the palms of his hands.

'It will pass.' I tried to comfort him and myself, neither of us believing a word I'd said.

'Are we working? I would like to. Even for free, so I do not have to think about all this.'

'Of course we are. If we don't, they win – and no need to worry, you'll be paid.' I answered.

'Get yourself ready and I'll drop you off. You don't want to be out and about today,' I said, and let him know I had an appointment with Philemon.

The streets were quiet on my way to Cobblers. A few cars but no one walking or biking. The hairs on my body continued to stand with the dread of the unexpected and dangerous. Cobblers too was empty except for Philemon in his corner.

'Morning.'

'Ah, hello, Rory.' Philemon's face was ashen, his tired eyes completing the haggard look of a person without sleep. 'Hope you don't mind. I ordered us both a coffee. Your shout.' He smiled in an attempt to lighten the moment.

'No problem.' I tapped his shoulder in solidarity and took a seat.

'A sad day, my friend. A sad, sad day,' he repeated himself.

'Indeed.'

Philemon wiped his face with his hand. 'This was always on the cards, but would they listen? No.' Anger replaced tears. 'Too busy filling their fucking pockets.' He apologised for his language after seeing me flinch.

'No need to apologise. I just haven't heard you use it before,' I answered him.

'I don't have the words to express myself. Not something I'm familiar with.' He smiled back.

'That's understandable,' I told him, then said, 'I'm not getting much from the news apart from their breaking story. How about you?'

Philemon lifted his phone. 'As you can hear, it hasn't stopped. The drums are beating, and it's not pleasant.'

'So, what are you hearing?' I asked.

Philemon gave a slight shrug. 'The riots started in Alex, as we know. Locals attacked migrants from Mozambique, Malawi and Zimbabwe, resulting in two deaths and many injuries. There are rumours some attackers have been singing Jacob Zuma's campaign song "Umshini Wami". 'Bring Me My Machine Gun'.

'Bloody hell, Philemon,' I whispered.

'That's not all. The hatred is spreading to other townships in the country.'

'But why?' I asked.

'So many reasons.' My friend sipped his coffee. 'There is fierce competition for jobs, commodities and housing. Dominance by authorities is taking precedence over psychological disorders.'

'Huh?' I gave him a blank look.

Philemon grinned. 'Not dealing with issues past and present for all.'

'Right.'

'There's also a sense of superiority towards other Africans. Exclusive citizenship – a type of nationalism that excludes others if you like.'

'Poor service delivery along with an influx of illegal immigrants from neighbouring states?'

'Unlawful or not has no impact on these attackers who perceive both to be unwelcome, Rory. But there is more to it.' Philemon paused for effect. 'Township politics. For the corrupt, community leadership leads to financial gain. To stay credible in a tough political environment, they encourage negative attitudes towards foreigners.'

'I've heard that before. All about deflection?'

'That same old chestnut Rory,' he agreed.

'So, what is there for us to do?' I asked.

Philemon heaved a sigh so deep that it seemed to come from his soul. 'All we can do as writers is share our experiences. Tell our stories as well as is possible.' He wrung his hands together, avoiding eye contact. 'If we cannot change today, we must document events for a history without prejudice.'

We chatted for another hour, digging deep into our consciousness. Despite our diverse backgrounds, we could connect through compassion and open-mindedness. Unlike the country.

'You know what, Philemon?' I said in a low tone. 'Today I once again experienced fear and isolation in person. Not the highfaluting theories that we debate in, but with the salt-of-the-earth people who live it every day.'

Philemon shut his eyes slowly, then reopened for me to continue.

'What's scary is I saw and lived it in Zimbabwe two decades ago, and nothing has changed. Maybe it's even worse now.'

'You are talking about your Themba?'

'Not just Themba, but everyone who got dragged into the civil war, especially the poor who had no say in it. Do you know what I'm saying, Philemon?'

'Believe me, I do, young man. I surely do.' Philemon placed his hands on the table and pushed himself backward. Don't forget, fighting at every level is necessary for change to occur.

'You're right, Philemon. I'm sorry. I didn't mean to disrespect the work you do.'

He laughed out aloud and tapped his mug, ordering us each another coffee. 'I took no offence, Rorke Wilde. It's an honour to see you questioning the status quo.'

The unrest extended to settlements in Gauteng Province and later reached Durban and Cape Town. The news also reported attacks in other parts of the country.

Sixty-two people lost their lives by the end of the riots. Police arrested fourteen hundred suspects in connection with the violence.

Authorities moved the victims to provisional camps after three weeks of staying in law enforcement offices and community halls. The opposition criticised the location and infrastructure of some of the new facilities, highlighting their temporary nature.

At first the government wanted to reintegrate the refugees into their communities, but later gave in to pressure and changed its policy to protect all asylum seekers, regardless of their immigration status. Instead, they were given a deadline of just a few months, after which they would have to return home.

After hearing of the refugee's plight on the news, Rose turned to me. 'We need to help, Rory.'

'We do,' I agreed.

'I don't mean money through a donation,' Rose added.

'I know. We have the time to get involved. Agreed?'

'Definitely. I'll text Philemon now.'

'Maybe also talk to Joseph. He knows what's needed as much as anyone.'

'Good call. I'll chat to him later,' I said, picking up my phone.

Their advice about what Rose and I could do to help was quite different, yet the goals were identical, as was their passion.

According to the latest radio report, the town hall was now a safe place for immigrants escaping danger. I passed by the building on my way home from a meeting in Johannesburg, concerned that the violence might spread to the suburbs and hence the family. The sight of the impoverished individuals pouring onto the streets erased any notion of self-protection. In the gutters, mothers nourished their children as toddlers in ragged clothes sat on the pavements. The pictures on television had not prepared me for what I saw.

A brief excerpt from my first memoir, *The Chameleon*:

I pulled over in my luxury car and headed towards the dishevelled congregation, who paid me little attention. A sense of walking among ghosts turned me cold. The large wooden doors of the old colonial hall in the high-street grated open. I took my chance and ducked inside, without hindrance, past the doorkeeper into the empty main entrance but for a small gang of conscripts cleaning. I approached a group who appeared in charge of proceedings; they greeted me with an unexpected exuberance. A young, fresh-faced man from the Salvation Army with a pleasant demeanour shook my hand. Two ladies from the Red Cross, one from the church and another in a private capacity, completed the band. A slim, well-dressed man, nicknamed Comrade, joined us along with our local council member, trailed by a brusque police officer.

Instead of focusing on the discussion, I studied the faces in our small circle. The holy lady talked ten to the dozen, touching each person's arm, and spoke to the anxious citizen who scribbled lengthy lists, insisting upon structure. The Red Cross team moved on, more concerned with sleeping arrangements and medication. The Salvation Army leader did his best to listen to everyone. A police officer laid down the law in a manner that made us cringe. His only concern was the safety of the terrified hordes. The councillor objected to the police officer's

*lack of political correctness and threatened to report him.
He pulled at the breast pocket of his immaculate suit,
searching for what resembled Mao's Little Red Book. I
scanned the officer's pockets, half expecting to find a copy
of Hitler's* Mein Kampf.

*Their passion re-ignited the embers of my burnt
African pride. Our modest group of diverse Africans was
here for a common cause, to aid those afflicted. Instead
of a halo forming above my head, I became depressed
and exhausted. No warm fuzzy feelings washed over me
at my perceived goodwill. A thankless vocation that only
the dedicated endured.*

I expressed my gratitude to Philemon through a message, as he had
recommended that I come here and help where needed. Little did I
realise that day I would reunite with my mentor, Themba Dube, after
twenty years apart.

I wondered how Rose was getting on doing the same, except she
and Sheila had gone to assist at a local woman's refuge. I looked
forward to catching up with her to hear how her day went.

Philemon's usual thumbs up emoji flashed up on my screen, and
a minute later Rose's text reassured me they were on their way and
would be home before dark.

'Hi, guys.' I opened the door to Rose and Sheila.

'Hi, my sweetie.' Rose flung her arms around me and sobbed, the
pain and anguish of her day escaping at last.

Ouma put the kettle on, consoling us after all we had been through.
'We are fortunate that we are all okay,' she said, buttering toast. 'We
must remain strong for those who cannot.' The bags under her eyes
revealed a sorrow. 'Come now, let's talk about what makes us happy
so we can rejuvenate ourselves for what tomorrow brings.'

We all wiped our tears just as Philemon turned up to collect Sheila.
He waved from the vehicle with no intent to stay - suiting all parties.

'Thanks, Sheila, see you soon.' Rose gestured with one arm, the
other around my waist.

We spent that evening in the family's company. There was a need for closeness and for a falsehood that everything was okay. After dinner, James and Chelsea went about their business in the privacy of their bedrooms. Ouma retired to her room, disgusted by the state of the world. Her anger and pain were profound at seeing her beloved country and its people in disarray.

'Fancy a hot toddy?' I asked Rose, slumped in her chair.

'You know what, Rory, that would be nice, thank you.' She sat upright. 'What a week. I hope it gets easier, but I doubt it. So much suffering.'

'I know. Tell me about your day,' I said, pouring a shot of whiskey into a tumbler followed by a teaspoon of honey and boiling water.

'Lemon?'

'Just as you like it.' I sat alongside her. Rose encouraged me to open up about my day first, which I did as best as my emotions allowed me. I also didn't want to upset her further.

When I finally stopped, I opened a large box of Smarties. The smell of the milk chocolate inside the rainbow of buttons made my mouth water. 'Your turn,' I said, smiling at my best friend.

Rose sighed and put her head on my chest. 'It was horrible, Rory. We went to a women's refuge centre in Soweto. I've never seen anything so terrible.'

Women endured most of the xenophobia attacks. In a patriarchal society like South Africa, the attackers targeted females because they represented the immigrants settling in the country. Rape was a common occurrence that often went unreported because the victims deemed the police were not impartial.

'You, okay?' I handed Rose a tissue.

She shook her head in denial. 'No, I'm not, and may never be again.'

We consoled ourselves in the silence and safety of our home, the sound of the TV separating us from the death and mayhem outside - if just for a while.

After the weekend, Joseph took us along another path that led to the same place. We drove into the squatter camps of makeshift buildings built from used tyres, wooden pallets and just about any kind of metal they could get their hands on. It reminded me of the stories Themba and his nephew Lucky shared around the campfire. *It was so good to catch up with him after such a long time.* I smiled recalling our reuniting at the town hall. Joseph looked at me aghast. 'It's a long story.' I dismissed his expression and continued on our way.

Running water was a luxury and a single outside tap servicing the camp for the squatters to get water for drinking and washing. It was a dour landscape of abject poverty. The stench of smoke in the air, fetid body odour, and disease at every turn. Malnourished children with bulbous eyes, looks of intrigue and, dare I surmise, a glimpse of hope? When charities ask for donations, they show the impoverishment on the television and billboards. If that makes you sad, imagine experiencing it with all your senses. It becomes embedded forever in your soul.

Joseph showed us the angels living in these shantytowns who devoted their lives to helping others that were suffering the same destitution as them.

'Hi, Joseph, we've got the supplies you asked for,' Rose said, climbing out of the truck. Donations we'd collected through our endeavours and contacts.

'Ah, Mrs Rose.' He clapped his hands in glee. 'You have brought much more than that. I see love and kindness, and above all hope is everywhere. Thank you.'

We hid our tears, but they did not go away. Instead, our hearts and souls wept. Once more, the question resurfaced, the one I'd pondered years ago while collecting Lucky from the AIDS hospital. *How is this possible? How is this allowed to happen?*

Silence was the only answer.

Chapter Twenty-seven

The xenophobia died down. Well, that's not true. The news coverage did, which is quite a different perspective. People also adapted to it, so it became part of the norm. The world was heading into a recession with oil prices climbing, a global drought, and the start of the world food price crisis that peaked later in 2007.

'Things are getting tough,' I said to Rose after a long day seeking new outlets to do business with.

'You can say that again. I just got off the phone to our supplier and they're putting their prices up.' Rose showed her palms in surrender. 'I told them the rand was weakening against the pound. They said they knew but they were facing the same against the US dollar.'

'Oh, shit. I was hoping they would help a bit.' I put the kettle on.

Rose shook her head. 'Do you remember when we started the business we paid six rand to the dollar? At this rate it might reach ten rand by the end of the year.'

'Crazy times.' I poured us each a coffee. 'The downturn is biting. This one will be tough.'

'Buying our products will cost more, even before they raise prices. Shipping container costs are through the roof, and consumers aren't buying as much.' Rose looked at me from over her mug.

'That's not all. The retailers are having the same problems, so they're searching for margin from their suppliers - us.' I shrugged. 'What do we do?' I wasn't really looking for an answer.

Rose remained silent for a while. 'Perhaps it's time to call it a day, Rory. I mean, it's just not worth all the hassle or the risk.'

'Could be.' I pondered the idea, a sense of relief enveloping me.

'The way the country is going as well…?' Rose did not finish her sentence.

'Are you saying what I think you are?'

'What do you think I'm saying?' Rose countered with a cheeky grin.

'Maybe you're right.' I paused, choosing my words. I could search for a new job while we explored opportunities abroad and got ready for the relocation.

'It will take a while to happen, but at least it's another option for us,' Rose said.

'Sounds like a plan.' I took her hands, pulled her to her feet and hugged her.

'There's not much else to do, Rory, especially now with Chelsea. In fact, the whole family.'

'Agreed. Let's do it.'

We closed our import business to a substantial loss, and began the slow struggle to pay back our debtors. Meanwhile I went back to job-hunting.

Finding a job with corporates wasn't any easier now than it had been back when we sold Cobblers. However, the same could not be said in private enterprise. The bureaucratic red tape of Black empowerment drove skills to the entrepreneurs, who took full advantage of the situation – employing the best person, irrespective of past injustices.

'Can't wait for the weekend.' Rose put down her phone after negotiating more time with an overdue payment. 'It's the only time they stop hounding us.' Her face showed the strain.

'I know.' I placed my arm around her. 'I wish I could make it all go away. Hate seeing you worry so much.'

'You're up most nights searching and applying for jobs.' She patted my chest. 'This isn't your fault. It's our problem and one day it will disappear.'

In the evenings we sought solace cooking in the kitchen or at the barbecue, escaping our situation and relishing phone-free silence.

Fortunately, within a few months I landed a job that offered a competitive salary and commission structure. It was at a growing franchise that dealt with solar power and diesel generators – both in high demand because of the ever-deepening energy crisis in the country. Insufficient electricity infrastructure had led to widespread power cuts, a classic repercussion of poor maintenance, lack of skilled labour and not investing in the future. A positive aspect was the use of enviro-friendly alternatives instead of burning fossil fuels to make up for the outages.

My job was to sell franchises. This meant setting up a stand at trade shows and selling a concept. The product, however, was in demand, which made it easier. Then came following up on leads, which involved visiting people in their homes. Part of the contract of becoming a franchisee was that they bought and installed a solar unit. They then purchased a trailer for the equipment, had a utility vehicle branded, and spent two weeks training.

These home visits gave me an insight into everyday people's lives. Most of my potential clients were aging couples investing their limited funds to support a meagre state pension, which was the equivalent of one hundred and twenty US dollars a month. The alternative, embraced by many, involved moving in with children or close family. Their homes were run down, lacking maintenance, and a heartbreaking sadness filled their eyes.

Youngsters who had left school and without any qualifications were also targeted. Excluded from jobs because they didn't fit under the previously disadvantaged labels in existence before they were even born, they could either start their own venture or join a small, existing business. Franchising covered both. Helping these young adults to finance the set-up costs proved stressful.

Each day after work I returned home exhausted from the ordeal of seeing people's struggles. Though they weren't in situations as dire as those in poverty or earning a few dollars a day, their fight was just as real. It further confirmed to me and Rose that Africa was not for us, nor our children.

Our focus, instead, was looking abroad for a country and a home we could immigrate to. We'd had the experience of living in England in the eighties, but now, twenty years later, with a family life, things were different. The United Kingdom was an option but one we decided we would not prioritise, since it didn't offer the lifestyle we sought.

Many South Africans were moving to America, Canada, nearby African countries, and Australia.

The people those countries needed more of were doctors, nurses, teachers and high-tech industry workers. Few were interested in what Rose and I could offer, despite us sending out numerous applications.

One Sunday evening while I was scrolling through Facebook, a message popped up on Messenger from an old acquaintance.

I see you guys are thinking of leaving SA.

He was referring to my posts on social media, put up in the hope of some help from friends, many of whom were spread all over the world.

'Hey, Rose, remember Paul from the baby stores? He's in Australia. Just messaged me.'

'Oh, wow. That's a while back. Say hello for me.'

Good to hear from you. Rose says hi. How's Oz? I typed a reply.

Same to her. I hear the Trade Barn is looking for management in New Zealand. Thought you might be interested. I read it out to Rose, who gestured I end the chat as soon as I could.

Appreciate the heads-up, Paul. Will take a look. I put my phone down and peaked up at Rose. 'New Zealand?'

'I know, right? I've heard a lot about the country. Quite a few South Africans are going there,' Rose said, appearing interested.

'Isn't it cold?' I scrunched my face in disapproval. 'Might as well go to England.'

'Not sure. Let's check online.'

'Good idea. We'll do it on the computer so we can both see.' I said, pulling a chair out for Rose to sit next to me. 'Every time I've watched the rugby in New Zealand on TV it's been raining, and so cold you can see their breath.' I searched the country on the internet.

'Perhaps that's because rugby is played during the winter. Summers seem all right.' Rose took over the keyboard, refining the search. 'Here it is.'

We read several blogs, ranging from Wikipedia to travel sites, becoming intrigued by the Land of The Long White Cloud, Aotearoa, New Zealand. Besides two landmasses, she had over seven hundred little islands. She had been the first country to grant women the right to vote and the first to establish a minimum wage.

Hours later, Rose leaned back in her chair and crossed her arms. 'Rory, this sounds amazing,' she said, looking at me.

'Absolutely. I never knew,' I answered, dumfounded. 'What was the name of the company again?' I searched on my phone. 'Trade Barn,' I mumbled.

With a brief investigation I found their vacancies page and the job I was searching for. I filled in the online form as well as I was able with help from Rose and uploaded my curriculum vitae.

'Your application looks professional.' Rose completed the last check. 'You have experience abroad which will stand you in good stead.'

'I hope so. What worries me is the piece that says applicants must be prepared to fly to New Zealand for a final interview.' I pulled a face. 'Expensive, especially if I don't get offered the position.'

'They wouldn't invite you over unless they were keen. Might be to make sure the person coming is the same one they are interviewing,' Rose surmised.

'Maybe you're right.'

'This bit's important.' Rose pointed to the screen. 'The job is on the New Zealand Skills Shortage List and the Trade Barn has preapproval from the immigration department.'

'I know, right? They offer a job, and the work visa is a certainty.' Nerves fluttered in my gut. *Here we go, Rory Wilde,* my inner voice announced to my brain.

Less than a week later, the Trade Barn sent me an email saying they had accepted my application, and the sender promised to be in contact to set up a Skype session. We had no clue what that meant, so Rose and I googled it and got the app.

Amid a busy week dealing with debts and collectors, the HR person emailed potential dates and times for the Skype interview.

'So exciting Rory. Which day are you thinking?'

'The sooner the better,' I answered. 'Look keen, make a lasting impression and the rest won't stand a chance.'

'Be serious, dumbass.' She laughed and gave me a playful push. 'Hang on.' She took over the keyboard. 'These times are GMT (Greenwich Mean Time).' She read each of the hours again. 'The earliest one is at midnight here.'

'Oh, crap. I don't want to wake the whole house,' I said. 'Maybe I should drive across to the office and do it there?'

'Not a bad idea. This is such great news. It's about time we had some luck.'

'Don't count your chickens. It's just another stage to get through.'

Rose shook her head. 'No, I have a good feeling about this. It came out of the blue. These things have a way of working out.'

I didn't have the heart to disagree, savouring the rare-of-late sense of hope.

We continued to duck and dive as we paid our outstanding debts. Some debtors were understanding, others not so much, demanding and hounding, and that we understood. We were at fault, but our intention was to pay back every cent plus interest.

On one occasion, the bottle store from where we'd purchased our spirits organised a meeting to sort out the owed amount. Not wanting to do it at any of our properties, I agreed to meet them in the carpark at Cobblers.

There I met up with a burly, bearded man wearing a voluminous sports jacket and with a cap pulled over his eyes. He lifted his chin in greeting, the corner of his mouth chewing on a stick.

Not wanting to escalate the situation, I apologised and bought an extra couple of weeks for a small interest charge. Business concluded, I bid him farewell, at which he suggested I was a nice person, but best I pay up before the agreed time. There was no doubting the look on his face. I knew only too well the owner's intention from my many visits to his bottle store over the years. The debt was old and patience was running out.

A week later and on the same day I was booked for my midnight New Zealand interview, we met again at the same place. I handed him a wad of cash that Rose had managed to raise. He took the money and stuffed it inside his jacket without even counting it, smiled, and climbed into his truck. Winding down the window, he thanked me for doing business, inviting us to buy from them again should the need arise.

Relief was an understatement and to this day, three decades later, I can still see, hear and smell that encounter. I chastise myself for going through with it. With more life experience, I would approach the situation in a different manner today.

After dinner that night, I researched the Trade Barn and watched online videos to improve my presentation. Since leaving Cobblers I didn't stay up much after nine-thirty and hadn't seen a midnight in some time. Showered and dressed smart from the waist upwards, I left for the other house where Joseph was still up and opened the gate. He offered to sit with me, but I sent him back to bed with thanks.

Sitting in the unoccupied house in front of the stock and business computer, I waited for the Trade Barn to connect. The screen flickered, revealing the human resources person busy at her desk.

'Hello. Can you hear me, Mister Wilde?' Her voice reverberated through the empty home. Upon seeing me, her frown became a broad smile.

Our accents hinted at the vast distance between us, and slight connection delays and freeze frames didn't help the flow of communication, but we both persevered.

'Well, thank you for taking the time to chat, Rorke. I appreciate the difference in hours made it even more difficult for you,' she said, concluding the interview. 'There will be a link for a psychometric test coming. If you could complete that as quickly as you can that would be great.' She smiled. 'Anything else you would like to ask or say?'

'No. I think we covered everything. Thank you,' I answered.

'You are welcome. The Trade Barn will be in touch soon. I look forward to meeting you in person one day.' We both said our goodbyes looking at each other with awkward glances. The screen went blank as I digested her last sentence. 'I look forward to meeting you in person one day,' I repeated out loud. *Calm yourself, Rory – don't read too much into it,* my heart warned. *Don't tempt fate.*

After checking it was safe, I opened the gate and climbed into the car. Before I closed the door, I caught out the corner of my eye a movement followed by a high-pitched scream and the crunch of running over the dirt drive. I froze, then realised it was only two feral cats fighting. My heart raced from the shot of adrenaline, relieved it wasn't a hijacking, and further confirming my determination to leave the country. This was no way to live. Always fearing what lay ahead or loomed behind.

'You look flushed,' Rose said, opening the door for me on my return home. 'How was the interview?'

'Good. In fact, it went well considering.' I changed, ready for bed. 'It's just a case of wait and see.' I decided not to share the Kiwi's last sentence with me and bear false hope.

'Outstanding work, Rory. I'm proud of you, no matter how this all ends. We did our best.' She kissed and cuddled close to me.

'We always have England,' I whispered. 'And our British passports give us access to Europe. So not a bad Plan B.'

'Not at all. We're very fortunate. Sleep tight.' Rose turned off the bedside lamp. 'The main thing is that we are out of here.'

Tomorrow was another day. The night was ours to rest and recuperate. My nightmares didn't cooperate. My darkness was filled with talking faces, windows pried open by invisible intruders, Chelsea being abducted by cats. And then a mysterious Immigration Department allowed Rose and me through but refused the children.

And so our lives ricocheted between protecting our credit status, staying safe, and chasing a dream we didn't really know if we wanted. Commonsense and emotional connections tugged us every which way. It would be easier to do nothing, like others, but that was not who we were.

To help ourselves, we worked with charities dealing with the aftermath of the xenophobia riots and supporting the homeless, injured and hungry. Guilt for our privileged lives played a huge part in our drive to assist the less fortunate and the targeted. By doing so, we discovered the true essence of humanity in the people and cultures we encountered but had never interacted with. That was our wrong, I know, and one reason for me writing *The Wilde Collection* series. My sadness today stems from my complacency in living a good life and neglecting this community. Do we only identify with issues we face ourselves? Shame on me once again.

Chapter Twenty-eight

Joseph was waiting outside the gates as usual, but this time was different. We were spending the day in one of the city's largest informal settlements – or, as the locals called them, squatter camps. Both names were feeble, as they were places that even Beelzebub would find alarming. Hellholes, for want of a better word, where predators preyed upon the innocent and fugitives hid. Not a place for Rose, but one where we could bring about change, albeit small and temporary. Her orchestration and coordination with Sheila made all the difference.

'Morning,' I greeted him, opening the car door from the inside. 'At least the weather is pleasant.'

'Morning. I'm looking forward to today,' Joseph said, smiling.

'What's so funny?' I noticed his smirk.

'The big boss spending the day in Alexandra Township.' He slapped his leg with one hand and snickered into the other.

'You find that amusing, do you?' I did my best not to smile.

'Too much. *Umlungu* – white person,' he translated. 'The place doesn't see your people often. They will think you lost.'

'Okay, okay, I get it.' I started the car. 'It is a bit nerve-wracking, though.'

'Don't worry. You have me and my friends to take care of you. No problem,' he said, proud of himself.

Can I trust Joseph? What if he... Shut the fuck up, Rory! My conscience cut my inner voice mid-sentence. I hit the steering wheel in anger at my instilled prejudice. I have found over the decades it never disappears. All we can do is oppose it at every turn whenever it raises itself.

'Are you okay, sir?' Joseph winced next to me in the car, watching my torment.

'Sorry, my friend.' I said, now smiling. 'I'm battling a little with all that is happening.'

'Aren't we all?' His tone was sharp, if not terse.

Touché, Joseph. Touché. My conscience admonished me.

Joseph and I sat without saying a word, the radio playing a soundtrack to our journey.

Over the rooftops, rats scurried about, jumping over the small distance separating the temporary shacks. The nauseating stench of trash and exposed sewage made me feel sick. Other sections of the township were quite a different prospect – buoyant and alive with sellers and tourists experiencing Alex on guided tours. Amenities in place and some law and order, albeit citizen led. The good, the bad and, yes, the ugly.

Rose and Sheila from Cobblers had joined forces in finding donations of clothing, basic foods, and medicine, which now filled the back of the *bakkie (*utility vehicle) a kind-hearted person had loaned us.

'Almost there.' Joseph said, winding down his window to speak to someone on the side of the gravel road we were traveling along. With the amount of people, our speed didn't reach fifteen kilometres an hour. 'Turn this way on the next road.' He showed to his left.

'What are we looking for?' I asked. Every building looked the same, with rusty corrugated walls or chipped concrete blocks.

'There will be a car outside with a red cross on it.'

Sure enough, through the golden dust swirling around the makeshift village I could see a white Kombi with the familiar sign on it.

'Over there.' Joseph said, closing his window and preparing to get out of the vehicle once it stopped.

Supplies filled the darkened room without windows. Two volunteers helped organise the next load of essentials. Care was being taken that the donations did not fall into the wrong hands to be sold for profit. An all too familiar occurrence by people without morals, which even a hardened criminal might battle to fathom.

We unloaded our wares and packed them where we were told to. Once finished, I texted Rose that we had delivered our haul and were on our way back.

Joseph had an alternative plan. 'Can we stop for a beer?' he asked with large, pleading eyes.

'What?' I looked around for an inkling where that might be. 'Where?'

'At the shebeen – an unlicensed, informal bar – just over there,' he said, pointing to a small group of men sitting on bricks out the front of a shack.

'You've got to be kidding me, Joseph.'

'Don't worry, it is perfectly safe. They are family.'

Still feeling guilty from our earlier discussion, I stopped a short distance away, turned off the engine, and reluctantly followed him.

The men raised their arms in greeting, slapping Joseph's hand in a warm shake, caterwauling in delight and calling to the proprietor for beer. An enormous woman of both height and width brought a fistful of quart bottles filled with lager, handing one to me.

'Cheers.' they called out, laughing at their attempts at an English pronunciation.

I saluted them back and took a gulp, to further banter by the enthused group.

Half an hour later I bid them all farewell, leaving Joseph with kin and friends. He looked happy, as did they all. I exited the shantytown, forsaking the cluttered dirt roads for the open highway, feeling perplexed by what I had experienced. These were destitute people not just in money but in all necessities. Yet contrary to what I had always been taught to believe, they could laugh and welcome strangers, even former enemies.

Doubts about quitting Africa raised apprehensions in my mind. Oh, the dilemma, the angst of leaving something so dear to our hearts. A passion that ran through our veins. Our place of birth.

That same year, a couple of months after I'd started my new job with the franchise, we put our second house on the market. Whether or not we were emigrating, we needed to free up funds. Our debts had been cleared and the nightmares of our import business and Cobblers Bar and Grill were gone, but we still had a bank overdraft. The proceeds from the sale would take care of that with a bit to spare.

Joseph helped spruce up the property and the garden for the estate agents to market it.

A week later he called around to our home, saying he had some important news for me. Refusing to come inside the gate, he removed his floppy hat and wrung it in his hands.

'What's up, Joseph?' I said, trying to help him say what it was he wanted to.

He looked upwards and then down at his feet scuffing in the dirt.

'Is something wrong?' I hoped it was nothing to do with his relatives.

'I have some difficult...terrible news, Rory,' he stuttered, hastily adding when he saw the alarm on my face, 'Not in that serious way, but about us.'

'I am listening.'

'I have decided to return to my family in Mozambique,' he said in a soft voice. 'Everything is changing here, and I can see you are also preparing for that.'

How did he know? We've never spoken about emigrating in front of anybody.

'That's okay. You don't have to feel bad about it. I have seen it in your eyes for a long time now.' He gave me a coy smile. 'Without you and your family I have nothing here, and these people don't want me in this country. Please don't be cross with me.'

With a laugh half-etched in pain, I answered, 'I can never be mad at you, Joseph. I respect your decision to go back to your family and your homeland.' We shook hands. 'I feel guilty that I couldn't help you more.'

We sat under the tree just outside the garden and chatted about his plans. Our families' peace would bring contentment to our hearts, replacing broken dreams with shared hope. Themba had done the same,

Two weeks later I picked Joseph up and drove him to the train station, having paid for his trip home – not to ease his woes, but to placate our guilt. There we stood on the derelict platform until it was time for Joseph to embark. With his worldly possessions in his backpack, we shook hands for the last time. I handed him an envelope of cash to see him through. In return, he handed me a photograph he'd taken of him and me with our arms around each other's shoulders posing in front of the house we'd worked on.

Without either saying a word, he hauled himself up into the carriage and found himself a seat, not daring to look at me. His pain evident. I would never see or hear of Joseph again. I'd known him just a little longer than six months, but like Len he left an indelible mark.

'That is so sad, Rory.' Rose pulled a sorry face on my return. 'We will miss him.'

Not wanting to discuss it, I accompanied Chelsea outside on her beloved trampoline. Seeing her joy as she bounced, with the dogs chasing her from underneath, would usually lift my spirits, but not this time.

'You okay, Rory?' Rose joined us in the backyard, hugging me from behind as I sat on the garden seat.

'I'm fine.' I sighed. 'I just wish we didn't have to make this decision.'

'I know, but I think we have done so already.' She rubbed my shoulders. 'The sooner we accept that, the better, but it won't ease the hurt, sweet Rory.'

'I know. You're right, of course.'

'Tell you what. I've got to spend the morning in town tomorrow. Why don't we meet for lunch at Cobblers?' Rose said, looking me in the eye with a cheerful face. 'Maybe give Philemon a shout to join you beforehand.'

'I might just do that. For old times' sake, hey?'

'Oh, Rory, don't be so glum.'

I smiled.

Since I hadn't heard from Philemon the next morning yet but didn't want to stay home, I took a walk to Cobblers a few hours before meeting Rose for lunch.

Inside, I didn't recognise any of the staff nor the customers frequenting the place. I knew Gary had moved to Durban's coastline, hoping to start over. That or to be a surfer or beach bum, whichever was easier. Sunette had returned to college to complete her studies. I headed to the room's far corner, Philemon's preferred spot, and took a seat at the empty table.

'What can I get you?' the bartender called from behind the bar.

'A Guinness, please.'

'We haven't had that here for some time.' He gave a short laugh. 'Plenty of lager though.'

'That'll do. Thank you.' I hid my surprise, noticing most of the Irish-themed paraphernalia had disappeared and that no keg beer was available.

'Here you go.' He plonked the bottle and glass on the bar for me to get for myself.

'Wow, things have changed.'

'They certainly have.' He missed my sarcasm.

I sat and watched the toing and froing of the familiar characters. Doom was working his charm on Kugel, and at any moment, I expected Weirdo and Balsak to walk in. I felt overawed by the future and depressed by the present. The past, as always, was unchangeable.

'I thought you might be here.' I heard the familiar voice of Philemon. 'Sitting here all by yourself. Fancy some company?'

'For sure.' I stood, shaking his hand. 'Great to see you. It's been a while,' I gushed. 'How the hell are you?'

'Good, thanks – and yourself?' Philemon said, signalling to the barkeep for a drink. 'Damn service here's just got so bad.' A look of irritation crossed his face.

'Sorry for not keeping in touch around our writing.' I offered to remove the elephant in the room.

'As much my fault as yours my friend.' He smiled and collected the drinks he ordered.

We chatted about his writing and my lack of doing so, our families, and politics around the world.

'Well, I have to go.' Philemon looked at his watch.

'Rose will be here soon. Why don't you join us?'

He hesitated. 'I'd like to see Rose so I'll stay for a minute or so, but then I must go.' He sat down again.

His unease concerned me.

'I have some exciting news.' Philemon blurted after welcoming Rose to the table. His eyes were brighter than I had seen before.

'Ooh, do tell us.' Rose loved to hear the latest gossip.

'I am to be published again.'

'That is wonderful news. Tell us more.'

I let Rose do the talking for both of us, but I was now sitting upright.

Philemon said, 'It is an English publisher, and they want Sheila and me to join them there for a three-book contract.'

Time froze, with nobody reacting, much less speaking, until Rose filled the void. 'Amazing, congratulations!'

I joined in with genuine felicitations, but felt the dread turn once more in my gut.

'I don't know much else about the move at the moment, but I'll keep you posted,' Philemon said, preparing to leave.

'I'm so happy for you. Let's have a farewell party before you leave,' Rose said as we waved goodbye.

We did not discuss the news, but decided after a drink that we were not in the mood to stay at Cobblers.

We missed Philemon and Sheila's farewell, or at least the one at Cobblers, for there were quite a few farewells to accommodate all their friends, colleagues and family. They planned to leave Germiston a week before their flight to England so they could spend time with relatives, and just before that I received a text.

Can we have a quiet drink at Cobblers before I leave?

I replied. **Sounds good. When suits...**

Friday around 11am? We move out over the weekend.

I tapped into my phone. **See you then.**

The exodus of people emigrating was alarming. Not a week passed without us hearing hear of someone doing so.

'Try not to be too glum, Rory.' Rose handed me the keys to the car. 'It's a big deal for Philemon and you don't want him to feel too guilty or sad.'

'I'm going to kick his ass. That's three who have upped and left us. Themba, Joseph and now him.'

'Idiot.' She kissed me and sent me on my way. Once more, her strength and sense of humour grounded me.

Inside the pub, Philemon was sitting in his corner, this time with no scribblings or laptop. He was bolt upright and staring at nothing in particular his face showing no expression and his eyes unblinking.

'Mister Dlamini.'

'Mister Wilde.'

'How are you, Philemon?'

'I am not good, Rory. I am fine, but I should be full of joy,' Philemon said in a monotone.

'I hope not on my account?' I sat opposite him at the table.

'Indeed, you are to blame.'

'Okay, let's cut this farce,' I said, joking but meaning it.

We laughed and ordered drinks, slipping back into our usual repartee.

'Last rounds, folks. The bar is closing in half an hour,' the barkeep yelled.

'Gosh, is that the time? Where did the day go?' I said, looking at my phone. 'One more?'

'One more, my friend.' Philemon emptied the last of the beer from his glass.

'One more indeed.'

An awkward silence fell on us as we waited for our drinks. I looked at Philemon and asked, 'Where will all this end?' referring to the country and its current plight.

'Ah, Rory Wilde, an unsolvable puzzle, my friend. We writers can warn of possibilities, and those of us who prove to be right will earn a place among the classics.'

'A tad melodramatic, now where have I heard that before?' I replied.

'Perhaps, but that's our prerogative.' Philemon smiled. 'In answer to your question, only time will tell. Our lives are a mere flicker, so it will be up to history to judge that.'

'I guess,' I answered with a sigh.

'We have a role to play,' Philemon reflected. 'Our challenge as scribes is technology, particularly the internet and artificial intelligence.'

'Artificial what?' I looked at my friend, confused. 'That's an oxymoron. Intelligence cannot be artificial, for it has no boundaries and is ever changing. Surely?' I asked.

'Indeed, but often intellect is a perception of others. The world has many examples of supposed brains that do not end well.'

I nodded in agreement as another disquieting moment lingered. 'It's tough gig this leaving.' I offered.

Philemon wiped a tear. 'My only advice is talk to your family, allow them to share their concerns and above all respect their decisions and advice. It is done with love albeit not always what you want to hear.'

We finished our drinks in unison and clinked our empty glasses. 'I await your debut publication, young man,' Philemon said with a wink. 'Write what matters to you.'

'I will try.'

'No, do not try. Do it. Only then will you know,' Philemon cut in. 'Farewell, my brother.' He leant forward, gave me a hug, and disappeared.

'Goodbye Philemon Dlamini,' I said under my breath.

The stench of Cobblers Bar and Grill filled my lungs, the emptiness of a soulless shell chilling me to my core. Overwhelming sadness permeated everything and everyone in this hellish place. Every recess, room, and space stirred horrors in my mind.

I left for the last time. Never to return, or to see people in the same light again.

Less than a week afterward, I sat my psychometric test online with a company working on behalf of the Trade Barn. Twenty-Four hours later while eating dinner outside with the family, an email pinged on my phone. I showed Rose the notification before opening it.

'Dear Rorke Wilde....' she mouthed the words and looked at me with the same mixture of excitement and nervous enveloping me. 'Don't let them see it - not today. Either way, they will be upset.'

I dropped my hands below the outdoor table, with Rose peering down with me. Before tapping the link, I glanced around at the family, enjoying themselves at the barbeque. Some were cooking, others chatting, all oblivious to what we were up to.

Unable to contain herself, Rose tapped my phone and after what seemed an eternity, the email opened.

Dear Rorke Wilde.
We have selected you to move to the final stage in the selection process. We shall be in contact to arrange a mutually beneficial date that we can meet you here in Auckland, New Zealand....

The phone turned off, but we had seen all we needed. Rose kissed my cheek and gave me a fierce hug before mingling. I joined her with our loved ones, my emotions a pendulum of emotion. *This is getting serious. We might just be emigrating one day soon.* My mind raced. It was all I could do to stay focused on the evening.

'It's all very exciting,' Rose said, drying dishes as I washed them in the kitchen sink. 'I thought the evening would never end.'

'Me too, but the flight isn't cheap.' I gave her a worried look.

'I know, but we will manage somehow.' She gave me a playful flick of the tea towel. 'If this works out, it will be a pittance.'

'No pressure then?'

'You will be amazing, Rory. Of that I have no doubt.'

'Thank you.' I put my arms around Rose's waist. 'I wonder when they are planning to have the interviews?'

'We'll find out tomorrow night. Won't we. Can't wait?' She danced in exhilaration.

'When do we talk to the family?'

Rose thought for a moment before answering. 'Only when we know for sure. The kids first, so they are part of the reveal when we tell the rest.'

The twenty-seven-hour flight from Johannesburg flew via Dubai and Sydney before landing in Auckland. The City of Sails. A four-day turnaround to the other side of the world followed. The many online meetings, along with HR and psychological testing, left me fatigued. Joyful at a fresh start yet mixed with despair at leaving my beloved Africa. Proud to help my family.

After a rigorous interview process, I accepted the management position. I signed, sealed, and delivered the deal, which included a residence visa within two years as a bonus. Rose and I cried together via Skype. This time with relief — it was beyond our wildest expectations and dreams. We stood a chance.

On my return, Rose rounded up the immediate family in the lounge and shared the news that we were preparing to leave for New Zealand.

'Oh, great and I'm supposed the leave all my friends and family behind?' James showed little excitement at the prospect. 'In fact, count me out. I'm not going.'

Rose, about to answer, bit her lip, choosing not to push the issues so early on.

'We're not forcing you, James, and there is plenty of time to think about it.' I said after our son disappearing down the passageway in a huff.

So, we made a compromise. He'd join us when we found a place to live and got settled.

'That didn't go as planned.' Rose shook her head. 'And worse still, we tell the rest at the family braai this weekend.'

I raised my eyebrows at the prospect, but we were both surprised by the family's unequivocal support that never wavered then or now. They made our journey easier in so many ways and we miss them every day.

Chapter Twenty-nine

This reminiscence, *My African Rose*, is about where and when we started our pilgrimage together and tells of our commitment to change our lives for the better. It displays a steadfastness to realise our dreams and an unwavering dedication to our family. This journal documents our adventure, as our life was and still is. I hope it will live up to the love I have for you so the world might glimpse your amazingness.

You rekindled my joy at writing and changed my world forever. You taught me how to love and to be loved. This memoir expresses how you make me feel. It matters not what others may think about this, our story, my African Rose. My intention was to document our collective efforts, not to achieve bestseller status or pass judgment.

My first scribblings – long before I dreamed of writing this memoir – began sitting on the bed with you, pen and notebook in hand:

WHY?
No single reason
Each cause enough
Teasing eyes
Seductive look
Curvaceous line
Evocative touch
Adoring smile
Welcoming arms
Strength of character
Power of mind

This plus more
Sweetness of soul

As each morning's mist gives way to sunshine, so my love for you grows. During good times your joy infects us all, while your tenderness calms us on the harshest of days. I don't say it enough or very well, but I dedicate my life to showing how important you are to me. With each setting sun I am blessed to have you by my side. Your love and dedication are responsible for all our achievements in the past thirty years. What an honour to have you as my friend, my soul mate, my everything.

Twenty-five years ago, on a cold and quiet night at Cobblers Bar and Grill, I was trying to write while hiding my efforts from our resident writer, Philemon. I didn't want him to see me struggling to put a sentence together. Giving up after many attempts at starting a story, I stuck to short verse. A realisation of what our partnership had become.

Kindred Spirit
Unfathomed oceans of life
Exist in a perfect synthesis.
A union of celestial bodies
Unexplainably linked within.

Souls fighting the currents.
And battering waves of existence.
Murky waters disturbed by
The turmoil of daily survival.

The allure of mimicry
Scuttling endeavours of enlightenment.
Materialism corrupting virtues
Consumerism the new prophet.

Kindred spirit purifying
Dissolving reefs of self-preservation.
Revealing crystal-clear reality
Within each mate's soul.

What a life it has been and still promises to be, my African Rose. The years passing us by as if in minutes reflect our happiness. This book is a monument to all we have experienced together, a homage to what we stand for and battle towards. We've done more than others and we are not about to give up. The journey has included hardship and grief. That is part of life. Without it, we would not have lived to the fullest. Our bounty is always an abundance, and the returns are our reward. Our pain stems from a devotion that will feed a lifetime of memories. My successes are yours. My failures, my own.

A wee poem for you, my rose.

We must never take you for granted.
We have led large corporates and sipped on Dom Perignon.
We have lived the life of Riley.
We have opened our own restaurant and dined in the finest establishments.
We have taken on paper rounds in our forties to make ends meet.
We have not known when the next meal might be.
We have faced abject fear and uncertainty.
We now live in tranquillity and satisfaction.
We never forget where we come from.
We always know where we are heading.
We are what makes it all possible.

As this memoir draws to an end, my heart is full. Contentment settles within my soul while weariness creeps into my eyes. The *My African Rose* story has proved to be the easiest of my three memoirs to write. Checking my phone at night to see if it was time to wake up. Excited at the prospect of recalling our experiences and living through the joys again. On more than one occasion tears cascaded down my cheeks, remembering those we have lost or left behind.

The world is going through another of her transitions, just like those we have witnessed before. Not something new or more evil than past growth spurts. The universe carries on. It's our responsibility to create our own path towards our goals. Time does not wait; nor are we owed anything. We make of it as we will.

Being someone to everyone
is being no one to anyone.
One must be true to oneself.
to be truly something to another.

To recognise pain in others
is to accept one's own.
Guilt a human
poison of the mind.

Companionship fades with absence
whilst blood thickens.
Subconscious desires searching
collusions of select friendship.

Substitution is pseudo love.
unconditional in its entirety.
Stimulation from all sources
forges true enlightenment.

Inspiration from within
ensures salvation.
To agree to less
is treachery of the soul.

I began this chapter intending it to be full and to document my feelings for you but I have failed in my attempt. As has always been the case, I must leave that to the ambiguity of poetry. For words are not adequate to show my love, so I continue the search for what may.

We have the advantage of age now – a rare commodity to cherish. My greatest delight of late are our moments when the brain plays with us. Entering a room and forgetting the reason. Putting something down but not knowing where. Repeating ourselves without recollection of saying it before. Our bodies are not responding in the way we are used to.

There is no shame in those follies, my precious Rose. It means we have lived life to the fullest. Our brains have become crowded and have already answered most of our questions. Our hearts have taken us to the places we had to be. Both deserve to slow down and rest, as they will be needed soon.

Ripening Fruit
Age begins the conflict between body and mind
Each blaming the other when youth fades
The soul, the intermediary, reassures both
Self-imposed limitations, as dreams slide into obscurity
Intensifying one's sense of mortality and fruitlessness
Lack of acknowledgement of goals achieved
And often finding solace in repeating mistakes.

Reconciliation of these two powers
Rejuvenates life's remaining chapters
Drawing strength from knowledge
Wisdom from experience
The contentment of memories
Replacing the arrogance of youth
To savour the ripe fruits of age

We have found our paradise. Aotearoa, New Zealand, is our Nirvana, for she has blessed the family with everything we need. Shielded us from what we thought we wanted. There is a stark contrast between them. No excess to be ashamed of, no shortage to worry about. We do not diminish our yearning for Africa by the appreciation we have for our home here beneath the long white cloud.

My African Rose, you make me complete, and I relish with such anticipation what future we have left together. When our time comes to an end on this Earth we will travel through eternity as one and revisit our loved ones and relive the moments we treasure. Our journey has just begun. The genuineness of our devotion blesses us.

And so, my Rose, the clicking of the clock moves us along. Time and life are one, as are we. With the approach of our retirement, we enter our fourth quarter well prepared. This book is now complete.

I need to hurry to the next; it yearns for freedom.
    Thank you, my sweet Rose. Thank you.
    All my love.
    Rory.

Chapter Thirty

As I get older, I feel the misery of loss. Loved ones who have passed for whom I could have done better. I now understand that once strange look I noticed in mature people. A deepness in their eyes showing a soul filled with memories both joyous and painful. The realisation that we are flawed and, above all else, mortal. There is an inevitability. I contemplate the reality that woman live longer and whether that is because of genetics or a bravery for the challenges old age promises.

But as I have said, the rewards of living a long, full life are boundless. I'm filled with pride passing on the traditions my sweet African Rose began. The children taking the batten and forging a future of their own is incalculable.

Life's reward is not about achievements or remarkable moments with my Miss Rose. It is in the sharing of everyday experiences, in the supposed mundane routine of shopping for a bargain. The love of cleaning our home, or in tending to the garden with its cherished remembrances. The sound of my African Rose singing and chatting to the birds, cats, and dogs. At peace - without fear of attack or an uncertain future.

Then there are the life puzzles to which we may never find the answers, no matter how long we live. I deem it most baffling that some people I have known for decades show no emotional intelligence and are incapable of growing. What was the purpose of your journey if you're the same person you were when you were young? Aside from being stagnant, what efforts have you made to contribute to the universe? I view them as the unequivocal mushroom feeding on archival mulch whilst hiding from the unmistakable light.

The Wilde Collection comprises three memoirs chronicling my journey from the 1960s to the 2020s. My life has been neither exciting nor inspirational, just like most, and by all accounts my means of living has been rather basic, but I make no excuses for that because it's the path I chose.

What is extraordinary, however, are the times I lived through and how that has affected the way we interact and live today. Regardless of recriminations, all eras are equal. When screen entertainment was an hour or two on a black and white television set and the world faced nuclear threats while man conquered the moon. Now, in a time where we are dependent on technology and flirting with AI, we're faced with the promise of climate change. As I have said on more than one occasion before and despite the possibility of sounding repetitive, artificial intelligence is an oxymoron if ever I've heard one.

The Wilde Collection series does not follow a logical timeline, but rather navigates steppingstones towards my final work in the collection.

The Chameleon is my story of growing up in Rhodesia in the 1970s. To survive apartheid, I had to mimic my chameleon pet. My dad was a member of the British South Africa Police, and my mother was a clerk in the tax office. My best friend and father figure was the family's domestic worker, Themba Dube, an *AmaNdebele* of Zulu descent. Themba guided me through the turmoil of civil war, and introduced me to Lucky Ndlovu, his orphaned nephew from Johannesburg's squatter camp. The old man and boy shared stories of their post-independence poverty with me. These two and their narratives changed my perspective on Africa.

The Chameleon is a history-defying biography that addresses apartheid, colonialism, heartbreak, love and compassion. It shows how the worldwide diaspora has been affected by politics, greed and opportunity.

In **Where the Birds Don't Fly,** I speak of resilience, belonging, and the desire for inclusion.

The Wilde family left Africa in my second memoir, set during a time of global prejudice in 2009. The story centres on our isolation and struggle to adapt to another culture. We recognised the importance of acceptance for gaining approval.

In New Zealand we befriended the Ncube household from Zimbabwe, who understood the challenges of parenting in their unfamiliar country.

A strong bond developed between Tāne Williams and me. We explored the effects of immigration on indigenous groups. Meanwhile Fran White and Hugh Biggete intimidated employees who challenged the status quo.

Despite bias and mockery, our family persisted in our journey. We avoided fellow immigrants who resisted change and remained rooted in their past.

A string of islands that hold the world's highest number of flightless bird species, would this foreign country, Aotearoa, offer us a comparable refuge after our flight?

My African Rose starts in the mid-1990s when my wife Rose and I first met and follows our decision to leave corporate life and run a pub in a mining town in the southern region of Johannesburg, South Africa.

This was an era of political upheaval, violence and xenophobia when the notion of a Rainbow Nation waned. We were dealing with the consequences of a government's attempt to readdress apartheid by leaving out certain groups.

Retribution and lawlessness forced us to live behind security fencing and alarms, and children could not play in their gardens. The alternative to this restricted life was to leave Africa and seek a safe home abroad.

Through all this, Rose has been my rock and my soulmate. This recollection is my ode to my best friend, my partner in life, and the world she made better.

I am busy writing book four, the final in the series. It will reflect on my experiences at an English public school in the mid-1970s, punctuated by holidays back in Rhodesia.

I shall share stories of jocularity and mischief, celebrate friendships that have lasted a lifetime, and describe pain and suffering that may last longer than we do as our families continue without us.

Included in this book will be an ongoing debate about a new mental condition called boarding school disorder, which is being compared to posttraumatic stress disorder. Since PTSD is often associated with soldiers after a traumatic war experience, I know some see this new condition as being woke. I also know that some of the worst perpetrators of boarding school misery hide behind the idea that the experiences we suffered were intended to be for our benefit.

Derision from those who never understood what I was going through or clinging to the past to justify its shortcomings will not change facts. Even now, child labour in these schools persists while the world remains oblivious, or instead chooses to look the other way.

The four writings are free to be read, debated, enjoyed or ridiculed as the reader pleases – in the end they are simply my recollections.

Not everyone may find this genre as captivating as murder mysteries, thrillers or romances with their predictable plots. The industries' enforced commercial arcs ensure no writer strays beyond a prescribed norm of pigeonholes. Literature must be about pushing the boundaries. How else are we to capture the fickleness of humanity? Forgive my sarcasm. The lemming fortitude on display is mind-blowing.

The Wilde Collection series draws inspiration from classic twentieth-century novels, that explored the scandalous behaviour and wrongdoings of society. The books are similar to but not in the same league as the works of Charles Dickens that questioned the plight of orphaned children (*Oliver Twist)* or reflected on wealth, poverty and love (*David Copperfield* and *Great Expectations)*. Dickens was a social critic who highlighted the shortcomings of the Victorian era with his larger-than-life characters – The Artful Dodger, Fagin, Pip and Miss Havisham, to name a few.

The burden belongs to the scribe. Now we duck and dive to squeeze into compartments that do not fit. Jump through hoops to garnish favour with agents and publishers. Flaunt jazz hands in the hope of commercial success. I fear this is true of all the arts. Despite claims, technology can only reproduce from existing databases and cannot think beyond established parameters. Pun once again intended. The brain is all we humans have that separates us and woe betide us when we stop using it. To create any works, the spark must come from within. Free from any influences other than the artist.

One of my favourite pastimes outside of my writing is watching reaction videos on the internet. Young people flabbergasted by the natural talent of musicians whose heyday came before they were born. Great songs, blissful voices without auto tune, and intriguing stage presences. It's wonderful to watch the youngsters' joy of discovery, though it's also worrying to see them admit that much of the music produced today is not up to scratch. Most arts are subject to controlled creativity. We cannot allow that to continue.

Change comes from accepting its inevitability. We cannot grow without embracing it and must transform ourselves before we question others, let alone judge what they do. We need to explore our inner selves, for there lies our preconceptions and prejudices. Once we realise we are part of the problem we will gain a respect for different views and behaviours.

Now I confront what I've avoided my whole life, no excuses. As a child, social survival meant not just fitting in but joining in. I can still see the broken faces of friends who were ostracised because they did not toe the proverbial line. Who remain excluded and sidelined because of their plight.

I aim to climb off the fence and defy those who assume they know me or how I should act. Yes, it has caused pain, but hurt feelings are not what is at stake here. They, too, disappear once we accept ourselves for who we are and what we have become.

At the risk of becoming too preachy, that is a topic I will cover in my next memoir. Where I recall my boarding school shenanigans, good and bad. The teenage years are an age of great joys and lifelong camaraderie that neither distance nor time can erode. But it is also tainted by an underlying malignancy of untold darkness and instilled shame – a ponderance of which impacted my early years.

As my mentor Themba Dube would say, *Hamba kahle* - travel well.

Until our next adventure together.

Epilogue

My African Rose is the third of my memoirs under *The Wilde Collection* series – a different journey in that I indulge in my love for Rose Wilde. She brings out a better side of me, completing and enhancing my life.

I shall not ask your forgiveness for doing so since my most considerable teaching from my partner is to share what you feel. All three books reflect almost six decades of holding everything inside – this latest one even more than the others.

The specifics of my past regrets remain untold, intertwined with this series. There are a couple of contritions I have yet to talk about, which will be in my upcoming and last memoir in *The Wilde Collection*. These revelations are not formidable, and my Rose is aware of them, as she knows me better than I know myself.

Spending a childhood living in the *stiff-upper-lip* philosophy of a British colony in the 1960s had its drawbacks. As did being sent to an elite boarding school that practised the renowned English public school system. A lesson in toughness. Their intolerance only allowed anger and rejected anything or anyone who did not conform.

Insults such as *sissy* suggesting you were more like a woman disrespected both genres, and *moffie* accused you of being effeminate or even gay. Today, derogatory sayings have shifted to labels including 'woke' and 'snowflake' with the same intended impact.

More on Boarding School Syndrome will be featured in my following memoir when I return to my life of education. Year one is in *The Chameleon;* the remaining six years are still to come.

The **Joker**. Your attempt at humour at others' expense was, and is, uncalled for. Your callousness intimidates those who are unsure of themselves.

The **Weirdo**. I know you have widened your influence, but your indiscretions in the past are catching up with your ilk. Even celebrities and powerful politicians cannot escape the long arm of the law.

The **Doom** and **Gloom** twins. You paint pictures of despair and feed off the resultant pain and fear others feel. I see your structured assault on the news, and your online manipulating of the public.

The **Sloth**. You are no longer rare in developed countries as new generations embrace your lethargy and disinterest.

Truther. You are the lead caricature of this band of despots. Your lies will haunt you, as they always do. Conspire at your peril.

Balsak the bully. You will live forever, for it is a human trait to dominate the meek and mild. However, your comeuppance will haunt you.

The **Kugel**. Partner to Balsak. Oddly enough, your modus operandi of self-entitlement and condescension has a positive impact on the world, inspiring the ordinary and good-hearted to rise.

Collectively, you all strengthened us and were no match for our determination to succeed. We lived through the pain you instigated and thrived on your personality types. I'm excited to meet you in the future, where we'll be more challenging than before.

As I finish this tale, I look at the bookshelf with *The Chameleon* and *Where the Birds Don't Fly*, and imagine my third book, *My African Rose*, joining them. Alongside the books is the small tin holding Themba's letters he wrote to me. I open the metal box as I did when I started this memoir and pick an aged note out, as if conducting a raffle. I unfold it and read.

Salibonani my son.
I have taken Lucky back to his family in the north.
We found a place on the bus.
It will drop us off before we reach the border.
From there, we shall walk the rest of the way.
You and I must do what is right for our family.
I shall tell Lucky of our friendship.

By the time we arrive home, the Ndlovu's will forever
speak your name.
My heart no longer feels pain, for it is beyond repair.
Before I rest with my ancestors, I must do this for Lucky.
Uhumbe kuhle, my son, Usale kuhle, Chameleon.
Never have I not had the courage.
Until now.
Forgive me for not having the strength to say goodbye to
you in person. Otherwise, I could never leave.
I am Themba Dube and must live up to my name of Hope
and the fearless zebra.
'Lisala kahle baba.'

There is nothing left to say.

My Rose
Life blessed me with a precious jewel
So beautiful it dimmed all others on earth
More dazzling than any diamond could ever be.
Warmer than the glow of the deepest ruby
More profound than the enigmatic emerald.
Fairer than opals at their milkiest.

From nature's treasure trove.
You captivate us all with your presence.
How I cherish your closeness
Your love for the family knows no bounds.
Our rock of unfailing strength.
A tender quality born out of resilience.

Your sparkle is visible even through my tears.
As I gaze at you by my side
My adoration for you is boundless.
I love everything about you.
I am undeserving
An extraordinary gift from above.

My love for you, my rose, is immense.
How amazing our life is!
Our shared history is unique.
We will always be one
Regardless of what lies ahead.
Even in spirit

Not the end.

Glossary

The below phrases and words are not direct or literal translations, but colloquialisms and slang. There may be variations for different areas and people.

Afrikaans
Bakkie – pickup truck, utility vehicle.
Ballie – old man
Balsak – ballbag, fool
Blatjang - chutney
Fundis - expert
Gaan huis toe – go home.
Kak - shit
Konfyt - jam, preserve.
Laanie - smart, posh
Lightie - youngster
meisiekind - young girl
Meneer - sir
Oke - guy
Ou - old
Poepal – foolish person
Skinder - gossip
Skomgat – scum of the earth
Snotneus – snotty nose, wet behind the ears
te Koop - for sale
Vrot - rotten
Wip jou gat - throw a tantrum.

Zulu

Eish – exclamation of surprise
Kulungile - that is right
Kwenzakalani - What is going on?
Lisala kahle baba – Goodbye, Father
Ma'gents - gentlemen
Ngiyesaba - I am scared.
Uhumbe kuhle - travel well
Umshini Wami - Bring Me My Machine Gun.
Umlungu - white man
Usale kuhle - stay well

Scottish

Auld – old
Crabbit - grumpy
Haud yer weesht - *be quiet.*
Peely wally – pale and sickly
Skinny malinky longlegs - children's song from Glasgow
Tae high doh - nervous
Yay dinnee like to blather - you don't talk rubbish.

Acknowledgements

To my family for tolerating my idiosyncrasies. Present in body but not always in mind. I'm able to pursue my writing because you are all in my life. Jody, Matthew, Toby, Michael, Chantelle and Amy. Without you all, I am an empty vessel.

Our fur babies provide another tier of inspiration.

Buddy, I miss you with each year that passes. You and Kitty, forever in my soul. Thank you for introducing us to Zelda, our SPCA rescue - what a joy she is. As are Morgana and Daisy.

To loved ones, we have lost along the way. Forever in our thoughts.

My thanks to Kingsley Publishers for running with all three of my books.

I am grateful to my editor, Lesley Marshall. *Member NZAMA (New Zealand Association of Manuscript Assessors), NZSA (New Zealand Society of Authors), IPEd; online tutor Applied Writing diplomas NorthTec/Te Pūkenga; NZ coordinator International PEN.*

About the Author

David Farrell, the author of The Wilde Collection fictional memoir series, lives in a rural village on the banks of the Mighty Waikato River.

While planning his next book, he walks through the magnificent landscapes of New Zealand with his new muse, Zelda, by his side. A Kiwi Heading Dog rescued from the pound.

With his partner Jeanne and daughter Amy, they now live a harmonious life after a challenging journey from Southern Africa

Connect with David on social media
he loves to connect with his fans
Instagram: davidfarrellauthor

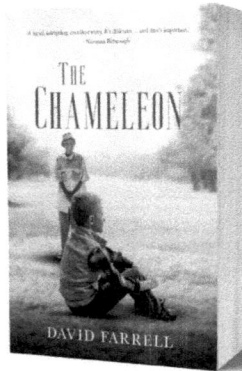

'A lucid, intriguing, excellent story. It's different ... and that's important.' - Author Norman Bilbrough

The Chameleon is the tale of Rorke Wilde, who grows up in Rhodesia. Rorke's need to mimic his pet chameleon, if he is to survive the racial discourse in a country divided by apartheid during the 1970s.

Rorke's father works in the British South Africa Police while his mother is a clerk in the tax office. His best friend and father figure is the family's domestic worker, Themba Dube, an AmaNdebele of Zulu descent. Whom guides Rorke through the turmoil of civil bias.

Themba introduces Rorke to his nephew Lucky Ndlovu, who lost his parents in the AIDS pandemic and who lives with his grandmother in a squatter camp (informal settlements) in Johannesburg.

The old man and boy share their experiences of a life of poverty post-independence where Rorke learns about the real Africa that he once saw through Panglossian glasses.

A fictional biography that challenges the norms of history. Of apartheid, colonialism, heartbreak, love, and compassion.

Many, if not all of us, have experienced the good and bad in the worldwide diaspora because of politics, greed, and opportunity.

Chapter One

I pressed my scrawny ten-year-old frame against the granite; the embedded lichen filled my senses. Veins of quartz and the glint of fool's gold brought the rock formations to life. With my airgun in hand, I peered over the ridge and selected a lead pellet from beneath my tongue. I was ready for my prey, a large rock lizard, to make a move.

I had forgotten to change after school with the thrill of the chase. Besides, the khaki camouflaged me here on the edges of the Kalahari.

Mum will be furious, but this is more important.

The heat burnt my lungs as sweat oozed from my *Worzel Gummidge* straw hair onto my brow and ran along the back of my neck.

That talking scarecrow looks nothing like me.

I flicked the flies from my eyes and spat out the bugs through chapped lips, cursing the unkind comments of the kids at school. The hunt had ended without success, so I sought shelter beneath the tree. I enjoyed the chase but not the kill. Guilt added to my self-loathing with every pursuit. It sounded glamorous in the cocktail lounge of the country club where my sister Cara and I messed around in the plush grounds while Mum and Dad attended soirees. Father, in his austere police uniform, oblivious to the kids pinching swigs of beer from the tables. More concerned with his waxed moustache as he twirled it between his fingers and patted the sleek blue-black hair. His efforts of a smouldering rock-and-roll stare was stranger than it was striking, without the complementary chin or impressive jawline. Mum always uneasy in a sleeveless floral dress preferring the freedom and functionality of slacks. On such evenings she puffed up her hair until it defied gravity, applied copious amounts of makeup and wore contact lenses, which turned her cobalt eyes red as the evening progressed.

In the valley below, I could see my home among a belt of steel roofs and terraced gardens. The granite contrasted with the yellow soil, whilst the collieries in the distance spewed coal dust into the Zambezi valley air. In the opposite direction was my Eden — the Wankie National Park.

Nowhere was I more secure than here in the arms of this leafless giant tree, fantasising about her bygone visitors. The San bushmen sharing tales around the fire and the pith-helmeted colonials with their enslaved porters. Reliving stories of today's guerrillas and freedom fighters in an escalating civil war.

'Hello, my old friend.' I hugged the soft bark of her trunk so shiny I could make out my reflection. I brushed the twigs and withered leaves from my favoured place amongst her voluptuous embraces.

With hands behind my head, I lay in the dappled light as I savoured the aroma of the sweet-spicy fruit of the Baobab protected beneath the hard shell of a green velvet husk. The dry pulp inside had a citrus flavour when chewed or added to drinking water, known as cream of tartar or monkey bread. Fabled to give strength and protection from the ever-prevalent Nile crocodile.

I hoped there was time to catch up with Bow. I combed through the bush on my approach into the valley, careful to look beyond the camouflage of nature's veil.

'Bow, where the hell are you? Don't fool around, man.' I clambered into a thicket, mindful of the thorns.

'There you are. You little shit.'

He co-ordinated his eyes, then edged towards me.

'I've brought food.' I offered a black and red beetle from between my fingers. 'Your favourite.'

With a flick of his foot-long tongue, the insect disappeared. Bow stood ten centimetres tall and forty centimetres from tip to tail.

'At least you're in a better mood. What happened?' I looked him in the face. 'The jacket you wore yesterday just didn't suit you.'

He focussed one eye on me, the other rotated back and forth in search of danger. Today he dined in a mustard suit to match the parched savannah.

'I guess something must have upset you. I can't stay mad at you, buddy. Watch out for the snakes and those nasty birds.'

Bow's back arched as I stroked him, and I swear he gave a wry smile.

'I'll see you tomorrow; it's getting dark.'

Twilight lasted but minutes. I kicked at stones and rustled the surrounding vegetation to secure my friend's safety, then slipped away into the blackening basin.

The last ray dipped beneath the horizon, bringing up a burnt-orange hue. The earth cooled. A symphony rejoiced at the close of day. Christmas beetles joined the sonata, as it surged to a crescendo of clicks and chirps. The double bass of the bullfrog entered the fray.

I paused on the slope, admiring my *kopje* against the kaleidoscopic blue and black of the night sky and the dying orangeness of the sun.

The smell from the kitchen confirmed dinner was ready. I muttered a hello to Themba, the family's domestic worker. A tall man of proud *AmaNdebele* heritage with thickset shoulders and muscular limbs. The kindest of faces that could frighten the bravest enemy if the occasion warranted. A wide forehead beneath his short-cropped hair sported a shaved parting that moved in sync with his emotions. His high cheekbones stressed the whites of his eyes and a nose which changed shape with his enormous grin. A Zambian from the north, disillusioned with politics, unfulfilled promises, corruption, and unemployment in his country of birth, he sought a better life in Rhodesia.

Themba Dube ran our home, from the cooking and cleaning to the laundry. In a house void of modern conveniences, he wax polished the wooden parquet floors on his knees, hand-washed the clothes in the bathtub and later dry-ironed them.

'Hi, Themba,' I said as he flashed me a toothy grin. 'I cooked your favourite food.'

'Sausage and mash? Wow, thanks, Themba.'

'Yes, and without gravy.' He waved a frying pan aloft and danced a jig.

'Dad will catch you again if you're not careful.'

Themba dished up dinner as he whistled.

Mum's old yellow Renault 12 sat in the driveway. Her sewing machine echoed through the walls of a house built of corrugated iron, louvre windows and an asbestos roof. Cut into the bedroom walls were air conditioners, which shook the foundations when turned on at the same time. Without them, the place became a giant convection oven and instead of tranquil African nights; we slept to their incessant drone. Our home, at the end of a row of identical houses, perched on the side of the largest *kopje* on the outskirts of Wankie town, confirmed our status as civil servants. It was temporary accommodation built for government workers before Rhodesia's Unilateral Declaration of Independence in 1969.

Dad arrived home early. Sometimes he never showed. If he wasn't in a criminal case, the political unrest kept him busy.

I fought the urge to rush to his police truck and hug him.

'Hi, Dad.'

'Hello.' His voice was monotone and without a glance, he headed for the bedroom.

I opened my closet and changed into a pair of shorts and tucked in a white T-shirt with an elephant waving a *Rhodesia Is Super* banner on the front. The skinny little boy glaring back at me in disgust caused me to stop for a moment.

When am I going to grow like the rest of my friends?

Knobbly knees, angular elbows dominated the image in front of me. The pudding bowl haircut of straight blonde hair covered the eyes and the sloping shoulders didn't portray what I saw in myself. The young lad in the mirror flashed two fingers and disappeared.

One day is one day. I'll get there, you'll see.

At 18:00 sharp, we sat at the wooden pot-marked dinner table in rickety chairs with threadbare cushions sagging through the frayed leather supports. The dining room a mere space between kitchen, the lounge, and the hallway leading to the three bedrooms.

Themba served as he and I pulled faces while my parents chatted. Meals were dour affairs with the minimal of tableware. On occasions there were salt and pepper shakers. For special celebrations, a jar of English mustard caked in dried mustard adorned the centrepiece.

'May I have a drink, please?' I asked.

'Your father doesn't allow it, dear,' Mum replied.

'Yes Rory, don't you know that?' Cara, my six-year-old sister, tutted at me. Her dishevelled golden tassels irritated me as it invaded every part of her delicate round face, doleful brown eyes, and dainty ears. In fact, her good looks annoyed me to no end.

It's just not fair.

"What are you looking at, creep?" She added with a devilish look.

'But it's hot and I'm thirsty.' I ignored her.

'You heard your mother, no water. Now finish what's on your plate.'

'Yes, Dad.' I avoided eye contact with Themba.

After the meal, we retired to the lounge, where Dad changed the radio to his favourite evening talk show. Mum settled into her chair with a romantic blockbuster in hand.

Why does she read those silly books? They're all the same, full of daft grown-ups, dressed up — fainting and kissing — ugh.

Bored and in no mood for adult company, I traipsed along the passage to my sister's room. Through the crack in the door, I watched Cara bossing her dolls around for wrongdoings. A look she often used on me after one of our spats.

'What are you doing?' I asked.

'Nothing, stupid, what do you want?'

'Nothing, stupid,' I replied and retreated, not keen for one of our battles.

She flicked her long, messy hair and resumed her make-believe. The dolls bore the brunt. It was time for bed.

The sweet tunes of wild birds woke me. I flipped off the air conditioner, pulled back the curtains, and took a deep breath to shake off the airless night. I sat and watched as morn ascended the horizon and lit the scorched lawn into a pasture of diamonds. It replaced the monochrome blanket of night by the orange of the sun, exposing a spectrum of blues from ultramarine to the azure of the African sky. Creatures quenched their thirst to prepare for the day's tussle with the elements.

Dad tended to his uniform, a splendid colonial outfit — pompous and impractical. Meticulous long socks turned at the knee, khaki shorts, a grey-cotton shirt, and polished belts crisscrossed his chest. Medals adorned his breast. A peaked cap and the three bars of inspector sat on his shoulders. Being the member in charge's son filled me with pride. I respected the position and what it commanded, despite the lack of financial reward.

'Rory, open for me,' Dad said.

I ran and opened the cast-iron gates. He reversed out of the driveway, too busy on the police radio to return my goodbye.

The walk to school took me through the arid *veld* with its centre parting of olive foliage that grew along the banks of the *spruit*. The alternative was a laborious, mine-sponsored bus through town. On foot, I crossed the town's revered, if not sacred, golf course. A weird place guarded by even stranger people. The greenkeeper and his henchmen patrolled the fairways, looking for any breach of their beloved turf by non-members, infidels, or rebellious children. I was never brave enough to cross on my own.

My best friend Alan waited on the corner of the street next to the golf club. His thick mop of curls wafted in the breeze. He was a heavy-set lad, with flawless olive skin, better suited to the climate than my freckled infested lilywhite hide.

We chose a dusty path that led into the bush and would bypass the clubhouse.

'Take it easy. One false step and it's over,' I said.

Alan nodded and scuffed through the gravel. 'I know, don't want to get near those thorns either.'

At the bottom, we peered through the undergrowth. To our left, a tractor offered no immediate threat; to the right, two golfers were teeing off.

Alan whooped and bolted like a warthog.

'Bloody hell,' I added as I followed.

Halfway and with little grace, we swallow dived into a sandy bunker to catch our breath. The thud of a golf ball landing nearby set us off in another wave of panic as we headed towards the far side of the fairway. Hysterical, we gasped a lungful of air.

'How cool. Bloody close though, hey?' Alan said.

'For sure. Check. I got their golf ball.'

'Shit!' Alan shouted. 'What are you doing with that?'

I shrugged. 'Don't know. Seemed a good idea.'

'Get rid of it, *now*.' Horror etched across Alan's face.

'But we can get fifty cents at the caddy shack.'

'Bugger the money, check out those golfers.'

Over my shoulder, a man dressed in plus fours, followed by a caddy, strode towards us. I lobbed the ball back and slithered into the scrub. Capture was beyond comprehension. Punishment meant washing the dishes in the cafe or cleaning the pool. Worse still was being sent to retrieve golf balls on the driving range.

Closer to school, we crossed a barren piece of land once earmarked for sports fields. Despite the attempts of the ground's staff, it remained a wasteland. This mystical land oozed, like puss from a boil, from which a pungent smell of boiled eggs rose from its shell — the by-product of ancient forests fossilised into rich deposits of coal and gas.

'Catch,' I said as I tossed Alan a box of matches.

'Thanks, hope it works.'

We scratched the surface and collected the powder.

'That'll do,' I said as I added the sulphur to the matches.

'Quick, before school starts.'

'Okay, okay.'

'Are you ready?' We slid a lit match in with the others and ducked to safety.

'It won't work,' Alan said.

'Maybe not.'

The cocktail burst into a ball of fire with flames shooting in every direction.

'Did you see that, man?' Alan danced and gripped me around the neck.

'You'll strangle me, dumbass.'

'Sorry.'

We lumbered into the school grounds.

The buildings were of military design with red-face brick, white-steel windows, and the usual asbestos roof. Our town was too small for a secondary school, so the townspeople sent their pre-teens to boarding schools, the closest being hundreds of kilometres away.

Shrill laughter stemmed from the classroom. Inside, a blackboard with a numerical black and white clock perched above covered the front wall. Chalk dust spattered the wooden floor, showing the teacher's imprints as she wrote on the board. Dusters littered the bottom shelf complemented by a disarray of coloured chalk.

'Settle down and take your places, children.' The schoolteacher handed out forms, her jersey covered in the same powder. 'Give these to your parents to fill in and make sure you return them tomorrow; any delays will reduce your chance of being given the school of your choice. Make a list of where you want to go to in order of preference, please.' She paused, then pointed to the boys. 'You lot get an extra sheet to register for national service.' She looked at us with slanted eyes from the tight bun of hair tied on top of her head. Her coloured cheek bones a curious red vied with the dollop of lipstick on her wafer lips.

My stomach turned at the prospect of military duty.

'Who cut the cheese?' a voice said and reduced the class to wails of laughter.

'Let's not go there today class.' The teacher crossed her arms.

A change in wind direction bore the odour of the sulphuric fields. This time, the aroma eased the nervous tension, much to the student's relief.

On my way home, I studied a dust devil's lethargic effort to cross the road.

Should I go into the hills or visit Themba?

I headed for his shed at the rear of our garden.

'Hi, Mr Rory. Do you want lunch?' Themba asked me.

'Nah.'

'Tough day at school, huh?'

'Why can't things stay the way they are?' I asked.

'Change is life, my young friend.'

'I have to leave for boarding school soon, and I also have to choose which regiment I want to enlist with.'

Themba blew hard. 'How can they ask the innocent to fight their wars?' It was a rhetorical double-edged question that I didn't understand.

'Never mind. Come, join us for lunch,' Themba said, changing the subject.

'Thanks, but what about Mum?'

'Don't worry, she's out shopping, and then she'll be staying late at the library.'

'Great.' I perched on one of the tree stumps the family used to sit around the fire while Themba disappeared into the house in search of his wife.

Their home comprised a fireplace between two whitewashed rooms discoloured by years of soot. Tin doors and exposed light globes hung from rafters without ceilings. One a bedroom, the other ablutions with a shower and a hole in the floor for a toilet, flushed by a rusty chain dangling from the roof.

While maize-meal was cooking over a wood fire, the acrid aroma of carbolic soap wafted from laundry hanging on a makeshift clothesline. The bare earth shone from the relentless brush of a straw broom.

Themba re-emerged wearing slacks and a T-shirt.

'Come, Mr Rory, let's rest and talk awhile. My wife and daughter will prepare us food.' He chose the largest of the sawn-off trees. 'A man's life is tough.'

Uncertain what he meant, I nodded, noticing a gaunt teenager wearing tatty shorts and a stretched t-shirt, approaching.

'What are you doing here?' he asked me with a scowl and pursed lips.

'Your dad invited me. Why?'

'Thought your parents didn't want you here.' He stamped the ground with giant feet.

'They're not me, are they?'

'Sit beside me and let us enjoy each other's company,' Temba said.

Sipho glared at me, in two minds. 'Okay Father, but only because you ask.'

Themba manipulated the conversation to avoid delicate topics, aware of Sipho's demeanour of late, while his wife, Precious, a stunning woman with an ample bust and wide hips, brought mugs of sweet tea with the youngest of their children strapped to her back.

'Hi Rory, how you?' she asked me.

'Fine. How's the baby?'

'We're good thanks.' She gave one of her infectious smiles that lit her oval face. Her chocolate brown eyes emphasised by pencil thin, mesmerising eyebrows.

Custom dictated that she served Themba first, the guests next, then the children and the woman last.

'When you're finished, wash up for lunch,' Precious said.

'Quiet wife, the men are busy.'

Precious chuckled and said, 'What fools' men are.'

Themba gave an impish grin. 'If we brothers don't stick together, women will run the world.'

We changed the subject rather than go down that road.

I snuck out of the house and joined Themba's family for supper whenever my parents went out for an evening. Tonight, was no different. A hearty affair with a three-legged, cast-iron *potjie* brimming with cornmeal and flame-grilled brisket. Exotic spices, influenced by the spice trade, wafted up from enamel bowls. We rolled the porridge in our right hands and dipped the food into the thick peri-peri sauce — a seasoning made from ground bird's-eye chillies introduced by early Portuguese settlers.

Idle gossip wound down the meal before Themba's side-splitting belch, accompanied by an appreciative rub of his belly, declared an end to proceedings.

His wife and daughter cleared the dishes and brewed mugs of tea for everyone except Themba. Instead, he accepted the first carton of traditional beer, an opaque brew fermented from sorghum and corn, with regal poise. The letters *SHAKE, SHAKE* printed on the side, advised drinkers how to avoid a mouthful of sour gruel at the bottom. He threw back his head and swallowed with gusto. The low-slung canopy of stars etched his form against the night sky.

'Much better,' he said as he wiped away his cream moustache with the back of his hand and launched into ancestral fables and myths, each one more outlandish than the last.

'That's not a fire...' He grabbed a pile of logs by his side and tossed them onto the coals. The flames created the backdrop while the empty cartons of beer strewn across the ground were the props to the spectacle. With each show, the alcohol brought the final curtain, followed by silence, but for the spit of the embers.

Trying not to break the trance, I peered from under my fringe at the whites of Sipho's eyes as he stared at me.

'Time to go home. Your mother will be here soon,' Precious said as she shook me by the shoulder.

With the evening over, we washed and packed up before I hurried home in time for my parent's arrival.

'Hi, Mum,' I said, wishing she had stayed out longer.

'Hi Rory, how was school, my boy? Please help Themba get the stuff out of the car.'

Themba arrived as Sipho vanished into the darkness.

Days later, I summoned the courage to approach my father, choosing a quiet evening without the usual family dramas.

'Here Dad,' I said. 'You must fill in these for tomorrow.'

At first, he didn't respond.

'Dad?'

'What is it, boy?'

'I've got the forms I need for high school and my national service.'

'Well, have you decided yet?'

I shrugged.

'Typical. This boy of yours is so indecisive,' he said to Mum, who was across the living room.

'He's your son too,' she replied with disregard.

'Fine, get me a pen and let's settle this.' He snatched the forms from my hands and scowled over the top of his reading glasses. 'For starters, consider the police, not the half-baked conscripts' regiment.'

'How does the S.A.S. sound?' I asked and watched the disbelief cross his face.

'You were... you do? Not an awful choice. What do you say, Mother?'

'That's nice, dears.'

'What do you mean, *that's nice*? Our son has chosen the most elite armed force, the Special Air Service, and all you got to say is *that's nice*?' Dad turned back to me. 'Well, it's your decision, my boy. Who are we to stand in your way?'

'I tried for Plumtree School, too.'

His eyebrows rose further. 'Are you sure? Plumtree is a long way away?'

'Yes, but it's the best school in the country.'

'Splendid boy, perhaps you are a chip off the old block after all.' He leant forward to punch my arm but couldn't reach. 'This country needs every man to do his bit. We must stop the communist-backed infiltrators terrorising… ah! I want to listen to the end of this programme.' He turned to the radio station.

'Thanks, Dad. See you in the morning.'

'Bloody idiot has no clue what he's talking about,' he said as he threw his arms in the air at the words spoken by the voice on the wireless and knocked me aside.

'Goodnight, Dad. Goodnight, Mum.' Neither responded.

I lay awake contemplating my future, boarding school, national service, Sipho and the imminent civil war. It was all so far removed from the warmth of Themba, Bow and the safety of my baobab on the *kopje*. My mind raced, unable to grasp the magnitude of the impending fear. Sleep brought relief.

www.ingramcontent.com/pod-product-compliance
Ingram Content Group UK Ltd.
Pitfield, Milton Keynes, MK11 3LW, UK
UKHW042207170725
6956UKWH00001B/69